The Deepest Blue

by kim williams justesen

Tanglewood • Terre Haute, IN

Published by Tanglewood Publishing, Inc., 2013

Cover by Andrew Arnold
Design by Amy Alick Perich

Tanglewood Publishing, Inc.
4400 Hulman Street
Terre Haute, IN 47803
www.tanglewoodbooks.com

Printed by Maple-Vail Press, York, PA, USA
10 9 8 7 6 5 4 3 2 1

ISBN-13: 978-1-933718-90-3

Library of Congress Cataloging-in-Publication Data

Justesen, Kim Williams.
 The deepest blue / Kim Williams Justesen.
    pages cm
   ISBN 978-1-933718-90-3 (hardback)
 [1. Custody of children--Fiction. 2. Families--Fiction.] I. Title.
 PZ7.J985De 2013
 [Fic]--dc23
                                    2013022122

To Morgan and Ryan.
Your strength and courage in standing up for
what was best for you has proven to be
an invaluable inspiration to me.

chapter 1

We have been stocking and cleaning our fishing charter boat for hours and finally give in to tired muscles and hunger. Dad steers the truck out of the parking lot and waves to Jack Sutton, who's sitting in front of his boat, the *Lolly Gag*, bobbing side to side in the slip where it's docked next to our boat. The sky is clearing from an earlier storm, and the air smells like damp asphalt and pine. I roll my window down, letting the fresh breeze blow in.

"You did a great job getting the boat cleaned up and ready for tomorrow."

"Thanks," I say. My arms ache, and I stretch them up and press my fingers against the roof of the truck. "Maybe I can practice driving." My words are hopeful, but Dad shakes his head.

"We're running late as it is." He shifts gears, and the truck lurches a bit. "We'll go soon. I promise."

"Should we call Maggie and let her know we're on the way?"

"That would probably be nice of us." Dad pulls his cell phone from the holder attached to his belt and hands it to me. "Tell her we'll be about twenty minutes."

I punch in the number and listen. It rings a few times till I hear the familiar, "It's your nickel."

"Hey, Maggie." I can hear Rocket barking in the background.

"Hey, Mike. Hush, dog," Maggie says. "So are you boys on your way? I've got a chicken in the oven that's just about finished."

At the mention of chicken, my stomach growls loudly enough that I bet she can hear it over the phone. "Yeah," I say, "we just left the marina, and we're about twenty minutes from helping you out with that."

"Would you ask your dad if he'd mind stopping real quick for a loaf of bread and some lemons? I just realized I'm out."

"Maggie needs some lemons and a loaf of bread."

"No problem," Dad yells toward the phone.

"Okay, so I'll see you two in about thirty minutes then."

I push the OFF button and hand the phone to Dad. "She's making chicken," I say. Not that it matters much. I'm so hungry I could eat my own tennis shoes. My stomach rolls over itself again in anticipation. It's so noisy even Dad can hear, and he pats my belly and laughs.

"Worked up an appetite, did you?"

It's quiet for a few minutes, and then Dad clears his throat and adjusts the cap on his head that says MIGHTY MIKE—the name of our charter boat. He smiles, and I wonder if he's thinking about Maggie or the chicken in the oven. I imagine it's a little of both.

I smile, too. Maggie is a great cook. Dad's smile makes me wonder, and I decide to ask something that I've been thinking about for months. "You ever gonna marry Maggie?"

Dad steers the truck along the road in silence, and I am almost sorry I said anything. Then he sucks in a deep breath. "Funny you should mention that, Mikey."

"Dad, I'm almost sixteen. Don't call me Mikey."

"Right. Sorry, Mike." He shifts in his seat and clears his throat again. "So as I was saying, it's funny you should mention that."

"Really?" I turn to look at him. He likes to tease me all the time, so I don't want to get my hopes up just in case he's messing with me.

"Well . . ." he says, dragging the word out like he's letting out a trolling line.

"Seriously, Dad, are you thinking about it at least?"

Dad gives me a quick glance and then shifts the truck into a lower gear as we turn onto the Atlantic Beach Bridge that leads from Moorehead to Atlantic Beach, then to North Carolina Highway 58.

There's still a lot of water on the road from the earlier storm, and I can hear the tires splash as we turn. I roll up the window so I can better hear whatever Dad might say.

"I always said I'd never get married again because I'd never get divorced again."

I sit at full attention.

"But I never thought," he says, and then he pauses and his voice gets softer. "I never thought I'd meet someone like Maggie. And I sure never thought she'd be interested in a guy like me."

There is something in his voice that almost makes me sad. Why wouldn't a girl, well, a woman like Maggie be interested in him? My dad is a great guy: strong, capable, able to fix anything.

He takes off the blue cap and runs a hand through his black hair. I can see flecks of white speckling around his temples, but I've heard more than one of the local ladies describe him as a handsome man. I hope women think he's good looking, 'cause I look just like him—without the white speckles, of course.

"So," I say, impatient for a real answer, "is that a 'yes I am' or an 'I don't know but I'm thinking about it' or what?"

"It's an 'I'm giving it some serious consideration, but I thought you and I should talk about it first.'"

"What's there to talk about?" I practically jump out of my seat. "She's a great cook, she likes you a lot, she likes your kid, she puts up with the two of us sticking our stinky feet on her furniture, and did I mention she's a great cook?" I catch my breath and then go on. "What more could you want?"

Dad lets out a big laugh. Then he grips the steering wheel tight in both hands as the truck fishtails. "Whoa," he says, the laughter gone from his voice. We drift dangerously close to the bridge wall, and I can see the white-capped waters of the channel below.

I grab for the arm of the door. My fingers wrap tight around the plastic handle. I take a deep breath to control the shaking I'm scared will show in my voice. "Slick?" I ask as Dad gets the wheels straightened out and maneuvers into the far right lane.

"Going a little too fast. A lot of water still on the road. We hydroplaned for a second, but I've got it under control."

I turn around in my seat and look at the road behind us. Water stands in big puddles on the bridge, and passing cars shoot up rooster tails in the air as they pass. Then I let out the air in my lungs. Dad has it under control. He's always got it under control.

We pull into the Food Lion parking lot, and I wait in the truck. I flip on the radio and scan through the stations. I settle on a classic rock station Dad and Maggie like. Okay, I like it, too. My heart is sort of thumping in my chest, partly from sliding in the truck, partly over Dad's hinting about Maggie.

For ten years, it's been just me and Dad. He runs fishing boat charters for tourists during the spring and summer and works a handyman business in the fall and winter. A few years ago, he let me start coming along on the boat as his first mate. I cut bait, get lines ready, clean up after tourists, and help Dad with whatever he needs. Some of the clients have been coming to Dad for almost ten years. He doesn't spend a lot on advertising—word of mouth is all he's ever needed really. Then about five years ago, we met Maggie. I thought she was the prettiest and nicest lady I'd ever met. I still think so.

After a few minutes, Dad saunters across the grocery store parking lot. He pulls on the door handle and slides back into the truck. "Now listen," he says, "don't say anything to Maggie just yet. If I'm going to do this again, I'm going to do everything the right way. No mistakes this time. No rushing in and going too fast."

"You've been dating for five years," I say. "I don't think anyone could accuse you of rushing anything."

"Okay, smart guy, but listen." Dad puts a hand on my knee, firm enough for me to know he's serious. "On Tuesday, since we don't have anything chartered, I'm driving up to Raleigh. I know a guy who's a jeweler up there. He's done a couple trips with me. He makes custom stuff, real nice, and that's what Maggie deserves. So the story is, I'm going to Raleigh to get some supplies for the boat. Cheaper for me to drive up and get them than to have them shipped. I'll be gone overnight, so is it okay if you stay with Maggie?"

"I can stay by myself, Dad." Visions of hanging out on the computer all night and playing games or messaging Rachel begin weaving their way through my head.

"Not overnight. So can you play along? Not let on there's anything up?"

I let out a long sigh. "Yeah, supplies in Raleigh, stay overnight with Maggie. Gotcha." There is no point fighting about staying home alone, even though I know I'm old enough.

Dad shoves the truck into gear and pulls out of the parking space. "Good. Now let's go eat."

I'm disappointed at not being able to stay by myself, but right now, that's not my biggest worry. I'm wondering how I'm going to keep this stupid grin off my face once we get to Maggie's. I make myself frown, but that only makes me laugh, and that makes everything worse. *Think bad stuff. Think English papers and chemistry tests. Think about failing your driver's license test.* It doesn't matter. I just feel like a big Cheshire cat with a goofy smile. As we near Maggie's house, my heart starts racing, and I doubt I'll be able to keep from blurting out the secret the minute we arrive.

chapter 2

"Hey, guys," Maggie says, her warm smile beaming. She tucks a curly strand of dark hair behind her ear as she pulls the door wide. Rocket, Maggie's Irish setter, bounces and barks behind her, trying to get at us to say hello. His tail winds around like a propeller and sweeps clear anything it comes in contact with.

"Hey, buddy," I say, walking into the brightly lit room flooded with the smells of chicken and homemade biscuits. I rub behind the dog's ears and then kneel down next to him. He rubs his muzzle against my head, snuffling at my ear.

"I hope you're hungry," Maggie says. She moves into the kitchen and slips thick padded mitts onto each hand. They look like kitchen boxing gloves. As she opens the oven, my mouth begins to water so much I'm afraid I might drool like Rocket does. Maggie slides a pan out that holds a golden-brown chicken the size of a small car. Steam floats up from the bird and circles around the lights overhead.

Dad sets the grocery bag on the kitchen counter, pulling out the lemons and the loaf of bread.

"When do we eat?" I ask.

"As soon as you go wash your grimy hands. Your dad's going to wash his and then carve the chicken while I put everything on the table."

I look at my hands. "They're clean."

Maggie takes an oven mitt and pops me on the head with it. "Go wash up or I'll give your plate to Rocket."

I head down the hall to the bathroom and take a bar of soap and some water to my hands. I scrub my knuckles and around my nails. Maggie will check, so I try to get them to a passable level of clean for her. I head back to the kitchen and plunk into the nearest chair, holding my hands up for Maggie's inspection. She nods and smiles. Rocket lies by my feet.

Dad's cell phone rings. He pulls it from the holder and checks the caller ID. "It's for you," he says, handing me the phone.

"If you'd get me my own phone . . ." I take the cell from Dad. "Hey, Rachel."

"Any chance you can come to the arcade tonight? Trevor and Caitlyn will be there, and Mandy's dad said he could give us a ride home."

I put my hand over the phone. "Can I go to the arcade after supper? Mandy Wilcox's dad said he'd give everyone a ride home."

Dad looks at me for a moment. "The Robertsons, 6:30 charter in the morning, remember?"

"Yeah, but the arcade closes at nine. I'm home by nine fifteen, nine thirty max."

He adjusts his hat and then shrugs. "Okay, home by nine thirty," he says.

"All set," I say to Rachel, "but I've got to be home by nine thirty. We have a charter in the morning."

"Man, it bites that you have to work all summer." Rachel lets out an exasperated sigh. "We're all meeting at six. Will you make it by then?"

I check the clock above the stove. It's five o'clock now. If I eat fast and run to the arcade, I should make it. "I'll be there."

"I'll see you when you get there," she says. "Bye, Michael." She hangs up before I can say goodbye.

Maggie sets a plate of chicken on the table.

"Trouble in paradise?" Dad asks.

"I don't know," I say. "I don't get what's up with her. One day she's calling me every five minutes, the next day she won't answer when I call her."

"On behalf of all females who went through puberty, I sincerely apologize for our hormone-twisted behavior." Maggie brings a plate of biscuits and sets them next to the steaming chicken.

Dad is already shoveling slabs of white meat onto his plate. I look down at my hands in my lap, still holding the cell phone. I set it on the table next to my plate. My stomach growls and lurches like an alien might suddenly bust through and steal some food off the table.

Maggie laughs out loud. She hands me the biscuits,

and I take two. Dad slides the plate of chicken to me, and I stab a few large, juicy pieces. I hand the plate to Maggie and begin stuffing my mouth. I wolf down the chicken, then rip open a biscuit and slather it with butter. I don't even bother putting jam on it. I stop long enough to gulp down some iced tea, and then I tear into the other biscuit.

Maggie slides an ear of corn onto my plate. "Maybe this will slow you down a little."

I realize I'm eating like a wild animal, so I take another drink, swallow, and look up at Dad. He is working his way across an ear of corn dripping butter down his chin. He looks at me and smiles. "Sorry," I say to Maggie, "I was really hungry."

"Apparently," she says. "There's plenty here, so just take your time and try to actually taste your food."

"I'm sort of in a hurry, too. I told Rachel I'd meet her at the arcade at six, and I figure I'm going to have to run to get there."

Maggie spoons a pile of green beans onto her plate and then adds a scoop to mine. "Rich?"

Dad looks up from his corn. "No, thanks."

"I meant, can't you drive him?"

Dad looks at Maggie, then at me. "Well, I've had kind of a long day." He sets down the corncob and wipes his face with a napkin. "He's young. He can walk."

Maggie wrinkles her nose. "It's starting to rain," she says. Then she looks at me. "I'll take you when we've finished."

I pick up my fork again, skewer a few beans, and then pause before I take a bite. They are sweet and fresh, right out of Maggie's garden.

"Before I forget," Dad says, "I need to go to Raleigh on Tuesday to pick up some equipment for the boat. Cheaper if I go get it than if it's shipped. Do you mind keeping Mike overnight for me?" He picks up a biscuit and slices it through the middle.

Very smooth, I think as I watch him spoon raspberry jam first on one half of the biscuit and then the other. *Got it under control.*

"Normally I wouldn't mind, but I'm working late on Tuesday night. We have a board meeting, and I won't be done until later." Maggie looks at Dad, and disappointment paints a dark cloud in his eyes.

"Well, I guess maybe he's old enough to stay alone," Dad says, though his tone suggests he doesn't really believe that.

My heart begins racing. Maybe at last, I'll get to have the house to myself for a night.

Maggie pats her mouth with a napkin and looks at me. "You're okay to hang out till I get finished, right? I could pick you up around nine?"

I shrug. A few hours alone are better than none, and then I think about why Dad is really going to Raleigh, and I have to fight to keep the dumb grin off my face.

Maggie looks at Dad. "More storms are headed this way on Wednesday according to the weather man on channel nine. Just go slow and be careful."

"We rode out that storm a few years ago, and that was supposed to be a hurricane. A little thunderstorm isn't going to bother me."

"Okay then," she says. She looks at me. "Plan on me picking you up around nine."

We finish supper, and I help Dad clear the table. Rocket gets a few scraps before he curls up on the sofa for a quick nap.

"Take the cell phone," Dad says as he rolls up his sleeves to start washing dishes. "If there's a problem with Mandy's father getting you home, give me a call here."

"You know, if you'd get me my own phone, we wouldn't have to swap this one around so much."

"You know," Dad replies, though I know what's coming next, "when you're old enough to have your name on the bill, I'll consider it."

"You know," I say, still pushing the issue, but Dad interrupts.

"You know—"

Maggie claps a hand over his mouth. "Boys, that's enough. We'll resolve this issue later. Right now, Michael has a date, and I don't want her angry at him because you two were bickering over a cell phone."

"Is Mandy's dad dropping me off here, or should I have him take me home?" I ask.

Dad removes Maggie's hand from his mouth. "Just head for home, and I'll be there after I spend some quality time with Rocket."

On hearing his name, Rocket lifts his head for a moment and then lays it back on the sofa cushion when he realizes no one is offering him food.

We climb into Maggie's green Subaru. Her hair is extra

curly. I figure it's because of the humidity. It hangs in little twists around her face. "Let me pull back this mop," she says all the time. But it doesn't really look like a mop. The guy at the health food store in Jacksonville who has dreadlocks, he's got a mop.

"So what's Rich headed to Raleigh for?" Maggie asks.

My stomach tightens, and I try to keep my voice steady as I answer. "Uh, some part for the boat. Maybe for the fish finder. I don't remember."

"Got other things on your mind," Maggie says.

"Yeah, I guess so."

"Listen," she says, "I'm sure Rachel is a nice girl and all, even though I've spent maybe twenty minutes around her. But a girl who won't treat you with respect is a girl who doesn't deserve your time and energy. Do you know what I'm saying?"

I'm glad Maggie thinks I'm worried about something other than Dad buying her a ring. "Yeah, but it's not like this is a big place with a lot of girls to choose from. And it's not like a lot of girls are gonna be interested in me." Maggie is a little unclear on the realities of living in a small beach town.

"Why not? You're handsome, you're intelligent, you're gainfully employed." She chuckles. "Those are all the things I love about your dad. Well, the employed thing is just a bonus."

"But you didn't grow up here."

"So?"

"I mean, I guess girls around here are looking for

something else."

"Like what?"

"I don't know, that's the problem. If I did, maybe I'd have an answer. But that still wouldn't solve the problem that this is a small town. When the tourists all go home, my choice in women gets dramatically smaller."

I watch the trees go past the window, occasionally backlit by the flashes of lightning from the approaching storm. The rain has started falling with authority now.

Maggie pulls up to the arcade. "The thing is," she says as I reach for the door handle, "fifteen-year-old girls don't know what they want. They're checking things out just like you are. They're confused, they're self-conscious, and they just want a guy who makes them feel comfortable." She brushes her hair from her eyes.

"I don't think that's Rachel's problem." I know it's not. I have an idea what some of it is, but I'm not completely sure.

"Then maybe you need a girl with fewer problems." Maggie beams another smile at me. Her smile is beautiful, and I smile without thinking about it. I totally love Maggie. She's like my mom. Not like my *real* mom, but like what a mom is supposed to be. Like what you'd design a mom to be if you could pick all the things you wanted.

"Maybe so," I say as I climb out of the car. "Thanks for the ride." I shut the door and dash through the rain to the arcade. As I reach the entrance, my stomach knots, and I wonder what kind of mood Rachel will be in. I take a deep breath as I open the door.

chapter 3

I shake my head like a wet dog, flipping rainwater every-where. The Jungleland Arcade is crowded with little kids, mostly tourists, probably trying to find a way to kill some time and wait out the storm. Bright, colorful lights flash, and the machines make electronic noises and music that compete with each other for the tourists' attention. A little girl, maybe two years old, wanders around with a ball from the Skee-Ball machine, threatening to throw the heavy, wooden sphere at anyone who tries to take it away from her.

I scan the crowd, looking for people I recognize. Over by the REDEMPTION CENTER sign, I can see Caitlyn Parker leaning on the glass case filled with plastic toys and cheap junk. Trevor Boone has his hand stuffed in the back pocket of her shorts, trying to grope her butt. She doesn't seem to mind. She is clutching a mess of red tickets spit out by the different machines, and I wonder how much that's cost Trevor already.

Trevor's dad runs one of the restaurants down in Indian Beach on the south end of the island. It's one of the oldest businesses, and it has a huge gift shop. Trevor busses tables or cashiers in the gift shop, and his dad overpays him. Trevor and I were best friends until eighth grade. I don't know what happened, but two years later, we're just acquaintances. My best friend is Jayden Stokes, only he's in Asheville enjoying the North Carolina mountains for the summer with his grandparents.

I head toward Trevor and Caitlyn. She and Rachel are best friends, which should mean Rachel would be close by. "Hey," I say. Trevor and Caitlyn turn at the same time.

"S'up," Trevor says.

"Seen Rachel?" I ask. I turn and lean against the glass case.

"She was outside on the bumper boats a few minutes ago," Caitlyn says. "She said she didn't think you'd make it until later."

I check the time on Dad's cell phone: 6:06 P.M. "Whatever" is all I manage.

Jungleland is more like a small amusement park with some weird tropical theme. There are bumper boats, miniature golf, and when the weather is nice, a go-cart track. Inside the arcade are all kinds of games, from classics like Skee-Ball and Pac Man to basketball and a zombie shooting game. The employees all dress in khaki shirts and shorts and wear pith helmets that I imagine would get really old after a while.

Mandy Wilcox stumbles in from the bumper boats,

dripping wet and laughing. Behind her, Rachel is wring-
ing water from her blonde hair, her green eyes reflecting
the flashing lights inside. Her pink t-shirt is stretched
below her hips from the weight of all the water, and it
clings to her body.

"When did they put in a swimming pool?" I ask as I
move toward the door where they stand dripping puddles
onto the cement floor.

"Maybe you didn't notice it is raining out there?"
Mandy says. Her tone isn't nasty. I think she just thinks
she's funny.

"I thought maybe *you* didn't notice," I say.

"I think they have the air conditioner set to North
Pole," Rachel says. I notice the goose flesh running up
and down her arms and legs.

"Come here." I hold out my arms to her. She lays her
head on my shoulder, and I pull her close. Shivers quake
through her body as she tries to get warm. I rub my hands
up and down her arms.

"Not so smart," she says, teeth chattering.

"Maybe not," I say. Her hair smells like chlorine. I pull
her closer. The dampness of her clothes soaks through to
my skin, but I don't mind. The arcade doesn't seem as
noisy as before. I close my eyes and hold Rachel.

We hang out in the arcade for a while, playing games
and exchanging our tickets for candy and temporary tat-
toos. When our arms are completely covered in bright-
colored skulls and butterflies, we look at each other with
blank expressions.

"Now what?" Trevor asks.

"I'm hungry." Mandy is always hungry.

Rachel looks at me. "You want to get something to eat?"

I don't want to say no, because things are going so well. Saying no would mean breaking the flow of the evening. "Yeah, sure," I say. There is a little snack shack outside that serves the typical, amusement park hot dogs and hamburgers. The tables are covered by huge yellow-and-orange umbrellas. The rain has eased off, and only light sprinkles still fall.

Everyone orders, and then we take our drinks to the tables. I brush the puddles from the plastic bench and tabletop with a handful of paper napkins. Mandy sits with Caitlyn, Trevor, and a boy named Bryce who just moved here from Charlotte. Rachel and I sit by ourselves.

"You have to work all week?" Rachel asks. She is playing with her straw, trying to sink the ice cubes in her soda.

"I have Tuesday and Wednesday off. Dad has to go to Raleigh and I'm staying here."

"So . . ." she says, dragging out the word, "will you be home alone?" The pitch in her voice stays level, but I can see the smile playing at the corners of her mouth.

My insides try to rearrange themselves. "I don't know," I lie. "I'll be home alone a lot of the time, anyway."

"So . . ." she says, again stretching the one syllable forever, "maybe I could come over to see you?"

"Um, yeah, I guess so. I don't know when, or whatever, but yeah, we could work out something. At least I think so." I can hear myself talking, but it doesn't seem like it's me. Rachel leans over and shuts me up by placing her lips on mine. Her breath is sweet, her lips warm and soft. My eyes roll back and the lids slam shut. I wrap my arm around her waist and pull her closer as blood rushes through my body and my skin prickles with heat. I open my eyes to watch her.

Her eyes open slowly and then grow wider. She smiles and whispers to me, "I love the way you kiss."

The kid in the snack shack calls our number, and I practically trip over the bench trying to stand up. My knees feel a little like rubber as I pick up the hot dogs and fries and bring them to the table.

Rachel squirts ketchup and mustard in swirls and loops across the top of the dog and then squirts a big pool of ketchup for her fries. She picks up a long fry, draws hearts with it in the ketchup, and points it out to me, grinning and giggling. On the one hand, I think it's kind of cute, sort of a sweet gesture. On the other hand, why do girls do such stupid stuff? Worse yet, why do they think it would mean anything to a guy? It's ketchup. Duh. I smile at her anyway, because the last thing I want is to have her disappointed that I didn't like her ketchup.

We finish eating, and an announcement comes over the loudspeakers. "Jungleland patrons, the park will be closing in ten minutes."

"Mandy, what time is your dad coming?" I ask. I'm eager to get home, not because I don't want to be with Rachel, but I've got an early morning, and lack of sleep makes the job twice as hard.

"Any minute. He said he'd be here no later than nine o'clock."

"Gawd, I'll be so glad to get a driver's license," Rachel says.

"And a car to go with it," I say.

"I can't believe I have to wait almost a whole year," she says with a slight whine.

"Only three more months for me," I say. "At least for the license part. I don't know what I'll do about the car thing."

"What do you do with all that money you make working on the boat?"

"Spend it on you," I say. I kiss her nose, and she pouts even though she knows I'm teasing. "Actually, I'm banking most of it for college. I've got a savings account in Moorehead. I check it online every once in a while."

"How much is in there?" she asks, dragging another fry through the ketchup puddle.

"There's more than eight thousand dollars in it, I think." There's a lot more than that in there for certain, but I keep that to myself. I already don't like the direction this conversation is heading, and I know how Rachel thinks.

"Eight grand would buy a great used car," Rachel says.

It would buy a lot of education, too, I hear Dad's voice in my head, but I ignore it.

"Why even go to college? You already have a built-in job with a future. You can take over your dad's boat when he retires and just work for him until then." Rachel swings her leg under the bench and kicks at the water by her feet.

"I don't know," I say. And I don't. I mean, I like working the boat and all, but it is hard work, and some years
we don't get as much business as we need. "Dad's good
with his hands. He can fix things, build things. I'm not
that good. If he didn't know how to fix stuff, some years
we would have had to move or go on welfare."

"Well, he must be doing okay now if you've got eight
grand in the bank."

"He's been putting that away for me since I started
being first mate. It took almost five years to get that
much." I don't tell her where a lot of it came from,
because I absolutely do not want to get into a discussion
about my biological mom in Seattle.

"Seems to me it's your money. You can do what you
want." Rachel has a kind of defiant look, like somebody
called her a liar or something.

"It is mine, it's just, I don't know what I'm gonna do
with it yet. I haven't made a decision, so it's not important." Then the light bulb switches on, and I know pre-
cisely what she's thinking. She wants me to use the money
to buy a car so that I can drive her and Mandy around.
Trevor's dad will buy him a car, and Caitlyn will drive up
and down the island with him. Rachel wants the same
thing. She doesn't want to look like she's less important
than Caitlyn.

Rachel looks up at me, blinking her eyes slowly. Now
she really has a pouty look, and it reminds me of the baby
with the Skee-Ball.

I close my eyes and let out a long breath. "I got three

months to think about it," I say. "I'm not making any decision about it tonight, so let it rest."

"Whatever." She spins sideways on the bench and crosses her arms. Her voice has that "you're an idiot" tone that makes me insane.

"You want a fancy car to ride around in, then get a job and save your own damn money. Don't be thinking of ways to spend mine." I keep my voice low so Mandy and Caitlyn don't look over.

"Who said I was trying to spend your money?" She sits up straight, arms still crossed, and looks me in the eye, challenging me.

"That's what you want, isn't it? You want me to bust into my college savings and buy a car so you'll have someone to drive you and Mandy around. Someone other than her dad, I mean."

"I did not. If you just want to pick a fight with me, then why are we even here?" Her voice is a high-pitched whisper, but I can see Mandy turning to see what's going on.

"I'm not trying to pick a fight, I'm just saying that the money I've got saved is not for you to tell me how to spend."

"I guess somebody has to tell you how to do things, 'cause you're obviously too slow to figure them out for yourself. If I hadn't kissed you first, you never would have had the balls to kiss me."

My temper flares, but I don't want to start yelling. I take a few deep breaths before I answer. "Maybe I'm just not in such a hurry. Maybe I don't see a good reason to move faster than I have to."

"That's why you'll be stuck in the same rut your dad is. You'll be running his boat, cutting bait until you fall over dead in the water."

Her words sting. My brain stutters as it tries to come up with something in reply. "Yeah, and ten seconds ago you thought having me run my dad's boat was the greatest idea ever." I'm confused—ticked off at her attitude.

"You're the one who wants to go to college because you don't think running the boat is good enough for you."

My head spins and my stomach tightens.

"By the time you make up your mind about things, you won't have any choices left." Her voice is almost a hiss.

I'm out of energy for this argument. I look at her, my eyebrows pushing together so hard I have to rub my finger between my eyes to focus. "What are you even talking about?"

"You think Maggie is gonna wait forever for your dad to make up his mind?" Rachel isn't even trying to disguise her anger now. She practically yells at me, even though I'm sitting right next to her. "She could have any man she wanted any time she wanted. And so could I. You and your dad will just sit and wait until there is nothing left to wait for. We will have moved on to something better."

"You don't know shit," I say. "My dad and Maggie are getting married." I'm immediately sorry I let this slip. "And you know what else? Being patient and waiting weeds out all the crap, so that all the valuable stuff is left for those who have a little patience."

"I'm crap, is that it?" Rachel looks really hurt.

A twinge of guilt pokes at my chest. "I didn't say that." I reach for her hand, but she pulls it away.

"Because I want to enjoy life now, because I want to live now and not ten years from now?" There are tears in her eyes, and I feel like an ass for making her this upset.

This much of what she says makes sense. I lower my voice a little. "I didn't mean it like that."

"But you said . . ." she lowers her head but doesn't finish the thought.

"Look, Rachel, you pissed me off, and my mouth went running on its own." I take a deep breath and try to calm down a little more. "I'm sorry. I just meant that taking things slower means you're sure you get what you want." I put a hand on her leg.

She backs up a little, but she doesn't really move. She tips her head and looks at me sideways. "All I want is you. You're the best thing in my life, and I don't want you to leave me to go to college, or to move away, or whatever."

"I'm not going anywhere anytime soon, except out on the boat to work and maybe into Jacksonville next week for supplies."

Rachel sniffs, and I move closer to her. She doesn't pull away. She lets me wrap an arm around her, and she lays her head on my shoulder.

"Besides," I add, "you'll get sick of me long before I'm ready to move on."

"Won't happen," she says. She almost sounds convincing.

"Time to go." Mandy pops up from behind us, pointing toward the exit where her dad's van is idling. The clouds have begun to break apart and scatter, and the sky is streaked orange and pink behind the blue-black clouds. I can smell the salt water from the ocean just a few blocks away mixed with the scent of pine kicked up by the storm. The air buzzes with the electric sound of cicadas.

I keep my arm around Rachel as we move toward the car. She climbs into the backseat. I slide in next to her. Caitlyn and Trevor take the middle seat, and Mandy climbs in front. Bryce stands at the exit and waves good-bye as we pull away.

We get to my house first, one of the few places in Atlantic Beach that isn't overrun with hotels and condos. It's an old beach house, just a few minutes' walk from the Atlantic Ocean. Dad has upgraded it, fixed it, added to it, changed it, and basically worked on it for the past nine years. The gravel drive is made up of broken shells dredged out of one of the channels.

Mr. Wilcox pulls in front of my door. The dome light in the car goes on as Trevor opens the door.

"Call me later," Rachel says.

I smile and nod, then climb out of the car. "Thanks, Mr. Wilcox."

"Welcome," he says in a friendly voice.

Rachel blows me a kiss as Trevor shuts the door, and the car drives off. As I climb the steps to the front door, I realize I have a headache.

I think about the argument with Rachel. My head

throbs. "Oh brother," I say to myself. I walk to my bedroom, tug off my shirt and shorts, and flop on my bed to wait for morning.

chapter 4

It's six o'clock in the morning. The sky is still dark as Dad and I start prepping the boat for the Robinson's charter. I make sure we have all the food and drinks we need for a group of four tourists, plus me and Dad. The water is calm in the marina, and the boat barely moves in its slip. It's quiet except for the soft sloshing noise of water against the hull as Dad and I move around getting ready.

I pull open the cupboard in the galley. There are four large boxes of saltine crackers, though I doubt we'll need them today. The red streaks of clouds across the sky last night were a good sign for fishing today, according to the old saying, anyway: Red sky at night, sailor's delight. Calm waters and a lot of active fishing lines are what I'm expecting.

"You have a good time last night?" Dad asks as he curls the hose he's been using to spray fresh water on the deck and sets it on the dock.

"Sort of, I guess."

"Hmm, well that's a little less enthusiasm than I expected. Everything okay?"

I shrug. "I dunno. Rachel is just being weird."

"Girls are weird," Dad says. "But that's part of why we like 'em."

"She thinks I ought to take my college money and buy a car when I'm sixteen." I come up the stairs from the cabin and grab a towel so I can wipe the water from the cushions on the sailfin chairs. "She thinks I'm just going to take over your boat when you retire and run charters like you do."

"What do you think?" Dad asks. He moves down into the cabin and brings out the big rubber trolling lures. They look like neon squids and have a huge hook inside for catching big-game fish like blue marlin and swordfish.

I finish drying off the last cushion and toss the towel into the cabin and then help Dad untangle the lures and get them connected to the trolling lines.

"Do you want to take over the boat, or do you want to do something else like go to college and study something important?"

I look at Dad. He stops hooking lures and makes eye contact with me. "I don't know what I want to do. I mean, I love working the boat and all, but I don't know if I'm as good at it as you are."

"Sure you are, or, you could be if you wanted. But that doesn't mean this is what you have to do. This is what I love. This is how I want to live my life. You might have another dream."

"What if I don't. What if I don't have a dream at all?" The thought of this makes the muscles in my neck tighten.

Dad makes a puffing sound like he thinks I'm ridiculous. "Of course you have a dream."

"There's really nothing that jumps out at me," I say. "There's really nothing that says 'This is what you're supposed to do with your life,' and it kind of makes me worried." I finish connecting the last lure, then pull out frozen bait fish. I get the big knife from the tackle box and start chopping the mackerel into thick chunks. I toss the chunks into a bait bucket so they'll be easy to get at when we switch to dropping lines for snapper and tuna.

Dad comes up next to me, and for the first time in a long time, he starts cutting bait with me. "I didn't know what I wanted to do until I was thirty years old. And then it took me nearly five more years to get here and make it happen." He tosses chunks of frozen fish into the bucket, pauses, then looks me in the eye. "One day, you'll wake up with this feeling in your gut that there is something you need to do. That's when you'll know. And if it doesn't happen until you're thirty, or forty, or seventy-five, or one hundred and twelve, so be it. But when it happens, you better do it, or you'll regret it for the rest of your life."

"So how did you figure it out?" I asked. "How did you know this was it?"

"One morning after you were born, you must have been—oh, I don't know—maybe three months old. I was sitting on the couch in front of the TV holding you, giving you a bottle, and flipping through the channels." He sets

the knife down and turns toward me. "You were such a
tiny little guy. Anyway, I'm surfing the channels, and I see
this program on one of the sports stations. There's a guy
who has hooked this marlin, and he is fighting it, and the
marlin is jumping out of the water, thrashing back and
forth." Dad pretends he's holding a rod and reeling like
crazy, pulling back against the fish. "And then I see the
boat, and the ocean, and I'm looking at you and thinking,
'Wouldn't that be a riot, Mikey?' And your little eyes lit up
like you completely agreed with me."

"I was three months old, and you're saying I helped
you decide this was what you wanted to do for a living?"

Dad lets loose a loud chuckle. "Yeah, that's how it
happened. For days, I couldn't get that image out of my
mind. Of course, I didn't know at the time that this was
going to cause me so much chaos. But I don't regret it."
He picks up the knife and starts cutting again. "I got
you, and I got my dream. I'm the luckiest man in the
world."

"And you got Maggie, too."

Dad grins from ear to ear. "And ain't that the icing on
the donut."

"So I guess I don't need to ask if you had a good time
last night."

"Guess not," Dad says, that cheesy grin stretching
farther across his face.

"Ugh," I say. "I don't want to know."

Dad wipes his knife on an old dish towel we use as a
clean-up rag.

"But what if I don't figure it out?" I say. "What if there's no TV show that gives me a clue?" The tension in my shoulders has worked its way down into my stomach and is worrying itself into a knot. "It's like I don't know who I really am," I say as I slap the last mackerel onto the chopping board.

Dad chuckles again. "You know who you are," he says with a matter-of-fact solidity in his voice that instantly makes me stand taller. "The fact you don't know what you want to do for a living yet is completely different from not knowing who you are."

I think on his words for a moment. "That's really deep, Dad," I say in a more-than-serious voice.

"Well, I'm a deep kinda guy." Laughing, we toss the last of the bait into the bucket as the four charter fishermen arrive.

The Robertson charter consists of a father, his two sons, and one son-in-law. They are from Toronto, Ontario, and I can tell right away that only the father has ever been on a boat before. The other three all look to be in their thirties, and they all look like they think Moby Dick is going to send them to Davey Jones's locker the minute we leave the marina. I decide we might need a box of saltines at the ready, and I break out a box just in case.

We head out about twenty miles off shore. The water is calm and the deepest blue—the kind of blue you see in pictures of Earth from the space station. Dad waves at me from the wheelhouse as I pull out lines off the big reels and get them set with bait or lures.

"On a day like this, I'd give anything to be a fish," Dad says as he climbs down the ladder from the wheelhouse to the deck.

"Not with the Mighty Mike around," I say. He claps me on the shoulder, and we toss lines into the deepest blue for the Robertsons.

It's a successful charter, one of our best of the season. We haul in red snapper, grouper, bass, and king mackerel. The time flies because we are so busy reeling in lines, baiting the hooks, and stowing fish in the hold—the big ice box welded to the back of the boat deck that keeps the fish from going bad. Seagulls flock around, flapping and calling as we pull in catch after catch. Even the son-in-law, who I find out after some joking and questions is a lawyer, has a grin on his sunburned face. There is cheering from the men as the fish slap and thrash on the deck until I can pull out the hooks and get the catch stowed.

As we make our way back to the dock, I feel the bone-tired sleepiness that wants to take over, but there is still so much to do. We back into the slip marked with our sign, MIGHTY MIKE DEEP SEA FISHING CHARTERS. Three women wait as we pull in. I help the four men out of the boat and then start unloading our catch. Dad finalizes the business details with Mr. Robertson, Sr., while I hang the largest four fish caught on the hooks beneath our sign for the trophy pictures. The biggest catch today is a black grouper, a huge ugly guy weighing in around eighty pounds. I have to struggle to get him hoisted, but I slide him on the trophy hook.

"And I thank you kindly," Dad is saying as he shakes the older man's hand.

"We'll look forward to seeing you next summer, then," Mr. Robertson says. "And next time we'll bring the ladies along." He wraps his arm around a thin woman with frosty, white hair. The men pose by the trophy fish, arms wrapped around each other's shoulders as the women snap pictures and smile. The son-in-law even pretends to kiss the grouper as his wife laughs and the camera flashes. They each thank us again.

"You folks have a nice evening and enjoy the rest of your visit," Dad says. And with that, they walk away.

"So am I loading this for the fish market or getting ice to take it home?" I look at the pile of fish on the dock.

Dad looks at the impressive catch. "I'll get the bucket and get started. You rest a few minutes. You've certainly earned it today."

Jack Sutton pulls the *Lolly Gag* into the slip next to us. Three kids climb off the boat before it's even tied up to the dock. Frank, the first mate, looks about ready to toss the kids into the water. He ties off the lines and then helps a younger lady off, followed by a man who looks like he needs a vacation from his vacation.

"You found the mother lode," Jack calls over to Dad.

"Neptune was kind to us today." Dad is pushing a large, rusted trolley—kind of like a wheelbarrow—over to the big ice machine behind the fish market.

I grab the freshwater hose from the dock where we left it this morning, turn on the water, and hop back on

the boat. It sways and rocks from the sudden shift of
weight as I begin washing blood, scales, and salt water off
the deck.

Frank is tossing the *Lolly Gag*'s catch onto the dock.
Some snapper, an albacore tuna, and a big trigger fish are
all they have to show for the day's work.

"That's a big trigger," I say as Frank hangs it up on the
Lolly Gag's trophy hook.

"It's ugly," says a girl who looks to be about ten.

Then Frank tosses out the best prize of the day. It
glistens blue and yellow, its blunt head looking like the
fish crashed into a wall as a baby.

"Nice dolphin," I say, tossing the hose onto the dock.

At that, the small girl begins to cry. Frank looks at me
as if I've called him some obscene name.

"It's not that kind of dolphin, honey," the woman is
saying to the girl. "This is a fish called a dolphin, not a
mammal. Remember?"

I look at Frank, a sturdy, muscular guy with dark hair
and skin like tanned leather. He rolls his eyes, shakes his
head slightly, and then hooks the dolphin in a trophy
spot—though I doubt there will be any pictures from the
looks of this group.

Jack finishes his business with the dad, and the family
scuttles away, the little girl still sobbing in loud, shrill cries.

"Swallowed the bait into its gullet," Frank says, his
voice flat and businesslike. "Pulled the hook out and
brought half its guts with it. Little girl kept yellin', 'Put it
back! Put it back in the water!' but it wouldn't do no

good. I tried to explain, but she didn't understand. Cried
like that the whole trip back."

I laugh. "Sorry." And I am sorry. We've all had a group
like that: a passenger who gets seasick and barfs in the
head instead of over the side; the whiny kid who gets into
everything he's not supposed to or hooks himself or
someone else with a big lure; the tourist who wants to tell
you all about his boat on the lake back home in agonizing
detail.

Dad comes back with the trolley loaded with ice, and
we start tossing in fish. "The Robertsons are taking about
half the catch, so I'll take it to the market. I'm selling
some of the snapper to the market, too, and I'll have them
clean some for us. We should make a few dollars with a
catch this size."

What isn't taken by the people who hire the charter,
we get first dibs on. What we don't take, we sell by the
pound to the fish market. Then they sell it to the stores
and restaurants. The arrangement works out well for
everybody.

The fish delivered, the boat cleaned, and everything
stowed, Dad and I hop in the truck. We toss the cleaned
fish into a cooler in the back, and I notice a big bag
labeled MAGGIE in Dad's lopsided handwriting.

"They tipped pretty good," Dad says, sliding into the
driver's seat. "The son-in-law even threw in a little extra
because he was so impressed with you."

Dad hands me a folded hundred-dollar bill. I tuck it
into my front pocket. It's one of the biggest tips I've ever

made, but I worked my butt off today, so I'm too tired to react.

"He says you've got a good head, and you'll be a good businessman one day."

I think over the conversation I had with the guy. "All I told him was a little about how we run things, and what I might do different if it were up to me."

"Hmm, and what would you do differently?" Dad pulls out of the parking lot and heads toward the main road.

"I'd advertise a little more, not just rely on repeat customers and word of mouth." Not that I'm trying to tell Dad how to run the business, it's just what I'd do, and I know he listens to me. Sometimes.

"What kind of advertising would you do?"

I lean back in the rigid seat, pressing my feet into the floor and arching my spine against the pressure of the seat belt, and stretch my arms in front of me. I let out a long groan. "I'd maybe do a brochure to put in the lobbies of the hotels—sorta like what Jack Sutton does, only nicer, with better pictures like a big marlin flying out of the water or one of the really good trophy pictures."

Dad drives on for a minute without responding. I look out the window as we reach the bridge and watch the water as we drive over it. A small boat is motoring toward a private pier, a large green net hanging off the back end where a man sits and steers up a narrow side channel. Further on I spot a sandbar where a white crane balances on one leg. Its bill rests against its long neck, and it seems at peace despite the noise of the traffic from the bridge and the boats making their way back to shore.

"You know," Dad says after clearing his throat, "those brochures can get a bit expensive. I'm not sure I'd even know how to make one or where to get one done." He shifts in his seat, grabbing the wheel with both hands and leaning forward to stretch his back. "I guess I could ask Jack Sutton, but I don't want him to think I'm competing with him."

"But you are," I say, though I don't have much enthusiasm in my voice. "Besides, I could probably design something on the computer that looks as good as his. Then all we'd have to do is find a printer somewhere who can do all the colors and print it on glossy paper."

Dad leans back and lets out a long breath of air. "Don't know if we could get it done before this season's up, but it might be something to think about for next year."

"It would only take me a day or two to pull it together, and maybe a day or two to call some printers up in Jacksonville or maybe Raleigh." I'm not trying to push. I just don't think it would be so hard. We have a ton of pictures on our computer from earlier charters, and I already learned how to do stuff like this in my computer graphics class last year. "I could probably give you something to take with you tomorrow, and you could get some price estimates while you're in Raleigh."

We pull up to the house, gravel and shells crunching under the tires as Dad coasts to a stop by the front steps. "Well, you show me what you can do, and I'll take it with me to see what I can find out about printing."

"I'll work on it in the morning," I say, because right now I'm so tired that just opening the truck door is a major effort.

As we climb the steps to the house, all I can think of is a hot shower and my bed. Then the phone rings.

Dad takes the cell from the holder on his belt as he unlocks the door. "It's for you."

I look at the caller ID and realize it's Rachel. "Don't answer it," I say. I'm so tired that I pass up the shower and head straight to bed. As my eyes slam shut, I worry that I've just given Rachel another reason to be mad at me, but right at that moment, I'm too tired to care. I'll just figure out how to deal with her when I'm not the walking dead anymore.

chapter 5

Dad stumbles into the front room around nine in the morning. I've been up and working on the brochure since seven thirty, and I've got a good draft to show him once he pries his eyes open.

"Coffee?" he asks. His voice sounds scratchy, and his hair shoots up in fourteen different directions at once.

"In the pot and getting old already," I answer.

Dad trudges into the kitchen, and I can hear the clatter of the ceramic mug on the counter as he pours a cup from the pot I made when I got up. I print a copy of the brochure, fold it into thirds, and take it in for him to look over. He is sitting at the table in a T-shirt and his boxers, leaning back in the chair and sipping from a red mug with black and brown dots that I made him for Father's Day when I was about seven. He takes the brochure from my hand and sets his mug on the table. He reads the information on the inside, flips to the back, looks at the picture on the front panel, opens it again, flips to the back again, and then looks at me. "How long did this take?"

"About an hour. It's not done. This is just a rough draft to see if you think it might work." I'm not happy with some of the layout, but I wanted to get something for him to see before he leaves for Raleigh.

Dad looks at me, his eyes wide open. "An hour?"

I nod.

"Son, if this only took you an hour, I'd love to see what you could do with a whole day, or a week."

"I don't like some of this." I point to the way the information on the inside flows around the bullet points I put in. "But I know how to fix it so it will look smoother."

Dad sets the brochure on the table, picks up his mug, and then looks at me again. "I just can't tell you how impressive that is." He takes a big swallow of coffee. "Not in a million years could I come up with what you've done there, and you've only been at it an hour."

It's hard to keep the smile off my face. "I really think this would help us. And if you can find a printer that makes us a reasonable offer, I think we could get them distributed within a few weeks." My excitement is building.

Dad takes another gulp and then stands and stretches one arm over his head. "I'm leaving in an hour. Fix what you think you can or need to, and I'll take it up to Raleigh with me and see what I can find out."

I sprint to the computer in the front room and get back to work. I can hear the shower running and Dad singing some old Eagles song. An instant message pops up on the monitor. It's Rachel.

Sweetthang101: U alone?

Mr.Mike2U: Not yet. Dad's leaving in an hour.

Sweetthang101: Can I come over later?

Mr.Mike2U: I guess. Call me around 12.

I don't want to be rude to her, but I really want to get this brochure done for Dad to take. I adjust the fonts I'm using and select different bullets. The shape looks better, but I'm still not satisfied.

Sweetthang101: Why 12?

Geez, Rachel, what does it matter?

Mr.Mike2U: Busy, call at 12.

I move a block of the text around, sharpen the picture in the background, change the color of some of the type, and zoom out to look at the whole page.

Sweetthang101: Busy with what? Too busy for me? Thanks a lot.

One of the things I am so totally confused by is how I can like a girl as much as I like Rachel, but how she can drive me nuts like nobody else at the same time. Does that even make sense?

Mr.Mike2U: Boat stuff. For my dad. Gotta get it done before 10. Then I'm surfing. Call around 12, ok?

I mess with a few more details. I can hear Dad crooning, "Welcome to the Hotel Cal-i-forn-ya." I hurry and print the brochure to see how it looks. I fold the paper in thirds and hold it up for inspection. I like it. It's not perfect, but I like it. Dad leaves the bathroom and heads into his bedroom. I take the brochure and follow him.

"Can I come in?" I yell when I'm about halfway there.

"Give me a second."

In the front room the computer chimes, and I know Rachel has sent me another instant message, but this is more important. She'll have to understand—or not. I'm starting to think I don't care which.

"Okay, it's safe," Dad says.

"It's not on glossy paper, or even card stock, but you get the idea."

His wet hair drips down his back. He has pulled on a pair of jeans and is tugging on a T-shirt with a marlin on the back and a picture of a boat called the *Water Witch* on the front pocket.

"Dad," I say, "it's gotta be eighty degrees outside already, and the humidity is way high. You're gonna die in those jeans." I hand the brochure to him.

He looks at me. "And you suggest?"

I tug on my shorts. They are yellow and black with white specks. I have on a black tank with a white skull and crossbones on it.

Dad nods. "I'm fine, thanks." He looks over the brochure. "I like this," he says, pointing to the inside bullets. "It looks better. Real professional."

"We can still make changes, but I wanted you to have something to show the printers." I sit on the edge of his bed, and it squeaks with its age and my weight.

Dad tucks the brochure into the front pocket of his shirt and then stuffs a pair of socks into a black duffle bag on the bed next to me. The round handle of his brush pokes out at one end, and he pushes it down as he zips the bag shut.

"Maggie's at work late, so she said she'll pick you up when she gets done."

"How late were you over there?" I ask. I came home from the boat and crashed. I didn't even eat dinner. I heard Dad drive off around seven o'clock, but I didn't hear him come home. I was completely wrecked.

"Not too late. I tried to be quiet when I came in. I hope I didn't wake you."

"I was dead," I say.

"You worked hard yesterday. You earned a good sleep." Dad grabs the duffle bag and heads out of the bedroom toward the front room. The bed squeaks its relief as I get up and follow. Dad checks the computer as he passes. "Who's that?"

I look at the screen. Rachel has sent another message that reads, "Can I come over at 1?"

"Rachel," I say. "She thinks she's coming over today."

"I think not," Dad says. He drops the bag on the sofa and then heads to the kitchen.

My heart rate picks up a little. I want to see Rachel, and I'd like to spend some time alone with her. Nothing too heavy duty. I have learned a few things of value from my dad. But I know what he's thinking, and there is no point to my arguing.

"That girl is starting to sound like trouble." He pours the last of the coffee into a travel mug and snaps on the lid. "I don't want you having girls over here when I'm not home."

"Not gonna happen," I say. "Rachel just wants to manipulate the situation. I'm not sure what her game is, and I don't want to know."

Dad looks me square in the eye. "I mean it, Michael. That temptation isn't worth the consequence."

"Dad—Not. A. Problem." I emphasize each syllable. "She's not all that, and I don't even think I'm going to keep dating her. She makes me crazy."

Dad laughs. "She's a girl," he says, as if that explains it all. "So what are you going to do today?"

"Surf, maybe. Watch TV. Play computer games. Basically hang out."

"No girls." He grabs the duffle in his free hand and walks down the steps to the truck.

"I'm not five, Dad. I heard you the first twenty times."

"Good. Maybe after twenty more, you'll listen to me." He hops into the truck, tosses the bag on the seat, puts the coffee cup in the holder, shuts the door, and waves. He mouths the words "no girls" one more time and then drives off.

I head to the computer to message Rachel.

Mr.Mike2U: You there?

Sweetthang101: Yeah. Where were you?

Mr.Mike2U: Getting chewed out by my dad, thanks to you.

Sweetthang101: What did I do?????

Mr.Mike2U: I told you he hadn't left yet. He saw your last message. He specifically said "no girls" so now I'm stuck here by myself.

Sweetthang101: It's not my fault he doesn't trust you.

My hands ball into fists, and I bang them on the desk.

Mr.Mike2U: Actually, yes it is.

Dad is normally pretty cool about things, but Rachel is kind of pushy, and she definitely has a big mouth. I know he just wants me to be smart about my choices.

I'm waiting for the computer to chime with another message, but instead the phone rings.

"Hello?" I already know who it is.

"It is not my fault that your dad doesn't trust you, and I resent the fact that you would even say that."

"Rachel . . ." I try to explain, but she won't let me speak.

"If you and your dad don't have a decent relationship, that is not my fault. If you have done something that has caused him not to trust you, then you did it and not me. Don't try to blame your problems on me. I am totally not the source of your problems, Mike. You are."

With that, she hangs up. I decide I'm going to go surfing before I rip the phone out of the wall.

I change into my black-and-green swim trunks, but I leave the tank top on. I keep my board in a storage closet under the steps. After looking for my sandals for several minutes, I remember I slipped them off outside the door. I fix a sandwich, throw it, some water, and a towel into my backpack, grab my board, and then walk the block and a half from my house to the public beach. The tide is on its way in, so the waves are picking up nicely. Iron Steamer Pier is not the greatest surfing in the world, but it's fun when you need to kill some time or blow off steam. There are the remains of an old steam ship about a hundred yards off shore. Sometimes when the tide is

low, you can see the very top of the wreck out in the
water. You can't surf there at low tide or you could seriously mess up your board. There used to be an old fishing
pier, too, but it blew down in a storm a long time ago; my
dad tells me stories all the time about fishing off the end
of the pier and getting his line caught in the wreck.

I spike my board in the sand, throw my towel out flat,
and drop my pack on it. The tourists are already out in
force, slathering themselves in sunscreen and flattening
out like lizards trying to soak up as much sun as possible.

It's times like this I wish October wasn't so far away,
so I could have my license and drive farther up the island
to a better spot for waves. But it will get here soon
enough. And I'm not ready to get through my summer
that fast.

I tug off my shirt and then pull my board out of the
sand and head into the water. The waves have a pretty
good surge to them. When I'm about waist deep, I float
my board and flop on top of it. I paddle out about thirty
feet, pushing the water with my hands. The ocean is
warm, but a little breeze is raising goose bumps on my
back, and I'm thinking my wet suit might have been a
good plan.

I raise up on my elbows and watch a few swells move
under me. I can feel the draw of the water pulling urgent-
ly out toward the ocean. It signals a rush of adrenaline in
me: a big wave. I start pushing hard with my arms as the
water crests beneath me. I hop on the board and fight
gravity to stand as the wave swells and begins folding over

on top of itself. Spray hits my face and my skin. I push
with my legs, guiding the board upward to stay inside the
curl, then coast off the edge and head behind the churning
froth as the wave breaks and rolls into the shore. I drop
back down to my stomach and paddle out again.

For about an hour, I paddle out and surf in. A few
more good waves arrive as the tide comes in, but most of
them are weak and shallow. I ride a few more, loving the
smooth feel of the water and the summer sun on my
back. I'm trying to decide if I might luck into another big
one, when I spot someone waving from the shore. I sit
up, shielding my eyes against the sun reflecting off the
water. It's Rachel. I ride a wimpy little swell most of the
way in before I pick up my board and cross the sand.

"What're you doing here?"

Rachel has on a red bikini top and white shorts.

"Looking for you," she says. "I figured this is where
you'd come if you were mad at me." She stands with her
arms folded across her bare stomach. "Besides, my dad's
home again."

I spike my board in the sand again. Rachel's dad has a
drinking problem, so she doesn't spend much time at
home. My anger eases a little, and I drop down on the
towel. She sits next to me.

"I'm sorry if I got you in trouble," she says. She
sounds genuine.

"Why do you have to be so pushy?" I ask. "I mean,
you know I care about you, but it's like you're in some
sort of race or something."

"I don't know," she says in a soft voice.

"You do, too, Rachel."

She sits in silence. A breeze plays with her hair.

"The other night at the arcade you were complaining because I didn't kiss you soon enough. Then you find out my dad's gone for the day, and you're in this big rush to come over to my house." I let out a sharp breath.

Her skin is pale except for the rush of color to her cheeks. I've embarrassed her, and I sort of feel bad. Maybe Maggie is right and girls don't know what they want any more than guys do. I feel stupid for getting mad at her.

"Maybe we should just do it right here on the beach," I say, trying to sound casual. "We could give the tourists a few vacation memories." I waggle my eyebrow at her. Rachel's eyes fly wide open as I untie the drawstring on my still-wet trunks and start sliding them down. I manage to get them to just about mid-hip when she grabs my hands.

"Stop it, Michael. Right now." She laughs, but her face flushes a deeper red.

"Aw, come on," I say. "They won't even notice." I nod over my shoulder at the pale bodies slowly roasting in the sun.

She giggles and then tries to pull up my trunks. "You'll get us in trouble. And the last thing I need today is to have a beach cop call my dad."

I laugh and sit beside her. I brush a strand of hair from her face. The waves crash and whisper at our feet. *I want this girl*, I think, but fear of the unknown stops me. Fear of the consequences, of not being any good at this,

of disappointing this girl and having her tell the whole
island what a failure I am.

"I'm sorry," I tell her.

"I'm sorry," she says. "I love you," she adds.

"I love you, too," I say before I realize what I'm saying.
But it's mostly true. I'll figure out the rest later. We lie on
the beach, listening to the water and the occasional gull,
and little kids who run into the waves and shriek as the
water races up to meet them. Rachel drifts off to sleep,
and I watch her breathe. She is so beautiful, and she can
make me so insane. I lie next to her. The sun bakes our
skin, but the breeze cools the air around us.

After a while she stirs and sort of blinks her eyes. I
smile at her. "I designed a brochure for the boat," I tell
her. "Dad took it to Raleigh to see about getting a printer.
He thinks it's pretty good."

"So do you want to take over your dad's boat?"

"I don't know. I don't want to be like Trevor, doing
what his dad tells him to do."

"You're better than that," she says. "You want something
more, even if you don't know what that is. And even if what
you want is to run your dad's boat, it won't be because that's
what your dad wants. It'll be what you want."

My stomach gurgles and rumbles. Rachel laughs. I sit
up and grab my pack, which she has been using as a pil-
low for the past hour or so. The peanut butter and jelly
sandwich I tossed in has become a peanut butter and jelly
decal: flat and sticky. Rachel giggles again.

"Wanna grab a burger somewhere?"

"Sure," she says.

"I need to run my board home first, but that'll only take a second. We can just walk to Sandy's or something, if you want."

"Sounds good," she says.

We brush the sand off each other and then head back to the house to drop off the board. "What time is it?"

Rachel looks at her cell phone. "Three forty-five, and I need to be home by six."

"Gotcha." We get to my house and stow my board. I run inside to grab my wallet, then we walk the two blocks to Sandy's Drive-In. We order burgers, onion rings, and chocolate-caramel milkshakes.

"Will you be online tonight?" Rachel asks between slurps of her shake.

"I'll be at Maggie's tonight, so I don't know. If she says I can, I'll get on. She usually lets me."

"How come you'll be at Maggie's?"

"Dad's staying in Raleigh overnight. He doesn't want me home alone, 'cause I might sneak a girl over or something." I wink at Rachel, and she smiles.

"Are they seriously getting married?" she asks.

I draw a deep breath. "About that," I say. "You can't say anything to anyone right now. I shouldn't have even told you. But yeah, I think so. That's why my dad went to Raleigh. To buy the ring. He hasn't officially asked her, though."

Rachel grins. "I won't tell anyone. But that is so cool! Are you excited?"

"I don't know. Maggie's been like my mom for so long now that it sort of seems like getting married is silly. Then again, I haven't lived with her full time, so I don't know what that's going to be like."

"I think it's great, and I think your dad should have done this a long time ago."

"Yeah. Me, too."

We finish eating, and Rachel calls her sister to come and pick her up.

"I'll try to catch you online," I say as she drives away.

I head back to the house and climb the steps just as the phone rings.

"Hello?"

"Hey, Mike," Dad says. "I talked to a couple of printers today, and I think we found one we can work with." He sounds excited. "He wants you to email what you've got to him so he can fix it up a bit, but he said it looked like a professional job."

A grin spreads across my face. "Awesome. Give me his email, and I'll get it to him."

"I'll bring it home with me tomorrow." He clears his throat and then says, "No girls at the house, right?"

"Not a one, unless you count the twelve I hid in the shower just now."

"Very funny."

"How was the drive up?"

"No problems. I picked up the ring first thing. It is beautiful, so Maggie better say yes." Dad chuckles.

"You got it under control."

"Be good for Maggie. I'll see you tomorrow."

I hang up the phone and decide to play on the computer for a while. While I'm reading my email, Jayden chimes in.

J-Dawg: Dude, wassup?

Mr.Mike2U: Not much, just hangin, waitin for Maggie to pick me up.

J-Dawg: Pick you up why?

Mr.Mike2U: Dad's in Raleigh. Staying overnight at Mag's

J-Dawg: Hey. Looks like I'm getting paroled early. Could be back next week

Mr.Mike2U: Totally cool, dude. What plans you got?

J-Dawg: None so far. Probably need a job.

Mr.Mike2U: If you want I can ask my dad about you working on the boat. We got tons of charters lined up. I know we need the help.

J-Dawg: Dude, that would be awesome! Will your dad be cool with that?

Mr.Mike2U: Let me ask, but I'm pretty sure.

J-Dawg: Seriously, man, that would rock. I owe you big just for asking.

Mr.Mike2U: No problems. It would be cool if we could work together.

J-Dawg: Totally. Hey, did your dad leave the phone for you?

Mr.Mike2U: No such luck. Trying to talk him into getting me 1, but so far he's not biting.

J-Dawg: Well, pretty soon I'll be close enough we

can hang out.

Mr.Mike2U: Get back fast, Jayd. I'm going nuts without you man.

J-Dawg: ASAP, dude, I swear.

I log off the computer and opt for watching a movie on cable instead, but there is nothing good on, so I grab my iPod and turn on some music. Heavy metal riffs scream through my head. At some point, the playlist runs out, but I have fallen asleep on the sofa. I wake when I hear Maggie's voice and feel her hand on my arm.

"Michael," she says, her voice scared or worried, I can't tell.

My eyes flutter, then open, squinting against the light. I sit up and realize Maggie has been crying. Her eyes are swollen, and dark circles hang under each socket.

"What's wrong?" I pull out my ear buds so I can hear her and I'm not screaming. My voice is froggy, catching like sand in my throat.

"Michael, it's your dad."

It takes a minute for her words to get clear in my head, and then my mind tumbles awkwardly through all the options of what that might mean. He's in trouble. He broke up with Maggie. He's in the hospital.

"Mike, your dad's been in a car accident. He was hit by a drunk driver."

"He's okay, right?" I search her face for some reassurance.

Maggie's mouth opens and closes like a fish out of water. She stares at me, eyes wide and glistening. Finally the words come out as sound. "The paramedics worked on him at the scene and rushed him to the hospital, but they couldn't keep him alive." Her hands come to her face to wipe the tears. I can see she is shaking.

I feel something surging in my chest. "No. No, that can't be what happened." My head throbs, and my chest feels like it might explode. I gulp air, desperate to fill my lungs, but there isn't enough oxygen. The room spins around me. I shut my eyes against the dizziness overtaking me.

Maggie wraps her arms around me. I grab onto her and bury my head in her shoulder.

"No," I say again. The word won't stop falling from my mouth. My brain tumbles and reels with voices, images, sounds, but all I can say is "no, no, no." He's always got it under control, he's always here, alive and here.

Maggie sobs, holding me and rocking me. The whole world has shrunk down into just this room, just the space: Maggie holding me, me holding Maggie. I see my dad's face—smiling and laughing and very much alive. I try to imagine no life in that face. I can't. But there's an empty feeling in my gut—a cold, hard place like I swallowed a stone. He isn't part of me anymore. I discover an emotion I have never felt before. It rises up and takes over me like a wave: I want to be dead, too.

chapter 6

I don't know how long we have been sitting on the sofa, maybe minutes, maybe hours. At some point Maggie's sobbing slows and then subsides into an occasional jagged breath. I find I can take in air now, though each deep inhale creates an ache under my ribs. I loosen my grip around Maggie. She pulls back to look at me, wiping tears from my face, her hands still shaking and her voice soft.

"There are going to be a lot of very difficult moments ahead," she says, and her voice trembles. "I'm not even sure what we need to do first."

"Do we need to go to Raleigh?" I ask. "Do we need to pick him up?"

Maggie takes a deep breath. "No, " she says. "I asked them to transfer him—" her voice breaks on the words, "to transfer the body to the mortuary in Moorehead."

Questions begin running out of me like blood from a wound. "What do we do now? Do we just sit and wait? Does someone call us? What about the truck? What about this place? Where will we bury Dad? Where am I going to live?"

Maggie waits with patience, her hand warmly wrapped around mine. When I stop babbling, she takes another deep breath, holds it a moment, lets it go in silence, then speaks. "I don't know all the answers right now, but I'll tell you what I can. When Chuck Marshall left the boat to go to law school, your dad promised to be his first client. When Chuck started his practice, Rich made good on his promise."

"We need to call Chuck then."

"I've called him already," Maggie says. "He's coming over in the morning to help us."

"Did Dad have a will? I mean, did he specify any of this, like what to do with the boat and the house—or me?" It suddenly dawns on me what I'm asking and what it must sound like. "I don't mean the stuff, Maggie. I don't mean I want his stuff. I just want to know if he made plans." I blink hard against the pressure welling in my eyes, but it does no good. I can feel the warm, wet trails being drawn on my skin.

Maggie squeezes my hand. "I know, sweetie." She reaches up and pushes my hair off my forehead. "You're a great kid. And you're scared to death right now because your whole world just changed."

"Yours did, too."

"Yeah," she says, her voice cracking, "yeah, it really did."

"You know why he went to Raleigh, don't you?" I ask. I want her to know. I want her to know how much my dad loved her.

"He went for boat parts and to find a printer for your awesome brochure." She forces a smile. "He stopped by the aquarium to show me."

"That's only part of it." The pain in my chest begins to spread to my solar plexus and into my stomach. "He went to see a jeweler. He went to buy you a ring."

Her eyes slowly open wider as she begins to figure it out. I manage half a smile, but it quickly falls as I watch Maggie move from understanding to devastation.

"I'm sorry. I shouldn't have said anything. I should've kept my big mouth shut."

Maggie's head drops to her hands.

I can't believe I'm such a moron. My head starts spinning again, and there's a throbbing between my eyes. A wave of nausea builds in my stomach. I bolt from the sofa, race down the hall to the bathroom, and vomit, my body retching and heaving. I sit hard on the tiled floor. I shake and tremble, and I can hear my own voice moaning, though I can't believe that sound is coming from me. I am embarrassed and ashamed at having puked and at the fact I'm sobbing on the floor of the bathroom like a baby.

Maggie comes in and kneels beside me. Her hands are cool on my clammy skin. "It's okay."

"How can it be okay? How am I going to be okay? My dad is gone. My dad is dead, and I want to be dead, too." My nose is running, and every inch of my body feels as if I've been stung by bees.

There is a knock at the door, and Maggie makes her way out of the bathroom. I can hear voices, and I try to pull myself together. I force myself to stand up and look in the mirror of the medicine chest. I look like hell. I blow my nose on a tissue from the sink, dry my face on a towel, then step out into the front room. Maggie is talking with Sheriff Oakes.

"I came when I got word from the mortuary. They want me to escort the body through Jones County and Craven County to Moorehead."

"That's very kind of you," Maggie says.

"Can I see him?" I ask.

The sheriff looks at Maggie. "I'll let you know about what time we expect to arrive, but I suspect it will be around six this morning."

The sheriff tips his hat to Maggie and then extends his hand to me. "I'm so sorry, son. I know what a mighty blow this is for you, but you let us know if we can do anything to help out."

I take his hand, shake it firmly, and then watch as he descends the stairs.

"Can I see him?" I ask Maggie again.

"Of course you can," she says. "As soon as he gets to the mortuary, we'll both go to see him."

I look at the digital clock on the microwave. It reads 12:32 A.M. "What do we do now?"

"You should try to get some sleep," Maggie says.

"Yeah, right."

Maggie smoothes my hair again and then pulls me close. She is warm and smells like rain. "Should we fix some tea?"

I nod.

Maggie heads to the kitchen and starts a pot of water boiling. She gets into the stash of herbal tea she keeps here because Dad only ever buys—bought—black tea. Maggie says black tea makes her jumpy, so she makes flavors like chamomile, or lemon, or peppermint.

My head begins to spin again, and I flop onto the sofa and press my skull between my hands. One thought begins forming at the back of my mind, but soon it starts pounding at the inside of my brain, just behind my left eye.

In the kitchen, the teapot lets out a whistle that builds to a high, shrill cry. I hear a chair scrape on the vinyl floor and footsteps move toward the stove.

"I want to live with you," I say as Maggie brings in a steaming mug of liquid that smells like lemon and honey.

She sits down beside me with her own mug, takes a cautious sip, then leans back. "Michael, I want that more than anything." She gives me a soft, barely noticeable smile. "But that may not be up to me."

I put the mug on the floor and sit up straight. "Why not?" The confusion weaving through me shows up in my voice.

"Because your real mother still has partial custody of you."

I lean forward. "I haven't seen her since I was five. I haven't heard from her in about four years. She doesn't pay support for me except when she feels like it, and she won't even talk to me. I don't know who she is and she doesn't know me, either, and it can stay that way."

"All that may be true," Maggie says. She sets her mug on the floor and leans toward me. "But the fact is that legally she is still your mom. Legally, I'm not anything."

A sudden urge to move takes hold of my body and makes me want to run out of the house and scream at the sky. I want to race down the street in the dark rain, dive into the waves, and let them drown me. "This can't be real. I can't lose my dad and you, too. I can't. I'd rather die." I am surprised by how calm my voice sounds.

Maggie scoots across the sofa and puts an arm around my shoulder. "Michael, I promise you will never lose me. No matter what happens, you will never lose me."

I am empty, hollow, and there are no more tears left in my eyes. The stone I've somehow swallowed is weighing heavy in my belly, threatening to pull me down. I lean against Maggie with all my weight, and she holds me, rubbing my shoulder and touching my face with her smooth hand. I feel like a baby. I should stand up and be a man. I should be comforting Maggie, figuring out what to do next, making whatever arrangements need to be made. I should be calling tourists who've chartered the boat. I should be figuring out their refunds. I should be contacting Jack Sutton to take on the extra charters for us. But right now, all I can do is lean on Maggie and let her love me.

chapter 7

Sunlight streams in through the front door. I am lying on the sofa, wrapped in a blanket from Dad's bed. My body is way too long for the ratty piece of furniture, and I have to stretch the kinks out of my legs and shoulders.

Then it hits: the lack of sound, the overwhelming emptiness. I sit up straight and my head begins to throb. "Maggie?"

I hear the kitchen chair scrape against the floor. "Right here, Mike."

I turn and look as Maggie rounds the corner from the kitchen. "Did you sleep?" I ask.

She shakes her head, though I could have seen she hadn't slept just by looking at the bags under her eyes. "Are you hungry? I could make you French toast or some eggs."

My stomach rolls and churns. "Thanks, but I don't think I could keep it down." I stand, but I wobble a little, so I sit back down until all my parts decide to work in harmony. "Any word from the sheriff?"

"He pulled up this morning about six thirty to let us know they'd arrived in Moorehead. I didn't want to wake you, so I just went outside to talk to him."

"So what now? Can we go see Dad?"

Maggie purses her lips, and a nervous look flits across her face. "We need to talk about that."

I feel off balance again. "What's wrong? Last night you said we could go."

"I know I did," she answers, her voice getting softer. "But I'm worried, Mike. Today may not be the best day for this."

Anger bubbles up in my stomach. "Why not today?" I say, trying to keep my voice even. "He's in Moorehead, waiting, and I want to see him today."

Maggie lets out a quiet sigh, clasps her hands in front of her, and looks at a spot on the floor. "I want you to really think about this," she says. "Seeing Rich like this— it won't be easy. It may even be the worst thing we could both do right now."

"I want to see him today," I say, my voice firm and steady. I try not to let the anger boil over, because I know Maggie is just looking out for me.

"You're old enough to make the choice," Maggie says, "but it needs to be an informed choice. You don't have to do this today."

I fold my arms across my chest. "I'll ride my bike over there if I have to."

Maggie gives me a faltering smile. "You don't have to ride your bike. We can go over anytime you're ready."

The anger subsides, and my stomach settles. "I need a

shower." I move down the hall toward the bathroom, stopping in my room to grab fresh clothes.

The hot water pounds against my head and neck, and I brace myself against the wall and let it pummel me. I hear Dad singing in the back of my mind, and I find myself crying again—softly at first, then growing more intense until I have to sit down in the shower with my head in my hands. After a few moments it passes, and I rinse the soap off my body, turn off the water, and grab a towel. I feel like I'm moving in slow motion, like walking in the waves and fighting against the current, my feet being sucked into the sand and making me fight for each step.

I get dressed, throwing yesterday's clothes in the hamper I share—shared—with Dad. Everywhere I look, he's there. I hear his humming as he changed clothes before going to see Maggie. I smell the cheap aftershave I gave him last Christmas. Then I see his Mighty Mike hat hanging on the bedpost in his room. Without thinking, I grab the hat and put it on. It smells like him, like his sweat, but it calms me for some weird reason, so I leave it on.

"Ready when you are," I tell Maggie.

She is washing out the mugs from last night. She shakes her hands, looks for something to dry them on, then gives up and wipes them on her shorts. "All set," she says, and I follow her out to her car. It is speckled with dust spots from the rain of the last few days. "I called Chuck and he will meet us there." We climb into the car and drive in silence.

It takes about thirty minutes to get to the mortuary.

The radio plays country music, which I hate, but I don't say anything. As we pull into the parking lot, Chuck Marshall gets out of his yellow VW. He shoves his hands in the pockets of his khaki pants and waits for us to park.

"Maggie, I am so, so, sorry," Chuck says, hugging Maggie and patting her back. "Mike, you too," he says, and he claps me on the shoulder and then hugs me in a sideways grip. "I'm here for you both. Anything you need."

"Thanks." Maggie fights back the tears that are brimming in her eyes.

"Yeah," I say, because I can't think of anything else to say.

"I've got copies of the paperwork," Chuck says, pulling a folded stack of papers from his back pocket. "We'll deal with the immediate things today. Then we can set a time to meet later on to talk about all the other issues."

"Like what?" I ask.

Chuck's lips press tight against his teeth, and then he lets out a puff of air. "Like what to do with the house, the boat, your dad's assets." He pats my shoulder again. "But that can all be dealt with later."

The early morning sun is heating the pavement, and a bead of sweat is gliding down my spine. "I won't go live with Julia. She's not my mom. I want to live with Maggie."

Chuck rocks back on his heels, looks at Maggie, bounces on the balls of his feet, then looks at me. "Okay, well, we don't have to deal with that today. Let's just take care of today, and then we can work the rest of this out later."

I sigh and blow at the hair that has wilted onto my face from under the hat. "Can we just get this over then?"

"Mike, this is going to be hard. If you're not ready to go in here yet, that's okay." Maggie looks at me with warm eyes, but her knuckles are white where she grips her pocketbook.

I don't know what I'm going to see. I've never had anyone close to me die, so I don't have any idea what to expect. I've never seen a real dead body before. Trying to imagine my dad this way—lifeless—I don't know if I can handle this, even with Maggie there. I don't know if I want this to be the last picture of my dad I have in my head. But I want to see him, and that feels more important than anything right now. I stare at the worn, leather sandals on my feet. After a moment, I tense the muscles in my solar plexus, relax them, and take a deep breath. "I'm ready," I say.

The mortuary is a low building that is dimly lit inside. The carpet is thick, and the whole place smells musty, like a library or a historical building you visit on school field trips. We are met inside the door by a balding man in a pressed, navy blue suit. He talks in soft tones. His name badge reads MR. SMOOT.

"We are so sorry for your loss. Of course, our purpose is to make this difficult time of transition just a bit easier for you all." He leads us to a small room with a large table made of dark wood. It is surrounded by lots of heavy, wooden chairs. There is a big, silver pitcher on the table and a stack of plastic cups. The pitcher sweats beads of cool water, leaving a puddle on the plastic tray it's on.

The word "easier" sounds like a joke to me. None of this is going to be easy.

Chuck says that Dad wanted to be cremated. That's news to me, but then why would Dad ever talk to me about dying? "He stated in his will that he wanted a small, private service. Family and friends."

Mr. Smoot nods, checks something off on a notepad, and scribbles some notes. He says something about facilities and transportation. My head is swimming again.

Chuck says something about the obituary, and Maggie gives him an answer. Blood is pounding in my ears. My eyes want to roll back into my head to see the underside of my skull.

The bald guy looks at me and Maggie. "Would you like to select an urn for the remains?"

My eyes refocus. I look at the man.

Maggie puts her hand on my arm. "After he's cremated, we keep the ashes, or we can bury them, but we need to find a jar or a box that they'll be safe in until we decide what to do."

That's a strange concept to me. I've heard of people doing this, but it's just weird having to face this kind of choice.

"You don't have to do this if you don't feel up to it," Chuck says.

I look at Maggie, and it seems like she doesn't want to do this alone. "I'll go," I say, and I follow everyone into a larger room filled with different types of caskets and containers that look like vases or jars with lids or even jewelry boxes. Some are wooden boxes with pictures of trees or fish or roses laser-etched into them. Some are metal and shaped like antiques you'd see at a museum. We wander around looking at each of them. I imagine Dad being burned to ash and poured into a jar, and the thought makes my heart race. I just want to leave now, but I tell myself to suck it up and be strong.

It is so quiet that I can hear my own heart beating, and I realize how fast it's going. I take a deep breath and then another, until my heart rate slows a little.

Maggie says something to Chuck in a voice so soft I can't hear her. Chuck nods his head.

"I like this one," I say, pointing to a vase and lid that are polished brass, shaped like something from China. I put my hand on it and touch the cool surface. It's a simple design, but it's nice.

"I like this one, too," Maggie says. "I think Rich would like it."

We head back to the smaller room. The bald guy pours water for us and then produces a pile of papers. He gives Maggie a pen and shows her where she needs to initial for this, sign for that.

"Chuck," Maggie says, "I think you have to do this."

The bald guy looks surprised. "Aren't you his wife?"

"No." Maggie looks at him with a sad smile.

"She was supposed to be," I say. "I mean, he went to buy her a ring, they just didn't have time to do it. Get married, I mean." I sound like a little kid, so I sit back in the chair with my mouth shut.

Maggie looks at me, and her smile wilts a little at the corners. "But I don't have any legal standing here. I can't sign anything because I wasn't added to the will."

I look at Chuck. He nods.

Mr. Smoot looks toward me.

"I can't sign anything. I'm only sixteen. Well, almost sixteen."

"That's why your father's attorney is here," Maggie says. "Chuck's the executor. He's responsible for signing any legal documents."

"Don't worry, Mike. I'm not going to do anything without talking to you and Maggie first." He nods at the stack of papers the bald guy is pushing toward him. "So if you say no, I don't sign anything."

We go through the paperwork one page at a time. Chuck reads it, waits for Maggie and me to agree, then initials it. He signs the last page and hands the stack back to Mr. Smoot. We pick a date and time for the service: Monday, 11:00 A.M., five days from now. Maggie asks me some more questions, but I've stopped listening, so I just nod to the question mark at the end of her sentences.

After what seems like forever, the bald guy leaves and then comes back with a folder he gives to Maggie.

"You may find some of this information helpful. And of course, we are always here to help in any way we can."

"Can we see Dad now?" I ask, thinking I'm ready to face this. The stone in my stomach is pulling me back, but I want to see him. I want to see him, but I'm scared. I'm really scared.

Maggie and Chuck exchange a glance. "Mike, you might not want to do this right now," she says. "This may not be how you want to remember your dad."

Anger hits me like someone elbowed me in the ribs. "I want to," I say, but my words don't sound as strong as I'd hoped they would.

Chuck watches me closely. "We can come back later," he says.

I look at Mr. Smoot. "Can I see him? Now?" I say before I lose my nerve.

"You may," says Mr. Smoot, "but please remember that we haven't performed any restorative work on him." He looks at the ground for a moment and then looks right at me. "I understand it was a car accident. You need to know that he is very bruised, and he won't look exactly like the man you knew."

Maggie draws a very shaky breath and takes my hand. Chuck follows behind us. The bald guy leads us down the hallway and through a swinging door. The room is as cold as the walk-in cooler at the fish market, and the light is almost blue, lending to a creepy feeling that causes my heart rate to speed up. Lying on what looks like a hospital bed is a body, wrapped like a mummy in a white sheet and blanket. I want to turn around, I want to run out into the heat of the morning, but I stay close to Maggie.

Maggie steps closer to me. We are still holding tight to each other's hands. In the middle of the blanket is a face, Dad's face. It is pale, a grayish color. There is a large gash that angles from the bridge of his nose, across his forehead, and back across his scalp. His eyes are closed, but the lid of his right eye is dark blue and purple. His nose takes a sharp turn about halfway down the bridge. His lips are closed, and at one corner of his mouth are a few dried specks of blood.

Maggie begins crying, making quiet noises. Chuck moves up beside her. She drops my hand and buries her face in his chest. But I can't stop staring at this body. It resembles my dad: the dark hair with flecks of gray, the strong chin, but that is not my dad. I take another step closer. I reach out and put my hand against his cheek. It is ice cold and feels firm to my touch, not soft and warm like my dad's face should feel.

"Mike. . ." Maggie says in a hushed voice.

I don't move, my hand still resting on his cheek. "Can I be alone?" I ask.

Maggie hesitates a minute beside me, then I hear footsteps and the door swinging open and shut.

I look at the bruises and the huge slash across his face. *Somebody did this to you,* I think. *I'm so pissed off that they did this, and I don't even know who I'm pissed at. I want the idiot who caused this. I want him in jail for this. I want him dead.* I see my dad, but he isn't my dad anymore, and while I don't feel scared by how he looks, I feel scared anyway.

This is a nightmare, I think. *A real one. Only I'm awake, and there is nobody who can tell me it will be all right.* My own voice echoes in my head. I'm shaking from the cold, from the emptiness. I have to get out of this room, but I can't pull myself away. My hands are balled into fists. I want to pound the walls and scream.

Warm fingers touch my arms. "Let it out," Maggie whispers. "Be mad as hell that he's gone. Be mad as hell that this happened. You have the right."

A groan forms in the pit of my stomach. It forces its way up, crawling out of my gut and emerging as a cry that doesn't sound like it comes from me. I drop to my knees, my head level with the edge of the bed and the white blanket. Maggie kneels beside me. I wail. I pound the floor with my fists until they ache and ask over and over, "Why?" Maggie rubs my back with a thin hand. I imagine my dad's hand, big and strong, patting my back or squeezing my knee. I hear his voice in my head telling me "I'm impressed, son," or "I got it under control," and I hear his deep laugh. It echoes in my head and then fades.

Maggie presses close to me. She sobs silently against my shoulder. We wait until the hurt subsides enough to move.

We walk outside into the bright sun. Chuck waits by the VW. "You okay, pal?"

I nod, squinting my tired eyes against the shocking light.

"Give me a call tomorrow, and we'll go from there."

Maggie hugs him. "I'll get you that list of names and numbers."

Chuck climbs into his car and pulls away. We get into Maggie's car.

"Are you hungry?" she asks.

"Not really."

"How about we stop for shrimp burgers and fries, take

it back to my place, and let Rocket eat anything we don't."

"Yeah, okay." I'm really not hungry, but I guess I should probably eat, and seeing Rocket sounds good.

We get our order at the Rusty Bucket: two shrimp burgers, two large fries, two large sodas, and a small burger for Rocket.

Maggie opens the door, and Rocket waits patiently for us to come in. He doesn't bark his greeting, but his tail sweeps the floor with a low-key enthusiasm.

"What's with him?" I ask, confused by the dog's silence.

"He knows something's wrong."

Maggie sets the paper bags with our food on the table. I put the drinks down and then scratch the dog behind his ears. He nuzzles my hand.

"Hey, boy." I lean down, and he licks my cheeks, jumps up, and puts his paws on my chest. I move away, and he follows on my heels. Inside the bag, I locate the small burger. "Want a treat?" I ask, unwrapping the yellow paper and holding out the burger. He wolfs it down in three bites and then looks at me as if I might have another one for him.

"Rocket, leave Mike alone." Maggie sits at the table and pulls out our lunch.

I check the time on the clock hanging above her sink. 1:45 P.M. "It's late."

"Time flies . . ." Maggie doesn't finish the sentence.

I unwrap my burger and take a huge bite. Hunger takes over, and I chow down my lunch almost as fast as Rocket did.

"If you're still hungry, there's chicken in the fridge," Maggie says.

"I'm good." Rocket rests his chin on my knee. Suddenly I realize I'm feeling sick—too much food on an empty stomach. I hope I don't have to throw up again. I've done enough of that for a while. I take a small sip of my drink, hoping it will help to settle the upset.

Maggie takes a drink of her soda. "Do you want to stay here tonight, or would you like me to come and stay with you?"

I think about being alone at home, and the idea weirds me out a little. "Can I stay here?"

"Sure," she says. "We'll run to the house later and grab a few things, make sure everything is safe."

I don't want to upset Maggie, but curiosity—or maybe vengeance—is driving a question through my brain. "Do they know who hit him?" I ask. As soon as the words are out, I realize I may not really want the answer.

Maggie swallows a bite, takes a drink, sets down her cup, and looks at her hands. "Hit and run. The Raleigh police are looking around, but there was only one witness, and he was drunk, too."

"How did you find all this out?"

"The sheriff. He told me this morning."

I pick up my soda cup and swirl the ice around. "We might not ever know then."

"Chances are good they'll find whoever did it. It might take time, but they'll find him."

"But what if they don't?"

Maggie sighs. "Well, then they don't. Does it change anything?"

I look from my cup to Maggie. "But I want the guy punished for what he did. I want him to have to suffer, too."

Maggie looks tired. "Mike, let's not worry about it right now. The police will do their job, but for today, there's nothing you or I can do about it. We have so many other issues to deal with."

Rocket inches closer to me, sliding his head along my leg. I look at him. His tongue pops out, licks his nose, and then disappears again.

"Can I get on the computer?" I ask. Maggie nods. I want to talk to Jayd, let him know what's going on. I log into my email. He's not online, so I send him a quick note.

Mr.Mike2U: Jayd — Not sure how to say this. Call me or something.

I stop and think. This is weird. I don't want to type in the words. I want to talk to Jayd, but I don't have his grandparents' number.

Mr.Mike2U: I really need to talk to you. Call me at Maggie's.

The phone rings with a loud chirping sound, and I jump a bit.

"Hello," Maggie says. "Oh, yes. Okay." She pauses and listens. I'm hoping it's Jayd, but I can tell it isn't.

"When?" Another long pause. "So now what?" Her voice sounds tense. "Okay. Thanks."

"Who was that?"

Maggie's shoulders tighten. "It was Chuck. He got

back to his office to start checking on some issues."

"And . . .?" I wait for her to answer.

"We don't need to worry about it right now," she says. She tries to sound relaxed, but it isn't working. She holds onto the phone with both hands.

"But what did he say?" I stare at her face, trying to read clues.

"Well, the state of North Carolina considers your mother to have legal right to your custody."

I bolt from my chair. "What?" I don't mean to yell, but this doesn't sound good.

"Chuck has to notify her that Rich has passed."

I go for the phone in Maggie's hands. "Call him back. Tell him no. Tell him he can't call her."

"He has to, Mike." She holds the phone close to her body.

"No, he doesn't. He can wait. He doesn't have to do this now." I hold my hand out, begging for the phone. "Please, Maggie, don't let him do this. I won't live with her. I swear, I won't."

Maggie looks like she is growing irritated. I can see it in the lines creasing her forehead. "Mike, stop it." She backs away from me and moves toward the sofa to sit.

Rocket is right under my feet, getting in the way of my walking.

Maggie sits on the sofa, still clutching the phone. "All he has to do is notify her. That doesn't mean anything other than call her. He doesn't have to put you on a plane and send you off today, okay? Don't overreact when we don't have all the information."

I untangle my feet from the dog and stand by Maggie. "Just let me talk to him. Just let me tell him I can't leave here."

"Mike, he knows what you want. But he has to abide by the law and your father's will. Your dad neglected to put me in charge of some things." Her voice has a definite edge to it. "But there is nothing we can do about it now. We have to go with what the law says. If we don't, we could make a bigger mess of things. Understand?"

"Just let me talk to him, please."

Maggie looks more tired than I've ever seen her. Her eyes are nearly slits, and there is no smile left to tug at the corners of her mouth. She looks at the phone, dials, then hands it to me. It rings, and a young woman's voice says, "Marshall Law Office."

"Chuck Marshall," I say. "It's Michael Wilson."

There is a click, followed by elevator music, followed by Chuck's voice.

"What can I do for you, Mike?"

"Don't call Julia. Please. Just wait a few weeks. A few days."

Maggie stands and puts her hand out for me to give her the phone. I turn my back.

"Son, I know how you feel. But I have to do this. It's the law."

Desperation grips at my chest like tiger claws. "Can't it wait?"

"Look, Mike, it's going to take me a few days to locate a number, so don't worry."

"But what about after that? What about after you call her?"

Chuck lets out a long sigh. "Mike, there isn't much I can do."

"Mike. Give me the phone." Maggie's voice is firm.

I hold up my free hand to her. "What if Dad and Maggie had been married?" I say more calmly into the phone.

"I don't know, Mike. Then I guess your dad could have asked Maggie to adopt you, but—"

I don't give him a chance to finish. "Then I want Maggie to adopt me."

Maggie practically yelps. "What?"

"Mike, it's not that simple."

"I want Maggie to adopt me," I say again. I turn to look at Maggie. Her face flexes with confusion and surprise.

"Give me the phone," she says.

I hand it to her.

"Chuck, it's Maggie." There is a long pause. "But is it possible?" Another pause. "Chuck, it's not about the money. Let me worry about the money."

My heart is banging off my ribs in anxiety. I pace and fidget. "What is he saying?"

"Shh," Maggie says, finger to her lips. "Okay, and then what?"

I walk across the room and back, then sit on the sofa. My knee bounces fast. My heel taps against the floor. I can't sit. I stand. I move to the window and look out at the yard behind Maggie's house that runs to the marsh. I feel the humidity of the post-storm air pressing on my skin. The sky is a dark, bruised blue with thick, white clouds hanging heavy in flight.

"And how do we do that?" Maggie sounds calm, regulated.

I stare out the window. A dragonfly hovers close by. Its shimmering blue body bobs near the glass like it's eavesdropping on us. I press my forehead against the cool pane.

"Then that's our next step," Maggie says with a note of finality.

I turn from the window and try to read her expression. She has her back to me. "It can't wait. So do whatever it is you need to do, and let's get going." Her shoulders are pulled up, as if she might curl into a ball and roll away.

"Okay then. Thank you, Chuck. I'll wait for your call."

"What?" I don't wait for an answer. I run to Maggie, take the phone from her hand, and stare her down.

"Let's sit down a minute, Mike. This is going to be a puzzle."

"Does that mean you will? I mean, you'll do it? Adopt me?"

Maggie maneuvers around me and sits on the sofa where she was before. She pats the cushion next to her. I slide into the empty seat, half anticipating and half dreading whatever it is she has to say.

"First, sweetie, there are a lot of different concerns involved in this, not the least of which is Julia."

"Forget Julia." The nastiness in my voice surprises me. "She's not my mom. She never has been."

"I know that's how you feel," Maggie says, folding her hands in her lap. "But how you feel and what the law recognizes are two very different things. This isn't like going to the shelter to adopt a dog."

"But if this is what I want, and this is what you want, then what's the issue?" It sounds simple enough to me.

"Well, first, like it or not, the law has to consider Julia in this."

My jaw clenches, but I stay quiet.

"Technically and legally, she is your mother. End of discussion."

"Then why are we still discussing it?" My temples begin to throb, and I rub them with my index fingers, pressing hard against the pulsing veins.

"We have one option open to us. Because of your age, you can request that your mother relinquish her parental rights and allow me to adopt you."

"So let's do it. Chuck can do the paperwork thing, and I'll sign away on that." I want to spring out of my seat and call Chuck back to get this plan in motion.

Maggie lets out a loud sigh. "It's not that simple," she says, her voice growing more frustrated. "According to Chuck, the best way to proceed is to first ask the state to appoint you an attorney."

"Why can't Chuck be my attorney?"

Maggie's hands are gripping tighter in her lap. "Because he represented your father, and he is my friend.

You need an attorney who represents only you. That person is called a *guardian ad litem.*"

"Then what? I get my own attorney, and they do the paperwork?" I'm not understanding why this is so complicated. Anxiety and frustration are swimming in my stomach, and I'm regretting having eaten my lunch so fast. I clutch at my middle and will my food to stay in there.

Maggie watches me and then closes her eyes. "Take a deep breath through your nose, and then let it out slowly through your mouth."

I do like she says.

"Good. Now take another one."

I do. The urge to puke slowly subsides.

"I think we both need a nap and some time to stop thinking." She puts a cool hand on my cheek. "I know I've had enough for one day."

The pain shooting into my left eye agrees with her, and I follow her down the hall toward my room. Rocket follows, too, and jumps on my bed even before I get there. I don't care, though. I sit on the edge of the bed, my forehead resting against the palm of my hand.

"I'll be in my room if you need me. I'm taking the phone in with me, just in case."

"Why don't you just unplug it?" I say. I ease myself onto my side and back up until I run into Rocket.

"That's a better idea," Maggie says. "We don't need to talk to anyone that badly for a few hours."

My eyes close. I hear Maggie's door shut. My head pounds in time with my heart, and my mind swims with a dizzying variety of emotions. The one parent who matters most to me is gone, and the one I care least about could be invited to waltz back into my life. I could wind up losing my dad, Maggie, my home, and Rocket without being able to say anything about it. As if he knows I'm thinking of him, Rocket's tail thumps on the bed, and he rolls over and rests his head on my legs. I manage to fall asleep.

chapter 8

Muffled voices in the other room cause my eyes to pop open. I strain to hear who's speaking. I recognize Maggie's voice, but the other one is lower. It doesn't immediately register as familiar. I sit up slowly. Rocket thumps his tail on the bed behind me where he has been napping with me. I stand and slowly twist the knob on the door.

". . . have it towed when they finish the investigation."

The other voice belongs to Sheriff Oakes.

"I'm so grateful to you," Maggie says.

Footsteps shuffle, and I hear the front door open and shut. Rocket maneuvers around me and noses the door open. I follow him into the front room. Maggie is sitting at the kitchen table, a small cardboard box in front of her.

"What did the sheriff want?" I ask.

The room is filled with the warmth and light of the late afternoon sun. I hear the sound of a car as it crunches down the gravel-and-shell driveway toward the street.

Maggie looks up with a start. "I'm sorry," she says. "I

didn't mean to wake you."

"It's okay," I say, sliding a chair from the table and sitting next to her. "What's this?"

Maggie rests her head against one hand, leaning hard on the tabletop. "It's some of the things from your dad's truck, things they found that they thought we might want and Raleigh police don't need for evidence."

I tip the edge of the box toward me. There are some papers with my brochure clipped to them, a white square box, Dad's travel mug, his wallet.

"Will you open that white box?" Maggie asks, her voice shaky and soft.

It dawns on me what might be inside, and my hands are suddenly sweaty. "Are you sure?" I ask.

"No," Maggie says.

I look at her. "We can wait till later."

She starts to cry. "I don't know, Michael. I'm so afraid."

"It's just a ring."

Maggie looks at me, her eyes flash like lightening.

I've said something wrong, but I don't know what. "Sorry," I say, but I don't know what I'm apologizing for.

"Just open it," she says—not angry, just very sad.

I take out the small box and open it. Inside is another box covered in dark blue velvet. It makes a cracking noise as I pry open the hinged lid. Inside is a broad gold band with a big square diamond set on prongs. It glistens and sparkles like the sun on cresting waves. I look at Maggie, but she is staring at the table.

"Wanna see?" I ask.

Maggie looks up, and I turn the box to show her. She reaches out and takes it from me, her hands shaking like an old lady's. She slides the ring from the box and examines it, turning it so she can see the inside of the band. Tears run from her eyes. "Today, tomorrow, always. Love, Rich," she reads. Quiet sobs shake her body, and her head drops. She holds the ring in front of her as if she's almost afraid of it.

I don't know what to do, what to say. Seeing Maggie hurt so much is making me hurt more. This kind of pain scares me, overwhelms me. I can't get enough air in my lungs, can't get the thoughts organized in my head. I want to scream, bang my head against the wall, try to wake up from this nightmare and be safe at home, in my bed, with my dad just down the hall.

I startle as the phone rings. Maggie puts the ring back in the box and sets it on the table. She wipes her face on her sleeve and then answers the phone.

"Hello?" she says, her voice trembling and tentative. She turns her head and sniffs. "Oh, hello Chuck." She listens, and I can hear the sound of Chuck's voice talking, though I can't understand what he's saying. Maggie takes a pen and notepad from the kitchen drawer and begins writing quick notes.

"Yes, I understand. I'll call as soon as I hang up with you."

An ominous clap of thunder sounds, and I look out the window. A collection of thick clouds has gathered, and fat drops of rain strike the glass with force.

"Yes, he's here now," she says, followed by a pause. "I'll let him know." Maggie hangs up the phone and looks at me. "I need to make a quick call, and then I'll tell you what Chuck said." Her voice is controlled, but she sounds frail, like she could crumble right in front of me at any second.

She punches a number into the phone. "Sylvia Young, please," she says. She sits at the table and pushes the blue velvet box away from her with the notepad.

"Ms. Young, this is Margaret Delaney. I believe Mr. Marshall told you I'd be calling."

I'm not used to Maggie using her full name, and it sounds odd to me.

"Yes, that's the situation," Maggie says. "Tomorrow at eleven would be fine." There is a long gap as Maggie writes more notes. She underlines something I can't read. Thunder booms above us, so loud and close the windows rattle against their frames.

"I'll be sure to explain that," she says. "I'm sure it will be just fine. Thank you so much for seeing him on such short notice." She says goodbye and then hangs up.

"This has something to do with me," I say. I feel jumpy, like I'm collecting all the static energy from the storm.

"Ms. Young is going to be your attorney. We have to drive over to Jacksonville tomorrow to meet with her."

I run my hand through my hair, realizing my dad's hat isn't there then dash to my room to find it. It's on the floor next to the bed. I pick it up, put it on, and then head back to the kitchen to talk to Maggie. "Why the rush? I thought we didn't have to worry about some of this until later."

Maggie picks up her notepad and looks at me. "Julia will be arriving Friday evening. She'll be staying until Wednesday or Thursday, at which time she plans for you to get on a plane and fly to Washington with her."

"What?" I say. "No way. No way am I going with her." I'm yelling, but I don't try to calm down. "How did she find out? How did she even freakin' know about any of this? I thought Chuck wasn't going to call her for a few days. I thought he didn't have her number? How did she hear about this?" The muscle in my thigh begins to twitch and bounce, and it feels like I'm losing control of my body and my mind all at once. "This isn't happening. This isn't happening," I say over and over.

"That's why Chuck found Ms. Young right away, so we could begin the process before Julia arrives."

"I won't go with her," I say. "I won't. I'll leave. I'll go somewhere she can't find me. I will not go with her. I don't even know her. She doesn't know me. They can't make me."

"Mike, this isn't helping," Maggie says. Her voice is calm, and she talks in a soft voice. "You need to settle down so we can deal with things in a rational way."

"Rational way?" I yell at her. "These people are talking about yanking me away from everything and everyone I know and care about. Do you get that?"

"You can be as upset as you'd like, but you will not yell at me like this. I can't help you if you can't settle down and deal with this rationally."

Blood pounds through my ears, and my arms and legs feel so twitchy they may detach themselves from my body. "There is nothing rational about this." My voice is a low, loud growl.

"Sit down, Michael." It's not a request; it's a command.

"No." I can't sit down. I can't be calm. I can't breathe. I head toward the door. "No," I say, half yelling and half snarling the word. I yank open the door and take off running. Behind me I can hear Maggie's voice. I head down a side road, through the trees, and across the main road. The rain stings my skin. The sky roars overhead as lightning rips through the air. I keep running. A car honks at me as I dash in front of it, crossing toward the beach. "You stupid jerk," I yell. "You jerk." I realize I'm not yelling at the car but at my dad. I find a beach access between two overbuilt hotels and make my way to the shoreline. The surf pounds against the sand and the water churns, turning gray and cloudy from the storm. I find a piece of a broken conch shell and hurl it at the water. "What the hell were you doing?" I scream. "If you had just married Maggie . . . If you had just gone to Raleigh two months ago, or two years ago, none of this would be happening." The words sting my throat, rain mixes with tears, and I am too tired to fight the storm anymore.

I sit on the beach, water coming down in sheets, and let the sobs overtake me. My body shakes from cold and running and emotions I can't even identify. I whisper to myself, "I can't do this. I can't do this." I can feel my body rocking back and forth, but I'm not in control of the motion.

My T-shirt is stretched from the rain and cold from the wind. The shaking grows more fierce as I sit on the packed, wet sand. I realize I've run farther up the island than I was aware of, and it will take me close to an hour to walk home from here, but I decide that's where I need to go. I trudge through the wet sand, moving down the shoreline until I'm sure I've passed Maggie's street. Then I move toward the main road and start the trek toward home.

"And I thought you knew everything. That everything you did was perfect," I say. "Give me crap about all my mistakes. Did you ever think about the ones you were making? You didn't have everything under control. That was a *lie*."

In my mind I can hear my dad's voice. "Now, son, I did the best I could."

A sarcastic and bitter laugh jumps out of me. "Ha! That was your best?"

I plod along, rain running off my body like I'm standing in the shower fully dressed. Cars drive by, spitting rooster tails of water off the street at me. I pass restaurants, big hotels, little beach houses, trailer parks. I keep walking.

"Son, I'm really sorry," I imagine him saying.

"You're sorry? Well a shitload of good that does me." I stay silent for a few minutes, and then I start laughing out loud. "I am totally crazy."

The rain begins to lighten up a little, and the lowering sun starts to shine through cracks in the clouds to the west, just off my left shoulder. To my right, the surf still pounds away at the shore. Traffic cruises by with the hiss of tires on wet asphalt. The air is a mixture of rain and pine and ocean. My legs feel like concrete as I make the last few dozen yards to the house. I climb the steps and head straight for the shower. My wet clothes leave a puddle on the floor, but I'll deal with that later. The hot water eases the shaking in my muscles. It pounds on my head and neck. I feel empty, like a shell tossed up on the beach after a storm. The sound of the pounding surf still rings in my ears. I let the shower run. My fists are clenched, and I raise my hands to the showerhead, coaxing my fingers to relax their grip. Steam fills the air and my breathing slows, gets easier. The warmth spreads through my arms, down my back, along my legs. I let the water wash away the salt of the ocean and the salt from my tears. It drowns out the screaming in my head, replacing it with the whisper of receding waves.

The water begins to turn cool, and I shut off the flow. I wrap myself in a dark-blue towel and sit on the floor. I can't cry. I can't scream. I can't think. So I just sit.

At some point I doze off, my body leaning against the tub and my head resting against the shower door. I don't know how long I sleep, but I hear a knock at the door. I figure it's Maggie, come to take me back to her place. I wrap the towel tightly around my waist and leave the bathroom. I open the door to find Rachel standing on the top step, ready to leave.

"I didn't think you were here," she says.

"Then why did you knock?"

She steps up to the doorway. "Can I come in?"

I push the screen door out of the way, holding it wide for her to come inside.

"Michael, I'm . . ." her voice trails off.

"What are you doing here?" I say as she steps inside.

"Sheriff Oakes was talking to my dad at the garage. I heard him say your dad had been killed." She stands in the center of the room, looking like she's lost. "I talked to Jayd online. He said you sent him a weird message earlier." Her eyebrows bunch together and make it seem like she's worried. "I'm really sorry," she says.

"So you talked to Jayd," I say. "Do you have a thing for my best friend now?" The words sound crazy the moment I say them, but my thoughts are so screwed up and everything else is going to hell, so why not this?

Rachel looks confused. "Why would you even say that?"

I head to the kitchen and pull open the fridge door. I grab two dark brown bottles of beer and carry them to the front room. Something inside—my conscience, my dad, I don't know—tries to get me to stop, but it is quickly silenced by some other voice, a new voice that doesn't care to discuss morals or values or appropriate behavior at the moment.

I twist the cap off one bottle and hand it to Rachel, who gives me a surprised look. I sit on the sofa, twist the cap off the second bottle, and take a long, cool swallow. It's not the first time I've had beer.

Rachel takes a tentative sip from her bottle. "Are you okay?"

"Dandy." The sarcasm scorches the air in the room.

"Look, Mike, if you don't want me here—"

"Stay or go. Your choice," I'm lying. I want her to stay. I want her here.

She sets the bottle on the floor away from her feet and looks me in the eye. "Why are you being like this? I just want to help. I care about you, and I just want to be here for you."

"Really?" I take another long pull from the bottle and swallow. The bitter taste makes my whole face pucker.

"Why else would I be here?" Her voice is almost pleading.

"Maybe you were thinking that Jayd might show up? I don't know. Why you do anything you do is a total mystery to me."

"Why are you stuck on that? He's worried about you, too."

"So the two of you are sneaking around behind my back? Great. That's awesome, because I needed another pile of shit in my life." The edge in my voice is sharp and vicious, and I hurl the words at her intending for them to sting.

She stands up and races toward the door, her expression tight and her eyes narrow.

My heart speeds up. I don't want her to leave. I go after her, grab her by the arm, and pull her next to me.

"Let go, Mike," she says in a low voice.

"No," I say.

"Let me go."

"No," I say again. The noise in my head is back, and it feels like the thunder and lightning have moved into my chest. I press my lips against hers and kiss her with force.

She slaps me hard. "Don't you ever do that again." Her words carry a threat, and I take her seriously.

"Rachel." I let go of her, but I'm begging her to stay.

"Who do you think I am?" Her face is twisted in fear and anger.

"Please, don't leave." My own voice sounds scared and distant and small. "I'm sorry," I say, hushed and worried. "Rachel, I'm really sorry. I don't know why I said what I said or did what I did. I don't understand anything that's happening to me, and it scares the hell out of me to feel so out of control."

"What's wrong with you?" She stares at me like some odd piece of junk that has washed up on the beach—a curiosity, but you don't want to get too close because it might be deadly.

"I don't know," I say. "I don't know what's happening. I don't understand why everything is falling apart around me." There is a deep ache in the core of my body, but no tears come.

I go back to the sofa and sit on the edge, resting my head in my hands. The air is cool and prickles my skin with goosebumps. I run my hands through my hair and try to decide what to do. "I'm going to get dressed," I tell Rachel. "Stay if you want to. I understand if you don't."

I head down the hall to my bedroom. Clothes are strewn on the floor, and the sheets are still pulled back from when I got up on Tuesday morning. I look around for something close at hand that's not too foul to put on.

Rachel comes in behind me, wraps her arms around my waist, and rests her hands on my chest. Her body against my bare skin warms me. My heart beats a little harder, a little faster. I turn around, brush her cheek with the tips of my fingers, and then kiss her gently. She doesn't pull away. I kiss her again, and she touches my back, running her hands from my shoulders to my waist.

"We don't have to do anything," she says to me. "I just want to be close to you."

I don't know if I'm relieved, or disappointed, or just more confused. We move to the edge of my bed. Rachel begins undressing. I know I should turn away. Part of me even thinks I should tell her to stop, to put her clothes on and go home, but I can't. I don't. I just watch as she reveals herself to me. She looks like she is made of porcelain. She lies on my bed. Without thinking, I unwrap the towel and lie beside her.

Her skin is velvet against my hands, and I touch almost every inch of her. She kisses my hand and runs her fingers along my ribs, down to my waist, across my hip. But neither of us moves beyond this. She curls into a ball, and I wrap my body around hers, pulling the sheet over us both, feeling safe for the first time today.

"I love you, Mike," she whispers.

"I love you, too," I say. And maybe I do.

We stay like this until it's completely dark. I don't sleep, I just hold Rachel.

The digital clock on my dresser reads 9:29 P.M., and I begin to worry that Maggie may show up—or Rachel's dad. Either way, they wouldn't understand.

"Rachel," I whisper. "I don't want you to get into trouble."

"Hmm," she says, still mostly asleep.

"It's nine thirty," I say. "I don't want your dad to come looking for you."

She stretches like a cat, arching her back, and rolls over to look at me. Her hair is all over the place, her mascara is smudged below her green eyes. I don't think I've ever seen her look more beautiful.

"Okay," she says, smiling at me.

"Thanks," I say. I kiss her. "I really . . . I just . . . just thanks."

Her smile grows wider. "You're welcome."

I sit up on the edge of the bed and grab a pair of shorts from the floor. I slide them up as I stand, and suddenly I feel a little embarrassed.

Rachel moves over and begins picking up her things. I keep my back to her as she dresses, though I'm not really sure why. She follows me into the front room.

"Do you want something to eat before you go?" I start toward the kitchen, flip on the light, and then look at her.

"I'm okay," she says. "But thanks for the offer."

"Do you need to call for a ride?"

"I have to be at the Sand Dollar at ten o'clock for my sister to drive me home after work." She looks at the floor like she's embarrassed or something. "She closes tonight."

"Do you want me to walk with you?"

"Nah, I can get there okay." She smiles at me. "Unless you want to come with me."

I look around for my flip flops, find a pair in my room, and head out the door with her. We walk in silence except for the occasional car buzzing past.

Rachel clears her throat. "I know we didn't really do anything," she says, "but I'd appreciate it if you wouldn't say anything to Jayden or Trevor."

"I'm not telling anyone anything." I put my arm around her waist. "This is just between you and me." *Besides* I think, *who'd believe that we were naked and didn't have sex? That we just lay there, curled up with each other?*

"It's just . . . Trevor has a big mouth, and if he tells Mandy—well, her mouth is even bigger."

"I got it," I say.

The air smells like pine and fresh rain. I pull Rachel closer as we walk the last block to the restaurant where her sister works.

"Call me tomorrow when you feel like it," she says. "No rush. I know things are crazy."

"I'll call," I say.

She kisses me, and I don't want it to stop. But I don't hold her too long. I let her go, and we wave as she pulls on the door to the Sand Dollar. I back away, keeping my eyes on her for as long as I can, then I head back to my house at a jog.

As I turn up the driveway, I see Maggie's car parked out front, and for a split second, I think she must be here to see Dad. Then it all floods back. I don't want to climb the wooden steps to the house. I don't want to hear whatever she's going to say to me. I am half tempted to take off running again, but I know at some point I will have to deal with whatever is waiting for me, and I'm just too tired to run right now.

I yank open the screen door and find Maggie sitting at the kitchen table, the two beer bottles in front of her.

"Have a nice little party?" she asks. I don't think I've ever heard sarcasm from her like this.

"Notice how much we drank," I say, pointing to the almost-full bottles and trying to sound just a little sarcastic in return.

"Was Rachel here?"

I nod.

"Is there anything else you'd like to tell me?"

"You mean about the hookers and the drugs? Nope, I guess not." I turn and head toward my room.

"Mike," Maggie calls. She stands in the hallway behind me, and I pause to hear what's coming next. She lets out a long sigh. "Never mind." She returns to the kitchen, and I hear the clank of the bottles as she dumps the beer into the sink and drops the bottles into the recycling bin.

I step back into the front room, ready to battle with words. Maggie stands at the sink, her head down. I wander over to the computer and flip it on. It whirs, then chimes as it comes to life.

"I need you to pack some clean clothes for a few days and something nice to wear for tomorrow."

"Why?" I ask, shoveling a little attitude into my reply.

"Jacksonville? Lawyer? Ring any bells?"

I sit up a little. "Oh, yeah." I can hear her moving around the kitchen, opening drawers, shuffling through silverware.

"It's after ten, Mike, and we're going to have to leave early if we're going to make it there on time. That means you need to get moving."

I don't move. "Can't we just worry about this later? I don't want to think about all of this right now." What I want is to go back to being with Rachel, to feeling secure, to forgetting about the fact that my dad is dead.

"It's getting late. Let's just get some stuff to take to my place, and we'll worry about everything else tomorrow." Maggie sounds tired and strained.

Still I sit. I feel the tension returning to my arms and hands. I feel my shoulders tightening and climbing up my neck toward my ears.

"Mike, come on." Patience is draining from Maggie like air leaking from a tire.

I don't move. I can't move. I feel paralyzed by having to do anything other than let the computer take my brain away for a few hours. "I don't want to go," I say.

"To my house?"

"Anywhere. Your house, Jacksonville, Washington—anywhere."

"So you're going to sit here at the computer for the rest of your life doing nothing?"

"Maybe," I say. It doesn't sound so bad, actually. And

if I could have Rachel come over every once in a while, and maybe Jayd, my life might all be okay.

Maggie lets out a "shh" noise. "Okay, here's the thing: You're the one who wanted this. You asked me to become your guardian, so we have to meet with the lawyer for that. If that's not what you want anymore, I'm happy to hand you over to your mother and let you deal with her on your own." She grabs her keys off the kitchen table and walks with firm steps toward the door. "You know, you are not the only person suffering, Mike. There were a lot of us who loved Rich. We've all lost somebody special, too."

"But he was my dad. *My* dad." I hurl the words at her. "I had him longer than you did, damn it. You don't miss him more than I do. This isn't harder for you than for me." I'm screaming, the words barely understandable. My arms shake, my head swims.

"He was my future. He was my heart." Maggie's words are clipped. "I don't hurt more or less than you hurt. I just hurt in a different way." She takes a big gulp of air. "But that doesn't mean you get to think you're the only one who lost somebody, that you're the only one who is struggling or suffering." She pushes open the screen door, but then she pauses. "When you figure out just what it is you want, you let me know. Until then, I'll contact Family Services."

"I'm fine by myself. I'm better off that way," I say. My heart beats in my throat.

"As evidenced by your excellent decision making and mature behavior." Maggie lets the screen door slam shut.

The car tires spit gravel at the steps as she speeds onto the road.

I stomp down the hallway and fall onto my bed. My head spins like a washing machine that's off balance. From somewhere in my gut, a growl crawls its way out, and I scream until I run out of air in my lungs. Everything is so screwed up. Nothing makes any sense. Maybe I am better off alone. I'm damned sure not going with Julia. I look around for my iPod, stick my earphones in, and then lie down on my bed, trying to drown out the noise in my brain.

chapter 9

I awake with a start. I was dreaming I was in the truck with Dad when the drunk driver hit him. I dreamed I saw the whole thing, and it scared me like the dreams I had about monsters when I was a little kid. I roll off the sofa and move to the computer to figure out what day it is. It's 6:12 A.M. and it's Thursday.

After I calmed down, I stayed up late last night calling our scheduled charters to cancel them. I called Jack Sutton first to coordinate with him. He hadn't heard about Dad, and he was pretty shaken when I told him. He said he didn't think he could take on all our charters, but that he'd see what he could do to help. He said he'd keep an eye on the boat for me.

I played computer games for a while, the whole time thinking about what Maggie had said about not being the only person who lost someone. I'm trying to understand that she is upset because I know she cared about him, but he is—was—my dad, my whole world.

I tried to see if I could live on my own. I did some research online. I could try to have myself declared an "emancipated minor," but that means you have to be able to support yourself and make enough money to live on. As much as I want to think I could run the boat, I know I couldn't do it alone. I'd have to hire somebody, and seriously, who would work for a sixteen-year-old boss? I wouldn't.

But I will not go to Washington. Julia is not my mother. Unfortunately, neither is Maggie, and she and I have some serious crap to deal with—like the thing with her freaking out because I had a swallow out of a beer, and her freaking out about Rachel coming over.

I tried to figure out all the bills I'd have to pay. Even if I could run the boat in the summer, I still want to finish school, maybe go to college. I couldn't support myself during the fall and winter. I'm not old enough to have credit cards or get loans or even buy my own cell phone. It took me until after midnight to get my head to settle down, but finally I accepted it: I can't live on my own. I need Maggie, and I really do want her to be my mom. Despite all the anger, all the weirdness of everything I'm feeling, I know that I want to live with her and be a family: me, Maggie, and Rocket.

At six thirty, I decide I'd better call Maggie before I miss my chance to set things right with her and try to get a plan in motion.

"Hey, Michael," Maggie says when she answers. I can't tell if she just woke up, or if she hasn't slept.

I run my fingers through my gnarled hair, pulling out a tangled clump between them. "So I'm gonna jump in the shower and get dressed nice for today, or as nice as I can anyway. I'm hoping you might know somebody heading to Jacksonville I could catch a ride with."

"Actually, I think Chuck will drive you."

I'm caught off guard by this. "Maggie, I'm really sorry. I didn't mean to be such a jackass last night."

"I know, sweetie, but you need to be able to speak your mind with this attorney, and I don't want anyone to get the idea I might have pressured you. I'd like to go, really, but Chuck said it would be better for him to take you, and I have to agree."

My stomach rolls itself into a knot and cinches up a bit. "But what am I supposed to say?"

"Whatever it is you feel you need to say, hon." Maggie pauses. "You say what you want. You say what you think is right and is best for you. The rest will take care of itself."

I swallow against the mild panic rising in my throat. "But don't you have to be there to say you'll adopt me? Don't you have to tell them why you'd make a great mom or something?"

Maggie chuckles softly. "That's up to you to do, honey. And it will be more important coming from you than from anybody else."

I think for a minute, and then I decide she's made up her mind, so I'd best just get ready. "Do I need to call Chuck and ask him to drive me?"

"I already took care of that last night."

"But last night I didn't even know—"

She cuts me off. "Just as a precaution. I didn't know what you would decide, either, but I asked Chuck to be ready, and he said he would."

"What time is he picking me up?"

"Be ready to leave by nine thirty. Chuck will not want to be late since this is a friend of his who's doing us a huge favor."

"Will I need to pay her money?" I feel the knot tighten a little more. I only have about sixty dollars left.

"All taken care of," Maggie says. "She's paid by the county to do this. Kids can't afford to hire lawyers, so the county pays the lawyers to represent kids who need them."

The knot eases up a little. "I'll call you as soon as I get back."

"Okay, bud. I'll be here waiting."

"Not going to work?" I ask.

She lets out a soft sigh. "Not for a little while."

I hang up and head to the shower. My pile of clothes from yesterday is still in a wet ball on the bathroom floor. I scoop them up and toss them out into the hallway, deciding I'll do a load of laundry when I get back from Jacksonville. After a quick rinse, I dry my hair with a towel and head to my bedroom to find something "nice" to wear. I don't have much opportunity to dress up, but I find a pair of khakis and a white, collared, button-down shirt. I even find a belt that isn't too beat up. I have one old, ratty pair of tennis shoes, a pair of water shoes I sometimes use for surfing or diving, and about thirty pairs of flip flops in varying conditions of hammered. I look under my bed for the woven leather sandals that will have to pass as nice shoes. I grab my wallet and flip it open: sixty-two dollars and some change scattered around on the floor and the dresser. I'll ask Chuck if we can maybe stop somewhere to look for nicer shoes than these. *I'll need them on Monday*, I think.

I fix a bowl of cereal, draining the last of the milk from the carton. I write "milk" on the magnetic notepad attached to the fridge that Dad and I used for our shopping list. Then I write "shoes" below that. I lose my appetite after just a few bites, so I dump the bowl down the sink. In my head, I can hear Dad yell at me about wasting so much food, and a twinge of guilt tweaks at my gut.

The clock reads 8:07 A.M., so I decide to get on the computer to kill some time. I check my email, hoping to hear something from Jayd, but there is nothing in the inbox from him. I poke around the Internet for a while then play a few games. At about nine, I decide to call Rachel. Her cell rings once and goes straight to voice mail.

"Hi, this is Rachel. I'm too busy to answer this call, so you'll just have to leave a message if you wanna hear back from me. Bu-bye."

I wait for the beep. "Hey, Rachel, it's Mike. Just wanted to say hey and let you know I'm going to Jacksonville today. Be gone a few hours. I'll call you when I get home. I love you, Rachel," I say, and I'm pretty sure I mean it.

I head back to my room and click on the television. I scan through a few channels and finally settle on some sports show. I try just sitting down, but I need to move. I pick up dirty clothes off my floor, make the bed, straighten books and magazines that are lying around. I grab the dirty clothes I threw in the hall, take the ones from my room, and then head through the kitchen to the laundry closet. It's not a laundry room, it is literally a closet with a sliding door. There's nothing in the washer, so I start a big load of my stuff. I've been doing laundry since I was seven or eight, so I'm pretty good at it; I just don't like doing it.

I pull open the dryer and find two pairs of my dad's jeans, a few dark T-shirts, and one pair of white boxers that accidentally found their way in with the other stuff. I laugh. "Nice goin', Dad," I say. The boxers look bluish gray now, and there is a blue splotch from the jeans on the left butt cheek of the shorts. Then I freeze. The color reminds me of Dad's skin at the funeral home: cold, empty, lifeless. I drop the shorts on the floor.

A car horn honks out front, and I run to my room to turn off the television. Then I head out the door to Chuck's car and climb in.

"Hey, Mike," he says in a serious tone as he claps me on the shoulder. "How you holding up?"

I buckle the seatbelt and look out the front windshield. "I don't know. I'm okay, I guess."

Chuck puts the car in gear and heads toward the highway. "I understand, man. I really do."

We drive in silence for a while, and then Chuck says, "You know, your dad was like a father to me, too." He signals a lane change and then looks at me out of the corner of his eye. "My dad left when I was about three, and I've never heard a word out of him since."

I think about what Maggie said last night, about how a lot of people loved my dad and lost someone important to them, not just me. I try not to be bothered by what Chuck is saying.

"When your dad hired me to work on the boat, it felt like I was working for family." He pauses and then continues. "He took good care of me, helped me get through college and law school. He was really a great guy."

"A lot of people thought so," I say.

"I expect a lot of the island will show up on Monday for the service. Have you thought about what you're going to say?"

"What I'm going to say?" I'm not sure what Chuck is talking about.

"For the service. I assumed you were going to want to get up as one of the speakers. Is that wrong?"

I scan my memory. Did I agree to do that? "I don't know. I haven't even thought about it. I don't remember saying I would do that."

"Yesterday at the funeral home. Maggie asked, and you said yes." Chuck shifts the car into a lower gear, and we come to a stop at an intersection. "You don't remember saying you'd speak?"

"I don't remember much of anything from yesterday.

But if I said I'd do that, then I guess I will. I'll think on it tonight and figure it out, write something down."

"You'll need something to wear, too."

"A monkey suit," I say, which is what Dad always called anything requiring a tie or a jacket.

Chuck smiles. I know he got the joke. "We'll stop somewhere in Jacksonville after your appointment. It won't take long—and I promise we'll get something you'll be okay with."

"I'd be okay with surf shorts and flip flops, but I bet more than a few people wouldn't appreciate my sense of style so much."

"Maggie asked if I'd find you something comfortable. She didn't specify what."

"I only have about sixty bucks."

"Not to worry," Chuck says. "Maggie sent enough to get you appropriately decked out."

"I'll buy my shoes." I'm not sure why it's so important to me, but it is.

"Your call," says Chuck.

I don't say anything else. Chuck turns on the radio to fill the silence in the car. He taps his hands on the steering wheel in time with some country tune I've never heard. It takes a little less than an hour to get to the office in Jacksonville, but it feels like half the day is gone when we get there.

Sylvia Young is a heavyset woman who looks like she's about Maggie's age, maybe in her midthirties. She has short, light brown hair that is super curly like a poodle's.

She is dressed in a denim skirt, a white-and-blue blouse, and a pair of white sandals that makes me wonder why I worried so much about shoes this morning. She has white, plastic, hoop earrings that match a white, plastic, beaded necklace and white, plastic bracelet.

"You must be Michael," she says, extending a pudgy hand with pink frosted nails.

"Yes, ma'am," I say, shaking her hand. Her skin feels doughy and warm.

"Come on inside, and let's you and I have a little conversation."

"I'll be back in about an hour," Chuck says as he heads back toward the car.

"Best make it two, just to be sure," Ms. Young says. "We've got a lot of work to get done today if we have to be in court Tuesday."

"Tuesday?" I ask. "This coming Tuesday? Why so soon?"

"Because your mother has filed a motion to have custody transferred to her immediately, so we had to file a motion for immediate adjudication with the court to get an emergency hearing on your case."

How did all this happen, and I don't even know about it? And why didn't anyone bother to talk to me about it or ask what I think?

Ms. Young pulls open the glass door that leads into the building. I follow her down a hallway to a wooden door on the left marked GUARDIAN AD LITEM. We step into a dimly lit office with a large desk piled to eye level with papers. There are no windows, and the room feels a little claustrophobic.

"So young man, sit down in one of the chairs here and tell me what brings you to Jacksonville this morning."

She has a funny voice, like she's really a funny person when she doesn't have to do all this legal stuff.

"Well . . ." I say, dragging the word out as I collect my thoughts, "my dad got hit by a drunk driver just two days ago. He was about to propose to Maggie . . . um, Margaret Delaney." It sounds weird, but I feel like I need to be sure I make everything clear. "So Maggie would have been my stepmom, because they would have gotten married pretty soon, I think. And that's what I want, for her to be my mom." My heart is beating hard, but I can feel the strength of how much I believe what I'm saying. "I want her to be my mom."

Ms. Young sits in a black office chair. She has picked up a yellow notepad and started writing. "What about your biological mother?"

"She's not really my mom. She hasn't been my mom since I was five. She just decided to try to creep back into my life now, even though I haven't seen her for, like, ten years. She thinks I'm moving with her to Washington, but I'm not. I won't go with her. She isn't my mom anymore."

Ms. Young looks up from her notepad at me. "You get to the point, don't you?"

"I understood there was a bit of a hurry to this," I say. I'm not trying to be a smart aleck, I just want to make sure she knows that I know how serious this stuff is.

"You're right, there is. I like your attitude. You're direct." She smiles at me, her bright pink lips framing perfectly straight, perfectly white teeth. "You and I are going to get along swimmingly."

My heart has slowed a little, and I take a deep breath. There is a musty smell to the room, like an old house filled with antiques and shadows. The smell reminds me of the mortuary in Moorehead, only not as sad and final.

"The court is going to ask you some tough questions. We have to be prepared to answer them." She looks back to her notes and starts writing again. "So let's spend a little time discussing this situation you're in."

I look at Ms. Young. "Okay, shoot."

"Why haven't you had any contact with your biological mother? Did your father keep you away on purpose? Did he speak ill of her or tell you things about her that made you want to avoid having any interaction with her?"

I feel my body tense and want to defend my dad, but I know she's only asking to help me. I take another deep breath, let it out slowly, then I start. "Dad and Julia divorced when I was about five. Julia decided she didn't want to be a mom. She told my dad that the whole thing—being married, having a family, all of it—had been a huge mistake, and she didn't want to do it anymore." I picture Julia's face, red and screaming, her finger pointed at my dad's chest as she yelled and cried.

Ms. Young scribbles on her notepad. "Did your father tell you this?"

"He didn't really talk about her," I say. "Most of it I remember from when I was little."

"Tell me what else you remember," she says, not looking up from the notepad.

"I remember them fighting a lot. It seemed like every day. It would wake me up at night sometimes. After awhile, my dad would come in to check on me and tell me that everything was going to be okay." I sink back into the overstuffed leather chair and rest my elbows on the padded arms. The cushion sort of squeaks as I shift my weight. "Julia never came in to check on me. In the mornings, my dad would look like he hadn't slept, and I'd see blankets and pillows on the sofa in the front room. Sometimes I'd find him there during the night, and I'd climb up on the sofa and sleep with him because I thought he was scared or had bad dreams like I did."

"Why did you go with your father instead of your mother after the divorce?"

"Duh," I say, not meaning to sound as obnoxious as I know I do.

Ms. Young looks up at me in surprise, but she smiles. "I know, Michael, but the court will probably ask about it."

"Dad and I left first. The divorce happened later. It wasn't really much of a choice. Julia made it pretty clear that she didn't want to be a mom. She told my dad that after she carried me for nine months, it was his job to make up for her sacrifice."

Ms. Young continues writing. "Did your father tell you this, or is this something that you heard?"

"Both. I remember her saying things like she lived with a parasite inside her, and now it was his turn to have it attached to him. Stuff like that. Dad told me one time that Julia resented him for the way her life was because she wasn't a happy person." I try to remember what Julia looked like when she wasn't angry: long, dark hair; almond-shaped eyes. I get a faint picture, but it is interrupted by the memory of Dad scooping me up and taking me out of her way so she couldn't hit me. I shudder, remembering how afraid I felt around her sometimes.

"What was that?" Ms. Young asks.

"I was trying to remember what she looked like, and then I recalled my dad having to pick me up and move me out of the way because Julia was going to hit me."

Ms. Young scribbles a lot, and I wait for her to finish. "Was she abusive? Was she ever reported for abuse?"

That's a word I had never applied to my situation before. "I don't think so," I say. "I mean, I didn't suffer a lot of broken bones or things like that." I think on the words for a moment.

Abuse.

Abusive.

Abused.

They don't seem to fit. They don't feel like my life.

"If we could prove she was abusive, the court would have to consider alternatives to sending you back to her." Ms. Young flips the page of her notepad and continues writing quickly. "Do you recall going to the hospital or the doctor for sprains or injuries she told you to lie about?"

I'm beginning to feel a little resentful about these questions. "I don't want to live with the woman, but I don't think she ever hurt me. I don't remember that. I just remember the one time."

"All it takes is one time," she says.

"But it wasn't like that. It was just . . . it was a lot of yelling. Both of them were yelling. It was shouting and name calling, but that's it. I can't remember anything else."

Ms. Young puts down the notepad and looks at me. "I'm not trying to upset you, Michael, I'm just trying to get all the facts I can so I can be better prepared."

I nod and sink a little deeper into the chair.

"When was the last time you heard from your biological mother?"

"About four years ago," I say. "She sent me a picture of her new son from her new marriage." I pause for a moment and then add, "And no, he didn't look abused."

"Good," she says without missing a beat. "What about holidays, birthdays, things like that?"

I think through the last ten years. "I got the picture. She never sent presents for any reason—not a Christmas card or anything. Dad told me when she got remarried, but he didn't tell me how he found out. I think I was about ten." I search my memory for any other meaningful contact, but nothing comes to mind.

"What about child support?"

"She was supposed to send a check every month. Sometimes she did. Sometimes she didn't. Sometimes she'd send $25 and sometimes $250. Dad used to stick it in my college savings account unless we were having a bad month. Then he'd ask me if it was okay to use Julia's money for groceries or something."

"Your father would ask you if he could use the child support money?" Ms. Young looks at me with wide, blue eyes. "You realize that the money was his per court order to use for your needs while in his care. It wasn't up to you to choose."

I blink. "He said Julia owed me, not him. He didn't think of it as his money. I don't think he wanted to feel like he might owe her something for it."

"So why do you want to live with Miss Delaney instead of your biological mother?"

This is easy. I sit up a little in the squishy chair. "Because Maggie is my mom already. She's been like my mom since I was about ten, and she's the only mom I've ever really had." I think for a moment, then I add, "Besides, she puts up with me when I'm being a jerk." *Which is happening a lot recently,* I think, but I don't say it aloud.

"And how do you know your biological mother wouldn't do this for you?"

"Yeah, right." The words snap out of my mouth before I can stop them. "She doesn't even know me. She didn't even want to know me until my dad died. She's just taking advantage of a bad situation to try to make up for something. Maybe for the guilt she has for ignoring me so long."

"But if she is claiming you as her legal offspring, wanting to be your parent full time, surely that means she must care about you."

"I don't know what her motivation is, but I doubt it has anything to do with love." I sink into the chair again.

"Maybe she's trying to impress her new husband or something."

"Why do you think living with Miss Delaney would be better than living with your biological mother?"

That's a big list. "Because this is my home. Atlantic Beach is my home. My friends are here. My girlfriend is here. My school is here. My life is here. Maggie is here. I don't remember too much about Washington. I don't have anything there." I can feel my shoulders riding up, the stiffness in my neck. "I don't want to lose my whole life after I just lost my dad by having to move all the way across the country to live with people I don't love and I don't know." My mouth is sticky and dry. "If she really loves me, she'll understand this and let me stay." I've moved to the front of the chair, and I'm leaning forward.

"That, Mr. Bryant, may be the most profound thing you've said today." She underlines on the notepad, and I can hear the paper tear from the force of the pen.

"Maggie has been around me forever, or at least for like the last five years or so. She loved my dad, and I know she loves me. She likes scuba diving and deep-sea fishing. She works at the aquarium. She's good with people, and she knows me better than my girlfriend knows me." I stop and realize what I just said. "Not like that. I mean, she understands me." I can see an amused smile on Ms. Young's face, but she doesn't laugh out loud. "Julia doesn't know anything about me, and I don't know anything about her except she has a little boy who is about four or five."

"All of this will be taken into consideration," Ms. Young says. "I think you're a very bright young man who has been put into a very terrible set of circumstances at a time when he needs all the love and support that a parent can give him." She rolls in the chair and moves behind the large, cluttered desk. She sets the yellow notepad on the top of a stack of papers and then stands and steps from behind the desk and comes toward me. "You make a strong case for yourself. I can see what Mr. Marshall meant when he called me."

"What did Chuck say about me?" I'm curious and a little worried.

"That you have a good head on your shoulders, which is clear from the way you present yourself and your interests."

"I'll take that as a compliment," I say, not sure if I should or not.

"He meant it as one, certainly."

We talk a little more about things like working on the boat, school, Rachel, and what I want to do when I graduate.

"I'd just like to get my driver's license first," I say, and Ms. Young chuckles at me.

"Good first step," she says.

She stops taking notes, but we continue talking. She fills out some paperwork that says I really am asking to have Maggie as my mom, and then she has me sign it. She guides me back into the hallway and outside into the bright light. I can see Chuck's VW coming up the road.

"Ms. Young, they can't really make me live with Julia, can they?" I ask as Chuck pulls into a parking spot.

"I don't see how that would be in your best interest, but sometimes judges make odd decisions for odd reasons. And the courts have traditionally sided with biological parents in many cases."

My heart misses a beat and drops three inches in my chest.

"However," she continues as we move toward the car, "you make a strong case for yourself. You're well spoken, bright, and aware of the decision you're making. I think you stand a darn good chance of getting what you want."

"What I want is my dad, alive and happy." I don't mean to be so sarcastic, but the words slide out before I can stop them.

"Well then," she says, "I think you stand a darn good chance at the next best thing."

Ms. Young and Chuck shake hands.

"I'll see you Tuesday," she says to both of us.

I climb in the car, and Chuck and I pull onto the street. I feel confused, uncertain, and more scared than I remember being in a very long time.

chapter 10

I spend about an hour telling Maggie about Ms. Young and the interview. Chuck talks about legal stuff, papers that have to be filed, life insurance claims, and junk I neither understand nor want to understand.

While they continue discussing paperwork, I grab the phone and head to my bedroom to call Rachel.

"Hey," she says when she answers.

"Hey," I say.

"You doin' okay?" The concern in her voice is kind of touching, but it worries me, too.

I close my eyes and squeeze them tight, then I sit on the edge of my bed and let my shoulders sag. "Yeah, I guess so."

"Can you get out tonight? Maybe go to Moorehead and see a movie?"

The thought of going to a movie doesn't appeal to me, but the thought of being close to Rachel does. "I don't know. I'll ask." I try to think through the logistics of it. "Except I'm just about broke because I had to buy a pair of shoes for Monday."

"I'll treat." Her offer is more of a plea, and it makes me want to see her even more despite how tired I am.

"I'll ask." I set the phone on the bed and walk into the other room. "Any chance I can be sprung to see a movie tonight in Moorehead?" I look at Maggie as she shifts a pile of papers from in front of her.

"Can I give you an answer in about twenty minutes?" she says without looking up. "I'm in the middle of something, and I can't think too clearly right now."

Boy, I hear ya on that one.

I go back to my room and pick up the phone. "Let me call you back in a little bit, Rach, and I'll let you know."

Rachel sighs. "Okay." She sounds disappointed. "Call me as soon as you know."

I close the door to my room. "Sorry. Things are really crazy and weird right now." Even as I say it, I realize I feel light-headed and shaky. All I've had to eat are those few bites of cereal from breakfast.

"I know, Mike. I just really want to see you, that's all."

"Soon," I say. "I promise."

I hang up the phone and walk into the kitchen in time to see Chuck giving Maggie a hug at the door.

"We'll get it all done, it just takes time." He shuts the door as he leaves, but Maggie stays standing at the doorway like she thinks he might come back in.

"Maggie?"

She turns with a start. "Sorry," she says. "Lost in thought." She moves to the table and gathers up some of the papers. She takes them to her room and then comes back to the kitchen. I stand with the fridge door open, looking but not really seeing anything I want.

"I can fix you a sandwich," Maggie says.

"I don't know what I want. I'm hungry, but I don't feel like eating."

"Me, too," she says.

I shut the fridge and lean against the counter. "I feel empty." The words seem to rattle around in my body, echoing off my skin. "I don't know what I want to eat. I don't know what I want to do. I just want to wake up at some point like six months or a year from now and have all of this be over."

Maggie looks me in the eye. "Some moments I feel like I'm holding together just fine so I can be strong for you. Other moments I feel like I might collapse on the ground and never get up again."

I nod. "How do we do this?"

She shrugs. Big tears slide down her cheeks, and she drops her head, raising a hand to her face. I step in front of her, wrapping my arms around her. I realize how small she is as she moves toward me, resting her head against my shoulder. I tip my head back, trying to keep the tears in my own eyes from falling because I know if I start, I won't stop for a long time.

Maggie and I stand there for what feels like forever. She finally stops gulping air in jagged gasps. She steps back from me, wipes her hands across her face, and lets out a deep sigh.

At that moment my stomach lets loose with an amazing gurgle, and we both allow ourselves to laugh.

"How does pizza at Luigi's sound?" Maggie asks.

My stomach lurches and growls.

"I take that to mean you like the idea?"

"Somebody in there does," I say. A little smile creeps across my face.

We head out in the Subaru, heading up the island about five miles to Luigi's for pizza and root beer. Pepperoni, black olives, mushrooms, and extra cheese arrive at our table, and even though I should be stuffing my face out of hunger, I can only manage a few bites. Maggie pulls the toppings off one at a time and eats them with her fingers. Then she pulls the cheese off in gooey clumps and takes small bites, licking her fingers when she's done. Finally, she nibbles at the crust, working from the small point of the triangle to the crunchy edge, which she folds in half and chews slowly.

"That's weird," I say after watching the entire process.

"You've seen me eat pizza before," Maggie says, smiling lightly.

"I guess I never really paid attention before," I say. "I mean, that's so . . . uh . . . methodical?"

She lets out a laugh. "I guess that's one way of looking at it."

I grab a wide slice and take another bite without thinking about it. Before long I've polished off two pieces, and I start to feel closer to normal, or what I think might be normal. I'm not sure I can tell what that is anymore.

Maggie licks tomato sauce off her fingers and then wipes her hands on a white paper napkin. "Better?"

"Better."

"At some point, when you feel up to it," she says, and I immediately get a knot in my stomach, "we need to talk about a few things. Important things."

"Mom things?"

She nods. "I don't know when the right time is going to be, so I need you to sort of help me out with that."

Next year, I think, but I know that won't fly. "What's wrong with now?"

Maggie looks around. "You sure you're up to it?"

I shrug. "As good a time as any."

She folds her hands on top of the table and looks down at them for a moment. "Mike, this is all new to me." Her voice is low, and she sounds a little nervous.

"Well, that makes two of us." I'm instantly sorry I'm such a smart ass.

Maggie's head jerks up. She looks confused—not mad— just like she isn't sure how to take what I said.

"Sorry." I lower my head because I can't look her in the eye right now.

"This is big, Mike," she says in a serious tone. "I mean, I've never been a mother. The most I've been around kids—other than you, mind you—is at work. And even with you, your dad was there a good part of the time."

I nod.

"This is all new to me, and I don't know the rules. I don't know what the right thing to do is most of the time, and I'm afraid I'm going to make some huge mistakes that wind up hurting you."

My heart speeds up, and I swallow back against that feeling of wanting to run again. "You mean, you don't really want to be my mom." The quiver in my voice gives away my anxiety.

"No," Maggie says, her hand shooting across the table to grab mine. "No, I'm not saying that at all."

Now I'm confused. "So what do you mean?"

"I'm scared, Mike. Terrified. You're a teenage boy, a young man. You're practically grown, and all of a sudden I'm supposed to step in and try to be your mom. It's a big order, and . . . I'm scared to death." She takes a deep breath and holds it a second, then lets the air slowly leak out in a *puh* sound between pursed lips. "All I know is that I love you. I loved your dad, and I really wanted all of us to be a family one day, but it clearly isn't going to be like I had it in my head."

No kidding, I think, but I keep my mouth shut.

Maggie releases my hand. "I guess what I'm trying to say, Mike, is that we've got our work cut out for us. We have to figure out the rules as we go along. We have to figure out how we're going to be a family of two. We have to figure out how we're going to live in the same house together, work out the shower schedule so no one uses too much hot water, decide who's going to take out the garbage. That sort of stuff."

"Where are we going to live?"

Maggie pauses for a minute and thinks. "Where do

you want to live?"

I think for a second. "At my house. Dad's house. But I know that might be weird for you."

"Maybe," she says, "but maybe not. We could do a little rearranging, make it 'our' house. I could sell my place and put the money into fixing up our house the way we want it." She emphasizes the word *our* like I might miss the point.

"Rearrange how?"

"I don't think I could stay in your dad's room." Her body shudders just a bit as she thinks through the idea. "But if you would be willing to move into his room, I'd be okay taking your room."

I let the idea roll around in my head. There is something comforting about the thought of living in my dad's room. "I think I could do that," I say. "But my room is a certified disaster area. It'll take a lot of work to make it suitable for you." I think about the holes in the walls, the broken closet door, and the pervasive scent of stinky guy feet.

"I think I can handle it." Maggie says with a smile.

"I'll have to help. It's my disaster."

She takes a long drink of root beer and then spins the ice cubes around in her glass. They rattle and tinkle as she sets the red plastic glass on the table. "I'll call a realtor next week, then."

I weigh this thought, and I decide it feels good to have resolved where we will live. And it feels good to know Maggie listened to me, and I listened to her.

"There's something else we need to talk about," she says. Her voice is softer, firmer.

"Okay," I say, hesitating just a little.

"Like I said, you're a young man, practically an adult. But we need to talk about Rachel."

I guess I knew this was coming.

"Nothing happened that night," I say, a little too defensively.

Maggie's eyes snap to my face. "Mike, I trust you. Just hear me out for a second."

I hold her stare, trying to read where this might be headed. With Dad I could always stare him down—or at least figure out how deep the crap was that I was in. Maggie gives nothing away. A knot tightens in my throat. My hands begin to sweat.

"Part of me wants to say that it's none of my business, but the fact is, it is my business now."

Sweat trickles down the back of my neck. I rub my palms on my shorts and grab the cool glass of soda to try and calm myself. She looks away for a split second, then stares at me right between the eyes. "Mike, this is a tough time for you. For both of us. I know you're going through a lot of emotions that are painful, confusing, and over-whelming." She is quiet for a moment, but she doesn't look away. "The thing is, running away isn't going to take care of the problem, and right now isn't the time to mak-ing life-changing decisions like having sex with a girl."

"Nothing happened." I say the words slowly. "I swear it."

"And I believe you. Really." Maggie reaches out and takes hold of my hands again. "I want us to be able to talk openly about anything. *Anything*," she says, stressing the word. "That may take time, I know, but Mike, I will never judge you or tell you something that isn't true. I promise you that you can trust me."

I believe that Maggie is being sincere, but the thought of talking about sex with her? Not so much. "I don't know," I say. "That sounds so weird to me."

"I'm sure it does. And I don't expect you're going to jump right in with both feet and start pouring out all your secrets. It will take time. But I just want you to know that I trust you, and that you can trust me."

I nod and then look away. "Really, Maggie, nothing happened between Rachel and me."

"I told you I believe you. I've known you long enough to know when you're lying."

I slouch a little in the stiff chair. "How do you know?"

Maggie smiles. "I just know. Like with your dad. I always knew when he was up to something."

"Did you know about the ring, his trip to Raleigh?"

Maggie draws another deep breath but lets it out quickly. "Nope. That time he got one over on me." She smiles, but it's a sad smile, like her face doesn't want to cooperate.

She isn't wearing the ring.

"Maggie, I'm sorry for being such a brat."

"You're not a brat. You're a great kid in a horrible set of circumstances, and just like me, you're doing the best job you can." Tears sparkle in her eyes, but they don't spill.

"I'm just glad you're willing to be my mom, or my guardian, or—okay," I say, exasperated. "Whatever it is you're going to be, I'm glad you're going to be it."

Maggie chuckles, stands up and brushes crumbs from her shorts, then comes around the table and hugs me. "Me, too."

We box up the rest of Luigi's pizza to take home, not that we need any more food. We drive back to Maggie's house and I'm caught somewhere between relief for how things happened, and some weird kind of guilt. I don't know why or where the feeling comes from, but it keeps me from being able to enjoy the evening. It's an awkward feeling, like having your shoes on the wrong feet and trying to walk. I'm off balance, and I wonder if I'll ever figure out how to straighten it out.

chapter 11

I decide not to go to the movie, and instead, Maggie and I rent movies and hang out eating popcorn with Rocket. The phone rings once in a while, but we check the caller ID and decide not to answer it unless it's Chuck, which it never is.

I sleep at Maggie's for the next few nights, Rocket by my side like a giant stuffed animal. It's comforting to have him next to me, and I'm glad I decided to stay over. I call and check in with Rachel. She is disappointed we don't get together much, but she seems to understand.

Sunday morning I find Maggie drinking coffee at the table and looking over more documents from Chuck.

"Did I wake you?" Maggie asks.

"Rocket woke me. That dog farts something foul."

Maggie smiles, but it's a weak expression that sags as quickly as it rose.

"I have a question about tomorrow," I say.

She looks at me over the top of her mug as I take the chair next to hers.

"I'm supposed to get up and say something."

"If you don't want to—" she says, but I interrupt her.

"It's not that. I do, but I don't know what I'm supposed to say."

Maggie sips her coffee, sets the mug on a white paper napkin, and runs her fingers along the grain of the wooden table. "Say what you need to."

I look at her, waiting for something a little more helpful. "Like what?"

"Whatever it is you need to say." She looks at me as if this is such a simple concept.

"Well, should I talk about him and the boat? Or about him and me?"

Maggie picks up her mug, wrapping both hands around it. I watch a ribbon of steam curl up and away as she looks at me. I wait for something, some clue as to what it is I'm supposed to do. I've been to only one funeral in my life, when I was seven or eight, and I barely remember it. I didn't know the person; it was someone from the docks that Dad knew. I just remember everyone crying, and I didn't understand why.

"If you could tell the people who're going to be there something about your dad, what would be the most important thing for them to know about him?"

I take in this idea and let it float through my brain a second. "That he was an amazing guy because of everything he did for me."

"Then that's what you should say." Maggie swallows a gulp of coffee. "You should tell people about the things Rich did for you, and what that meant to you." She tilts her head from side to side. Her voice sounds strained and tired.

"Okay." I spend most of Sunday in my room at Maggie's, writing and rewriting things about my dad, but what I write sounds stupid, hollow. I ball up sheet after sheet from the legal pad, wadding the wasted words into a sphere and chucking it at the trash can.

Maggie pokes her head in every now and then to make sure I'm all right, to wonder if I'm hungry, to ask if I want to go for a walk with Rocket. I nod or shake my head, saying little.

The day drags. An electrical storm creeps in from the ocean. The sky darkens, and lightning slices through the air, flashing in the corner of my eye as I stare at the blank lines on the legal pad.

Around five o'clock the phone rings. Maggie comes to the door. "It's Rachel," she says, keeping the receiver covered with her hand.

I come to the doorway and take the portable phone from her. "Hello," I say as Maggie heads toward the kitchen.

"How are you?" Rachel asks, and she sounds worried.

"I don't know," I say, and I really don't.

"If you feel up to it, some of us are going to the arcade again. I'd really like to see you."

I think for a moment, but I can tell the idea isn't one that appeals. I'm tired, and my dad's service is tomorrow, and I'm supposed to speak, and I haven't written any-thing. I would rather stay in at the moment. "I don't think tonight is a good night for me," I say.

"Just for a little while?" I can hear the disappointment in her voice.

"I'm sorry," I say. "I just don't want to be around Trevor or Caitlyn or Mandy."

"So you don't want to be around me, either." It's a statement, not a question.

"Rachel, I didn't say that." I'm too tired and too frustrated to start an argument right now. "I don't know how to make you understand. My dad's funeral is in the morning, and I just don't feel like hanging out right now."

"Okay."

I wait for her to throw a tantrum, start a fight, but it doesn't happen. "Look, I have to get through this week. I have to get through tomorrow. I can't think any further than that right now." I toss another ball of wadded paper at the trash.

"It's okay, Mike," Rachel says. "I understand."

I'm not sure if she does or doesn't, but I'm not going to get into it with her right now. "I promise, things will get back to normal soon." I don't know exactly when *soon* is, or even what *normal* is. I just know I can't pretend everything is like it was last week.

"Is there anything I can do?"

I pause. "Not really. I just have to get through the next few days."

"Let me know if you change your mind about tonight. Otherwise, I'll see you tomorrow."

We say goodbye, and I watch the storm roll past my window, a giant bank of clouds crawling over the tops of the pines. Soon the sun breaks through, and I pick up the legal pad and try again.

Maggie knocks on the door. "I've got ham and potato salad if you're hungry."

I'm not really hungry, but I know I need to eat. I shuffle out of my room and plop into a chair. Maggie brings a plate filled with ham and potato salad and sets it in front of me. I shovel a forkful of the salad into my mouth. I don't really notice the taste, like it doesn't have a flavor. I chew for a long time, swallow, and take another bite.

Maggie sits down and picks up a knife and fork. She cuts her slab of ham into small bites, but she doesn't eat, she just pushes the meat around her plate, staring at it as if it were some sort of game.

"Not hungry?" I ask.

She shakes her head.

"Me, neither." I set my fork on my plate and lean my head against my hand, resting an elbow on the edge of the table.

Maggie stares at something in front of her. "I don't know how I'm going to get through tomorrow."

"Me, either."

Her fork clatters against her plate as her head drops into her hands. Her shoulders shake and heave, but she doesn't make a noise.

I want to comfort her, but I don't know how. "It'll be okay," I say, but the words feel false. "It'll be hard, but we'll be there together." That feels better, more true.

Maggie wipes at her face and then rubs her hands on

her sweat pants. Her blue T-shirt is speckled with dark tear stains. "Together," she says. "That's the most important part."

"You don't have to try to be strong for me." I don't know why I say it, but somehow it makes sense. "I can be strong for me." *Time to get it under control. Step up and be a man*, I think.

"Maybe," Maggie says as she sniffs back the last few tears, "I can be strong for you and you can be strong for me, and together we'll be stronger because we have each other to hold on to."

I nod.

"How's the writing going?"

"Not so good."

"Yeah, I saw the pile on the floor."

"Everything I write sounds like crap, like it's fake or something." Frustration rises in my voice and in my chest at the same time.

"You don't have to write anything out beforehand," Maggie says. "You could just speak extemporaneously."

"Say what?"

"Impromptu?"

I stare at her.

"Off the cuff."

I blink. "You mean, just wing it when I get up there?"

She nods.

I don't remember agreeing to do this, and I'm not sure why I haven't taken the outs offered to me so far. The thought of getting up in front of people makes my stomach swim. But the thought of getting up in front of people without knowing what I'm going to say? That makes me feel like I'm being swallowed by a giant wave, getting sucked under and dragged out to sea to drown.

"I'll keep working on it," I say.

Maggie gives me a wilted smile. "Whichever way you chose."

I spend the rest of the night on the bed or in the chair trying to think of something—anything—that I could stand up and say to the people who were coming to say goodbye to my dad. I let the memories flood through me. I try to remember the smell of his aftershave, the way he slid his hat on his head, and how his hair stuck up at gravity-defying angles in the morning. I think about all the things he'd taught me—or tried to teach me—and all the times I'd tuned him out or thought I had better things to do. I miss his voice. I try to listen for him, but either he isn't talking or I can't remember the sound of it right now. Sometime late, I go out into the hallway and grab the phone off the stand. I dial his cell number and wait.

"Hi, this is Captain Rich of the *Mighty Mike*. I can't take your call at the moment, so leave me a message and I'll get right back to you."

There he is: alive and captured electronically. I hang up and call again, and again. Finally, I leave him a message.

"I miss you so much," I say. "I miss you, and I love you."

Rocket pushes his nose through the door and jumps up on the bed beside me. His tail thumps on the blanket, and then he rests his head on my chest as I turn off the phone and sink back onto the pillows. The morning will arrive, and I will stand in front of the people who've come to tell my dad farewell, and I will look like an idiot because I can't figure out one reasonable thing to say about the man who to me was the most awesome guy on the planet. More and more, I wish that I was the one who died.

chapter 12

The morning sun filters through the pines outside the window, as if it has a dimmer switch that someone is slowly turning up. I watch as the dark shadows beyond the glass morph into shapes with meaning. I've only slept about an hour or so, and I lie on the bed, brushing Rocket's fur with my fingers as he snores rhythmically by my side. Sometime in the middle of the night, I gave up trying to write something to say today about Dad, gave up trying to put words to something that I am barely able to understand for myself. I'll just tell Maggie I can't do it. I know she'll understand.

Rocket stretches, his body shuddering as his muscles stretch, then contract, and begin preparing for his day. My hand is covered in his reddish fur that clings to me with static. I try to shake it off, but it flies around briefly and then reattaches to my arm. I chuckle, and Rocket wags his tail, thumping it hard against my leg.

In the kitchen I can hear Maggie moving around and

making coffee. The faucet runs for a moment, then stops. Canisters rattle on the countertop, and I hear the coffee pot clank as she slides it into place. Then I hear her crying, loud sobs that she makes no effort to disguise. I throw my feet over Rocket and to the floor, pull on a pair of jeans and a T-shirt, and open the door to my room.

Maggie is braced against the kitchen counter, her shoulders curled and her head lowered. She wipes her nose on the sleeve of her faded green bathrobe as I step into the kitchen. She doesn't look up as I wrap my arm around her waist.

"What can I do?" I already know the answer, but the words leave my mouth as the only life preserver I can throw.

Maggie stands still, sobs pouring from her small body. A little puddle of tears is forming on the counter as the coffee drips into the glass pot and fills the room with an earthy aroma. She wipes at her eyes with the other sleeve of her robe but never looks up from the counter, never moves from her braced position. Rocket weaves between our legs, his tail wagging into the cupboard where Maggie stores the plastic wrap and foil.

I keep my arm around her, but I don't pull her. I know she'll let me know when she's ready to move. Rocket sits on her bare feet and looks straight ahead as though he were doing his best to protect her—just like I'm doing.

As the last bit of steam hisses its release from the coffeemaker, Maggie draws a long breath and stands up. She wipes her face again as she reaches for a mug from the cupboard above her head. She sets it on the counter and then grabs a second mug.

"Cream and sugar?" she asks.

"Just cream," I say. It's the first time Maggie has ever offered me coffee, but I figure now isn't the best time to make mention of it.

She spoons powdered creamer into each mug and then fills both with the freshly brewed coffee. But she stands firm by the counter, doesn't head for the table, doesn't look at me. She doesn't even push Rocket off her feet or tell him to get out of the way.

I feel disconnected from my skin, like I am moving around and doing things, raising my mug, taking sips of coffee, setting the mug down again, but it's not really me that's doing it. I'm swimming around inside myself, floating in this weird bubble. It's almost like I could close my eyes and everything would just keep happening around me—autopilot Mike.

Maggie finally steps away from the counter and walks to her bedroom like a ghost. The door closes with a soft click. Rocket waits for me to move. I take my cup and walk toward my room. There is a suit hanging in the closet that Chuck helped me pick out in Jacksonville a few days—or years—ago. Time is a confusing, sci-fi kind of thing. My own, personal monkey suit is charcoal gray, with a short-sleeved white shirt. I have a tie, too. It drapes over the shoulder of the jacket, deep blue like the water. Like the day Dad and I took the Robertson charter out.

That feels like months ago, though it's barely a week ago. But so much has changed. The whole world has changed.

I wander down the small hallway to the bathroom and splash a quick shower. I'm not even in there long enough to fog the mirror, so I can see the outer hull of me, searching in the mirror to find the lost part that's swimming inside my skin. I don't make eye contact. I just keep floating on autopilot.

I wrap a towel around my waist and drift down the hallway to my room, plopping onto the edge of the bed. Rocket is sprawled across the middle of it, or I'd stretch out on the blanket myself. There is a hollow place in my solar plexus, like a black hole that threatens to suck me into its darkness. In my mind I hear a voice echoing, "Why? Why? Why?" No answer comes back. The urge to cry swells in my chest, but I fight it down, breathing deep lungfuls of air and sitting straight-backed with the heels of my palms pressed hard into my thighs.

I take the towel from my waist and buff my head with it, running my fingers through to untangle the mess. "The black snarl," as Dad used to call it.

I put on everything except the jacket and tie, then pick up the brush that's on the small desk by the window. My hair is almost dry, and I decide it's good enough. Nobody is really there because of me, anyway. Except Rachel. The thought of her next to me makes me feel lighter for a second. I imagine her warm skin next to mine, the scent of her hair. But then I remember what the rest of my day involves.

In the kitchen I can hear Rocket pacing back and forth, waiting to be fed. I move from my room, find a can of dog food, and feed him. I wash my hands and then make my way to the sofa and turn on the television, clicking through channels without really looking to see what's on. I settle on some sports show. The noise is a distraction.

The clock reads 8:49 A.M. I heard Maggie coordinating with Chuck to be here at 9:15 to drive us over to the funeral home. I wander around and find my coffee mug from earlier, think about pouring another cup, change my mind, and rinse my cup instead. I turn off the coffee-maker and walk toward Maggie's room.

"Do you want more coffee?" I ask through the door.

"No thanks." Her voice is soft and muffled by the barrier.

"I'll turn it off then."

"Okay."

I go back to the sofa and sit down. I hear the door to Maggie's room open.

"You look handsome," Maggie says. She manages a half smile.

She is dressed in a black skirt made of some wrinkly material, a black tank top, and a lacy black sweater. She looks pretty in a sad way.

"You look really nice." I hope it's the right thing to say.

Car tires crunch on the gravel drive. Maggie moves to the door. Rocket starts barking. "Hush, dog," she says. He stands by her side, tail sweeping back and forth. Maggie opens the door. I stand, because I think I'm supposed to.

"Ms. Delaney, I'm so sorry for your loss." An elderly

woman stands in the doorway, a casserole dish in her hands.

"Thank you so kindly, Mrs. Palmer. Please, come in," Maggie says.

The lady squeezes in past Rocket and heads directly to the kitchen where she deposits the dish on the counter. "I can't stay long, but I wanted to bring you some supper for later. I know you won't feel much like fixing things on your own."

She moves back to the door and pauses to give Maggie a big hug.

"I appreciate this very much," Maggie says.

The old lady looks at me. "Young man, your daddy was a fine gentleman, and I know he is right proud of you. I'll be keeping you both in my prayers."

"Thanks," I say, nodding. It's an autopilot move.

As quickly as she came, the lady leaves.

"Volunteer at the aquarium," Maggie says by way of explanation. She shuts the door, and the phone begins to ring.

"I'll get it." I head to the small table near the hallway. "Hello."

Chuck's voice comes over the line. "Hey, Mike, how you holdin' up?"

"Uh, well, you know . . ."

"I'm almost there but wanted to give you guys a call before I just showed up at the door, make sure you were awake and all."

"We got up early." It sounds completely stupid. Why

would Chuck care what time we got up?

Maggie has moved to the kitchen and is rinsing her coffee mug.

"Tell Maggie I'll be there in fifteen."

"Okay." I hang up the phone. "Chuck's on his way," I say.

Maggie is drying the two mugs and returning them to the cabinet. She nods but doesn't say a word. I hear her take a deep breath and let it out in a long rush of air. A tightness cinches my chest because I know she is fighting tears—and now I am, too.

Dad would have known what to say to her. He would have had the words to make her believe everything would work out okay. I can't even make myself believe it. I'm pretty much worthless to her right now.

"You need help with that tie?" Maggie asks. "I know it's not a usual part of your wardrobe."

I head to the bedroom and return with the deep blue tie. It's silk and shimmers like the water on a calm afternoon. I know how to tie it, but I let Maggie do it for me because I think she needs to feel useful.

"There," she says, patting the knot she just slid to my throat. "You look like a right presentable young gentleman."

"Maybe I'll fool a few people," I say.

Maggie smiles a genuine smile. "Not me." She looks up at me, gives me a wink, then wraps her arms around my waist and squeezes me. I hug her just as hard.

We stand in the center of the room like that, hugging each other and not wanting Chuck to show up, not wanting the phone to ring, not wanting any of this to be true.

But the sound of shell-gravel being chewed by tires distracts us from the moment. Maggie pulls away, and I wander to my room to get my jacket.

We ride in silence to the funeral home in Moorehead. Maggie leans her head against the car door and occasionally lets out a sigh. Chuck has his country music station dialed on the radio. I watch the scenery go past the window, marking memories of Dad as we pass. The Food Lion where we did our shopping. The beach turn-off where he taught me to surf. The street to our house. The bridge we drove over nearly every day to get to the docks. All of it I shared with him, and none of it will I ever share with him again. The empty ache flooding my body makes it hard for me to think straight. My brain swims in memories and voices. I try to organize my thoughts, quiet my head. A shooting pain strikes above my left eye, sending a searing shock down my neck.

Chuck pulls the car into the parking lot of the funeral home, and I leap out of the tiny backseat of the VW and run. This morning's coffee leaps out of my stomach, and I spray it across an empty parking space. I try to push the tie out of the way to avoid splash damage. Maggie is by my side in a flash.

"It's okay," she whispers to me, rubbing my shoulders with one hand while she grips my arm firmly with the other.

The air is still and thick. Cicadas buzz in the trees. My head throbs, and I'm afraid I may hurl again.

"Here," says Chuck. He hands me a bottle of water and a yellow paper napkin from Wendy's.

"Take your time. Catch your breath," Maggie says, still holding my arm.

The shade from the trees is minimal, and the sun is pounding down on us. I feel the heat pressing on my skin like a wetsuit. "I can't—" I start to say, but I don't finish.

Sobs boil up from somewhere in my gut, and I can feel the tears rolling down my face. I'm hunched over, staring at asphalt between my feet, crying and sweating and feeling like I want to die. I can hear Maggie trying to comfort me, telling Chuck to get a cool towel from inside, but the noise in my head tries to drown her voice. All I want is to take off running again, get to the boat, and take it out to the water where it is the deepest blue. I want to dive in and let the water wrap around me, let it pull me under. I want to sink into the darkest part where it's cold, silent.

"Let it out," Maggie says. Her voice sneaks into the cracks of my thoughts.

I cry and yell and cry some more. Finally, the wave passes, the pain in my head begins to ease. I wipe my face and my mouth with the napkin. Chuck emerges from the building with a white towel that he hands to Maggie. She wipes my face with it. It's cool, damp.

"Try some water," she says.

I crack the seal on the lid of the bottle and sip. It's lukewarm but better than the bitter taste of bile and acrid coffee.

"You okay?" Chuck asks with genuine concern on his face.

I nod.

"Go ahead, Chuck," Maggie says. "We'll be right behind you."

Chuck heads back into the funeral home. He pauses in the shaded entrance and looks toward us. Maggie waves him in.

"We'll get through this," she says with confidence. "We can both get through this."

"I know." My voice isn't quite as confident as hers. I'm not really sure I believe what either one of us is saying.

chapter 13

The room is already filling with people. I recognize most of them. Jack Sutton from the *Lolly Gag* is sitting about five rows from the front, and Frank, his first mate, is a row behind him. I look around for Rachel, but she isn't here yet. A large table has been centered at the front of the room. It's draped with a white cloth and surrounded by flower arrangements. There are pictures of Dad on the table in frames of all different sizes. Some of them are from Maggie's house that I didn't notice had gone missing. Some are pictures of Dad with people from the community. There is an old photo of me and him on the *Mighty Mike* when I was about eight; Dad used to keep that in his bedroom. Maggie must have gotten it or sent Chuck for it. There is the brass vase that we picked out what feels like a hundred years ago in the middle of the table, big and more heavy looking than I remember.

"I'm so sorry, Mike," says Mrs. Clark. She is an elderly lady that Dad did handyman stuff for. She takes my hand in her soft grip and squeezes. "If I can do anything, just anything, you let me know."

I nod. She releases my hand and starts walking toward Maggie.

"Mike," says a voice behind me. I turn.

"Jayden, man, I'm glad to see you."

He reaches out to shake my hand, but I grab him around the shoulders. He doesn't back off but gives me a firm pat on my back. His hair is slicked back and looks darker than its usual light brown. He is dressed in a black suit with a purple tie that I think I recognize from prom.

"I'm really sorry, man."

I start to say something, but I'm not sure how to respond. "This totally sucks," I finally say. "There are no other words for this." The tears begin to well up in my eyes. "I can't believe he's really gone. I can't believe he's not here." My voice cracks a little.

Jayden looks at his feet. "I don't know what to say."

"You don't have to say anything. I'm just really glad you got here."

Jayden looks up at me. "Rachel here?"

"Not yet," I say. "But she said she's coming." I take a quick look around the room to make sure she hasn't walked in.

Chuck comes up beside me. "We're going to have a little family gathering before the service," he says. "In about five minutes you need to head over that way." He points to a small curtained area just off the main room.

I nod, but I don't know what we could be gathering for.

"So what happens after this?" Jayden asks.

"I think some of the ladies that work with Maggie are fixing lunch at St. John's."

Jayden grimaces. "No, I mean *after* after. Where're you gonna live?"

"Oh," I say. "*That* after." I take a long breath. "I'm gonna live with Maggie in my dad's house." The words sort of hit me as I realize we haven't really made any firm plans, we sort of talked about it over pizza. That would probably be the next step—after today, that is.

Jayden nods. "I guess that makes sense." He looks around. "What about the boat?"

"I have no idea. It hasn't even been a week. We haven't figured everything out yet." My voice comes out a little more harshly than I mean it to. Jayden backs up a step.

"Sorry," he says. He isn't mad. I think he just doesn't know what to say or how to act. *Welcome to my world.*

"No, dude, it's okay. It's just kind of overwhelming to think about it all."

"For sure."

I see Chuck waving me over to the side room. "I guess I have to go do the 'family gathering' thing."

"Yeah. I'll catch up to you after everything, okay?" Jayden grabs hold of my arm. "I'm just really sorry. I'm here for you, okay?" Jayden gives me a smile like I just biffed on my surfboard and I should get up and try again. I try to smile back, but only half my face cooperates. I take a few steps away, then turn and give him a sort of weak wave as I head toward Chuck and Maggie.

"I guess we're all here now," Maggie says to a tall man in a black suit. His thin, gray hair is combed over his mostly bald head. He is skinny, but his face is warm and sincere.

"We'll start with a brief prayer," says the man. I notice he's wearing a name tag from the funeral home: MR. STROUD.

He says a very quick prayer to which we all say "Amen."

"Did you get a copy of the program?" Maggie asks, holding a folded piece of paper out to me. I take the paper. On the front is a picture of a large tree near a river. Inside is a schedule of the service: someone is playing the organ, Chuck is speaking, everyone is supposed to sing a hymn. Then I'm supposed to speak.

"If you'll follow me," says Mr. Stroud. The organ is playing something slow and sedate. We all follow him and take seats in the front row. Mr. Stroud stands at a podium. The microphone squeals as he adjusts it.

I look around for Rachel, but I can't turn all the way around, so I don't know if she made it or not. The room feels chilly, fans spinning overhead and cool air spilling from vents near the floor. My jacket feels hot and binding, and the tie around my neck threatens to choke me. I reach up and hook a finger under the knot to loosen it just a little, and then I undo the top button of my shirt.

"Friends and family of Richard Wilson, we thank you for joining us today to honor and remember Richard and to celebrate his life." Mr. Stroud shuffles some papers on the podium. "Richard Leland Wilson, age forty-five, was called from this life on Wednesday, June 18. He was born and raised in Moorehead, North Carolina, lived briefly in Seattle, Washington, and most recently resided in Atlantic Beach, North Carolina. He was married to Julia Hanson, but later divorced. He is survived by his son Michael and his fiancé Margaret Delaney."

I look at Maggie. Margaret doesn't fit her. The word "fiancée" hits me. She wasn't—isn't—really, but she would have been. She should have been. She has her hands clasped in her lap, her knuckles showing white against the dark fabric of her skirt. Her eyes are glued to Mr. Stroud, her lips pressed together as though she is afraid of saying something inappropriate.

The organ begins playing some song that sounds like it belongs in a church. The organist is a thin woman with silver hair. She gently presses the organ keys. I notice there is no sheet music in front of her, and she plays with her eyes closed as though she can see the music on the inside of her eyelids. When she finishes, Chuck stands and heads to the podium.

"Rich was an amazing guy. He was a hard-working guy, and he expected the best from everyone. But he was fair, and he was funny." Chuck clears his throat and then tips his head back slightly. I can see him struggling to maintain his composure. "I never had a better friend, and I'm sure many of you feel the same way." He grips the edges of the podium as if he is holding it in place. "Rich did everything from his heart. From raising his son," he raises his arm and gestures toward me, "to helping people around town, he approached everything with integrity, with honesty."

I glance to my left. Tears stream down Maggie's cheeks, her eyes glued on Chuck. I put a hand on her arm and can feel her shaking. A burning ache rises in my stomach.

"If Rich believed in something, he believed one hundred percent. He didn't hold anything back. When I told him I wanted to be a lawyer, he believed in me. He helped me get through law school. He helped me get my practice started. Hell, he was my first client." Chuck lets out a heartfelt laugh, and a few people in the room release a laugh, too.

"I always knew that Rich would be there for me if I needed him. He was loyal like a dog—fiercely loyal. You always knew that he had your back, no matter what. It was an honor to know him, and in everything I do, I will continue to strive to be more like him."

Chuck wipes at his face with the back of his hand as he leaves the podium. Mr. Stroud takes his place with a black hymnal in his hand. "Would you please turn to page 173 and join in singing 'Eternal Father, Strong to Save' for our hymn?"

We all sing in disparate voices:

"Eternal Father, strong to save, Whose arm hath bound the restless wave,

Who biddest the mighty ocean deep, Its own appointed limits keep;

Oh, hear us when we cry to Thee, For those in peril on the sea . . ."

After two more verses, we stop. Maggie nudges me, and I realize it's time for me to stand up and say something. I make my way to the front, adjust the microphone, and look out at the faces. The room is filled. I hadn't noticed all these people coming in, but there are at least a hundred, maybe more. So much for the small family gathering. My heart races. I scan the room for Rachel, but all I can see is a blur of people. I spot Maggie, and she looks at me with an encouraging but worried smile.

"I'm supposed to say something great about my dad," I say. My voice echoes in the room. Papers rustle. Someone coughs. "My dad was my best friend. He was everything to me." My throat begins to tighten, but I see Maggie's smile, and I swallow hard. "And he wasn't the greatest at everything. He wasn't perfect. He couldn't make macaroni and cheese without turning it into soup." I smile as I remember all the runny, orange goo that Dad would try to call dinner. "He wasn't good at laundry, either. One time he washed all my white T-shirts with a pair of red shorts and turned everything pink." I laugh a little as a tear slips from the corner of my eye, and I hear laughter from people who would recognize my dad in the story. "But he was great with people. All our charter customers loved him. They came back year after year because he was so good. And all the little old ladies in Moorehead loved him because he could fix their roofs, or their leaky pipes, or their broken hinges on their cupboards." I hear someone sniff. "And people at the dock loved him because he was nice, and he was generous, and he was honest and fair." I look down at the top of the podium. "He loved Maggie a lot. He loved her because she took care of us. He loved her because she made him laugh. He loved her because she loved me. He loved her so much that he was going to marry her, but someone took that away from us."

Now I can't stop the tears from coming. I can't look up, not even at Maggie. I hear people sobbing and sniffing.

"But even though someone took him physically, they can't take away his love. He had so much of it. No one could ever take all that." I step away from the podium and sit next to Maggie again. She pats my leg. The organ begins playing again, something I almost recognize. The tune is full of sadness, but full of hope, too. The silver-haired lady who is playing has her head tipped to one side, eyes closed as though she is in rapture. She finishes with a flourish, then rests her hands in her lap and opens her eyes.

Mr. Stroud stands at the podium again. "The family extends their thanks to those of you who joined us today. You are invited to join the family at St. John's church on Beaufort Street for a reception. God bless you all and drive home safely."

He steps toward us and raises an arm, pointing up the aisle for us to leave. Maggie goes first. I take her hand. Chuck walks behind us. I can hardly see where I'm walking, my eyes are so blurry, and I can barely breathe. We step out of the funeral home into the bright heat of the day. The cicadas are buzzing in the trees like electrical static across wires. I become aware that I am inside the bubble on autopilot again. I know it's hot, and I'm aware of the buzz, but it comes through layers I can't see or feel. Chuck steps ahead of me and unlocks the doors, then he flips the seat forward so I can climb inside the VW.

Across the parking lot, I can see Jayden getting into the driver's seat of a white sedan. His mom climbs into the passenger side. I think about driving the truck with Dad, struggling to coordinate the clutch and the brake and the gas all at once. Inevitably I would let out one or the other too fast, causing us to lurch forward and slam to a halt. Dad would laugh and say, "Ease it out, son," or "Lighten up on it slowly," or some other piece of advice that was, to me, meaningless in my fear and uncoordinated panic.

I watch the white car pull away from the mortuary, signal, and merge onto the main road. Chuck guides the VW out of the lot and into the flow of traffic. A bouncy country tune comes on the radio, and he quickly silences it. Maggie softly cries. I am completely numb.

chapter 14

There is a hushed crowd of people milling around the large gymnasium at St. John's. The floor is marked with basketball court lines, though the baskets are all raised. I sit in a chair at half court at a round table covered in a white paper cloth. At the far end of the room is a kitchen where ladies from their teens to their eighties are fixing trays of food and filling silver pitchers with lemonade mix, water, and ice. We arrived before they were completely set up, and now they scurry like squirrels to get platters and trays onto the long table in the center of the open space.

Jayden sits to my right, Rachel to my left. They talk about Asheville, about Jayd getting his license, about what kind of car he will drive. He tells Rachel that his grandparents may let him buy their Camry, and Rachel says something like it's a good car and gets great mileage. It sounds like I have water in my ear canals.

The smell of fried chicken and fruit salad mingles with the faint scent of antiseptic cleaner that was probably used to mop the floor. Shoes click and squeak on the wooden surface, and muted voices echo off the high ceiling.

Maggie sits one table away, smiling politely at each person who touches her shoulder and offers his or her condolences. Chuck had been sitting next to her, but he's walked off somewhere.

"Mike?" Rachel says, a look of concern furrowing her forehead.

"What?" I say, trying to strain through the bubble to be part of the real world—for a minute, anyway.

"Jayd was saying we should go to a movie later this week. I think it's a great idea."

"Yeah, maybe," I say. I can't think past this second, so I can't make plans for the end of the week.

"We'll just check in later and see," Jayden says. "Maybe you won't feel like it."

I shrug. "I don't know." Because I don't. I don't know how I feel right now.

Jack Sutton walks toward me, barely able to meet my eyes with his own. His hands are shoved into the pockets of a suit that looks like its better years were sometime in the mid '70s. "Mike," he says, extending one hand to me.

I clasp his hand in mine with a firm grip. "Mr. Sutton."

"Son, I'm just so damned sorry. I just can't believe this whole thing." He lets go of my hand and wipes at his brow with a white handkerchief he pulls from a back pocket, then shoves his hand back into the front pocket. "I know this is all so fresh, so I won't bother you with business."

"The boat." I am thinking aloud more than anything.

Jack looks a bit sheepish, but it's no news that the *Mighty Mike* is the envy of many at the dock. She's less than ten years old, has two sport-fishing chairs in the back, and she's thirty feet long. Dad kept her in prime condition, too.

"I don't want you to think I'm trying to take advantage." Jack looks me square in the eye now. "I'd never do that to your dad. He was too good a man for me to try to take advantage."

"I don't know yet what we'll do with it," I say. "I know it's something Maggie and I will have to think about, but we haven't had a chance."

Jack nods. "No rush, son. Just want you to know I'm here to help."

Part of me wants to be angry about Jack asking, but he's a good guy, and he really isn't trying to overstep his boundaries. No doubt it took a lot for him just to say anything. I watch as he walks off. He wipes at his forehead again and then stops at the long table to gulp down a glass of lemonade.

More people mill around the gymnasium, filling plates with food and talking in hushed voices. Every once in a while soft laughter filters through the air, but it quickly dissipates in the heaviness of the business at hand. I only recognize about half the faces, and it amazes me so many people knew my dad. I'm a little annoyed they all seem to want a piece of my dad, like they can lay claim to him somehow, and I want to get up and yell that he was *my* dad, and what gives them the right? But

Maggie's words come back to me. My dad touched a lot of lives, but I can be proud that he was my dad—and no one else gets to have that.

Chuck returns and stands over Maggie, his back to me. Maggie sits up suddenly and looks around the room with panic on her face. I can hear her say, "Get him out of here," and I wonder who "him" is. Then she looks at me.

I look at Maggie, then at Chuck. He motions me to him. "What's wrong?"

Chuck puts an arm around my shoulder as if he's pulling me into a conspiracy against the kitchen ladies. "We might have a small problem . . ." he says. "Julia is here."

Instinctively I look around the room. *Yeah*, I think, *as if you might actually recognize her.*

Maggie grabs my arm and pulls me into the chair next to hers. "You don't have to see her. You don't have to talk to her," she says.

"How do you even know she's here?" I ask.

Chuck clears his throat. "I heard her introduce herself and ask where you were."

Again I look around the room, more crowded now as people from all over the Outer Banks region arrive to mourn my dad. I spot a woman in an emerald green dress with her hair pinned back, another in a beige skirt and brown shirt with long, dark hair. *She could be anyone*, I think. I try to draw a picture of her in my mind, try to visualize how she might look now.

Maggie touches my hand. "If you want to see her, that's up to you. I just don't think it's a good idea today."

My heart speeds up at the fear in Maggie's voice. "Maybe Jayden can drive me home," I say. "Or to your house."

Maggie looks at Chuck, searching his face with her eyes. Chuck looks down at me, his hand still resting on my shoulder. "It's up to you. Nothing's been decided, and we've got the court date. We just have to wait until we can get before a judge tomorrow and start the process."

"But I don't have to see her now, do I?" I can feel the panic rising in my chest and constricting my voice.

Jayden has moved to my left. "Is everything okay?" he asks, as if he somehow should be a part of the plot shaping up at our table.

"I'll explain later." I turn my shoulder to him.

"I heard you say my name. You need me to do something?"

I look at him, his brown hair flopping over one eye. He brushes it away with the sweep of his hand, but it falls back to where it was.

"Maybe, I'm not sure yet," I say. "Give us a second, and I'll fill you in."

Jayd nods and moves back to the other table. I can hear Rachel asking questions, but I look to Maggie instead.

"If you want to go to my house, I'll give you the keys," Maggie says. She digs through her small bag and fishes out the key ring. The keys jangle as she sets them on the table.

I look around the room again. The flood of people ebbs and surges. I feel like I'm on the boat in rough waters. "I think I'll go," I say. I turn in the chair and grab

Jayd by the elbow. "Can you drive me somewhere?"

"Yeah, sure, whatever you need."

"I need to go," I say. "Now. Check with your mom. Make sure it's okay."

"Yeah, okay."

"Can I come?" Rachel looks at me with concern in her eyes.

"I guess."

Jayden comes back to the table and gives me a thumbs up. I push Maggie's keys toward her. "I've got one, remember?"

She gives me an embarrassed smile. "Sorry." She stuffs the keys back into her bag. "I won't be far behind."

Jayden, Rachel, and I get up and head for the other end of the room and a set of wooden doors that lead to escape. I go first, hitting the crash bars a little harder than I mean to. Jayden and Rachel follow. We wind up at the far end of the parking lot.

"So what's up, Captain Mystery?" Jayd asks.

"My mom's here."

"Your who?" Jayd stops in the middle of the asphalt lot filled with cars.

"Julia, the wicked witch of the west. Chuck says she's here, and she's looking for me. I've gotta get out of here." I take a deep breath of the sweltering, humid air. I can't breathe. I yank off the tie and the jacket and drape them over one arm.

"What's she doing here?" Rachel asks.

I start walking, scanning the lot for the white Sable.

"Looking for me. She thinks she's taking me back to Seattle or wherever the hell it is she lives." My footsteps feel heavy on the pavement. I can't see the car anywhere.

"She can't just take you," Jayd says, trying to be the voice of reason. "She can't just pluck you out of your life like a weed."

"She thinks she can," I say. "We've got lawyers and judges and shit like that involved to try and prevent it, but she thinks she can just waltz in and yank me out of my home and haul me off like I'm some freaking bowling trophy or something." I can feel the anger rising in my chest. It bangs on my ribs like a gorilla in a cage, slamming around inside, looking for a way out.

Rachel scurries up behind me, her high heels clicking like an overwound clock. "Wait," she calls.

I stop, spin, and glare at them both for taking so damned much time. "We gotta go," I say, my voice low and loud.

"When are you going to court?" Jayd asks, calm and logical.

"Tomorrow." I turn and resume my stomp through the rows of cars.

"What time?"

"I don't remember right now." My head is pounding; I just want to get away from here as fast as I can.

Jayd jogs up beside me, raises a key ring level, points it at a white car, and presses a button that beeps. The taillights flash, and I head for the passenger door. Cars are still pulling into the lot, though other cars are already leaving. People wander to and fro, getting in and out of vehicles in the parking lot.

I grab the handle and yank the door open. Rachel clicks up behind me. "I left my purse," she says, her voice high pitched and apologetic.

"We'll wait," Jayd says.

I dive into the car, the heat pressing on me like a weight. I leave the door open, hoping for a rogue breeze to blow through. Jayden climbs into the driver's seat. "This is surreal," he says.

"Tell me about it." I drop my head in my hand, my eyes slamming shut.

"What are you going to do?"

"Fight like hell to stay with Maggie."

"How can I help?"

"I don't know. Just get me the hell out of here."

I hear the key slide into the ignition and the engine turn over. Hot air blasts from the dashboard vents, but gradually it grows cooler in the car. Air hits the top of my head and sifts through my hair. I lower my head and let it hit my neck.

Footsteps approach, high heels on pavement. "It took you long enough," I say.

"Ten years too long," comes a woman's voice.

My eyes fly open. I see beige shoes and white legs. I look up. A woman with jet black hair and wearing a pale pink dress stares down at me.

"We need to talk, Michael."

chapter 15

Late one night when I was five years old, my dad picked me up out of my bed and sat me on his knee. I was half asleep and had to struggle against my heavy eyelids to focus on him.

"If you could pick your three favorite toys, what would they be?"

"Choo-choo train," I said, yawning the last word. "Teddy bear, and . . ." I thought for a moment in the dark room. A slash of light leaked beneath my bedroom door. I could hear heavy footsteps down the hall. A door slammed and I jumped, my eyes wide and trying to adjust to the limited light.

"It's okay," Dad said in a comforting voice. "What's number three?"

"Legos."

Dad hugged me close, and I could hear him sniff. He was crying, rocking me softly. Suddenly I became very scared.

"You okay, Daddy?" I asked. I remember putting my hand on his damp cheek, wiping his tears on my pajama top, then wrapping my arms around his neck.

"Little man, this is a tough thing I'm about to tell you. I need your help." His voice cracked slightly at the last word, and in my five-year-old heart, I knew this was serious.

"Okay," I said, trying to sound strong and serious, too.

"Can you get those three favorite toys together and put them in your backpack?"

"But it's nighttime, Daddy." I felt confused and scared, but I wanted to help.

"I know, Mikey, but this is important. Can you do that for me?"

I nodded my head. "Yes."

"I'll turn on your lamp so you can see, okay?" The lamp with the miniature train circling its base switched on. The soft yellow glow hurt my eyes, and I squinted and covered them with my arm. Another door slammed, and I could hear my mom yelling something, her voice climbing higher with each word. I looked at my dad, my eyes still squinting against the light. His eyes were rimmed in red; his face was pale and damp.

"You get your toys in your pack, and I'll be back here in just a second, okay?"

"Don't leave, Daddy." My voice sounded more scared than I wanted it to.

"I'll be right back, little man, I promise." He smiled reassuringly, and I turned to my closet to find my favorite things.

My Legos were in a plastic tub with the lid sealed. I tried to wedge it into the pack, but it was too large for the small opening. I pried at the lid until it finally popped open and dumped the plastic squares and rectangles into the bottom of my pack. I heard something crash, something glass breaking into pieces and scattering. It sounded like it was in the kitchen, so I decided to put on my sneakers so I wouldn't step on a piece of glass if I walked in there. My mom yelled again: loud words, mean words, bad words that I would get my mouth washed out with soap if I said. I didn't completely understand what she said, but I knew she was telling my dad that she was unhappy, that she didn't want to be there, that he made her mad.

I found my bear and my train under my bed and put them in the pack. I had to fold the bear in half to stuff it in and make it fit. Then I sat on the edge of my bed and waited. I listened to my mom yelling. I felt tears welling in my eyes. I was scared, confused, and didn't know what was happening—I just knew that it wasn't good.

Time slowed to a crawl as I waited. Then Dad came in. He had a black bag with woven strap handles. He unzipped it and started taking socks and pajamas out of the top drawer of my dresser. He took T-shirts, underwear, and shorts out of the next drawer, and long pants and jackets from the bottom drawer. He took my other pair of sneakers out of my closet and put them with my clothes. He carefully put them all in the black bag and zipped it closed.

"Where am I going?" I asked, worried. "What did I do?"

"You didn't do anything, little man. You're a great kid, and none of this is because of you." My dad patted my knee, then sat on the bed next to me. "The thing is," Dad said, and his voice sounded so sad it made me start to cry, "the thing is your mom doesn't want me around anymore. She doesn't want to be married to me anymore."

I didn't fully understand, I just knew my dad was unhappy, and I would have given anything to make him happy. I reached over and hugged him, wrapped my arms around his neck tightly. "I still want you to be my daddy."

He rubbed my back and held me close. "I will always be your dad, no matter what." His voice sounded fierce but not scary. Behind me I could hear Julia slamming something into a wall—a chair maybe or a table. I was growing more and more frightened that she would try to hurt my dad.

"So it's time for us to go."

"Go where?" I asked.

Dad pried me off his neck and sat me on his knee. "I think tonight we'll stay in a motel. I'll figure out the rest tomorrow."

"Should I pack my swim trunks?" I asked. Motels always meant swimming pools, and I cheered up a bit thinking we might be headed on a vacation of some sort.

Dad gave me a weak smile. "Yeah, little man, grab your trunks."

I dashed to the dresser and pulled out my swim

trunks. I handed them to my dad, and he stuffed them into the bag. He looked at me with a soft gaze. His eyes looked tired, and his beard was coming back in scratchy stubs on his chin. "Is there anything else you really have to have if we leave?"

Suddenly I got really scared. "You mean, we might not come back?" The thought of leaving my home, my room, my toys, and my friends washed over me like a tidal wave, and fear froze my feet in place. I sucked in deep breaths of air, like I was drowning, and my heart pounded like a drum in my ears.

Dad pulled me close again, rubbing and patting my arms. "It's all going to be okay," he said. "I'm not going to let anything happen to you. I'll get you new toys, I promise."

My heart rate slowed a little, and again Julia smashed something on the floor. I jumped. I heard her screaming, her voice so out of control it sounded like a cartoon. The only words I clearly understood were ". . . ruined my life" and ". . . you wanted him, not me." They struck straight into my heart. A door slammed, and then I couldn't hear her anymore. I looked at Dad, tears spilling down my cheeks.

"Let's go find a nice hotel with a big swimming pool," Dad said, his words cheerful but his voice full of concern and sadness. He wiped the tears from my face with his thumbs. "Would you like that?"

I nodded.

Dad hefted the black bag onto his shoulder. I hoisted my backpack onto mine. Dad stood from the bed and grasped my hand in his. I looked up at him, wanting him to carry me, but he stepped toward the door, so I followed.

He pulled the door open slowly, looking down the bright hallway. I followed him through the door and into the hall, down the stairs to the family room, then into the kitchen. Shards of glass glinted on the floor, a chair was overturned by the table. I held Dad's hand even tighter. He opened the door to the garage. The July heat was trapped in there, and I moved quickly to the car, where I knew it would be cooler soon. Dad closed the door behind us with a soft click. I struggled to open the car door as Dad opened the garage. He pushed the big door slowly above his head. We were sneaking away like burglars in the night.

After he buckled me into my booster seat, Dad climbed into the driver's seat. Then he started the car and began backing into the driveway. He didn't stop the car to close the garage. He just kept backing down the long, cement drive leading away from our house.

As the rear of the car dipped and we pulled onto the street, Julia emerged from the kitchen, arms flailing, yelling loud enough that we could hear her with all the windows closed. The car lurched forward, but Julia dashed to the side of the car and began tugging on the handle. Dad had already clicked the locks shut, but she banged on the window and screamed for him to stop. He hit the brakes, and we jerked to an abrupt stop.

Julia pounded her fists on the window. "Don't you walk out on me," she said in a voice that was almost a growl. "Don't you run away from me."

Dad stepped out of the car, leaning over the top and yelling back. "You said you didn't want me. You said I ruined your life, remember?"

"But what am I supposed to do? How am I supposed to pay bills or take care of the house without you?"

Dad's fist hit the top of the car. I jumped. "Damn it, Jules, I don't know. I can only do so much, and if I have to be mother and father to Mike, then I can't take care of you, too. Get a job. Move back in with your mother, or your sister, or one of the ten guys you're always telling me would die to have you. But leave us alone. Let Mike be happy. Let me be happy."

He got back in the car, slammed the door, and sped away, leaving Julia standing on the lawn in her bare feet and a T-shirt with Donald Duck on the front.

I leaned against the car window and eventually fell asleep. I woke in the morning on a bed in a small hotel room. It didn't feel like Seattle, and it smelled different, too. There were no gulls calling out, no damp air that smelled like the ocean.

Dad was sitting in a chair, his head resting on one hand, his other hand frantically writing something on a piece of paper.

"Where are we?" I asked. He jumped.

"Hey, champ, how'd you sleep?"

I sat up and swung my feet to the edge of the bed. "Okay."

There were dark circles under his eyes, and he still

had on the same jeans and T-shirt from the night before. "Come on over here."

I ran for his arms. He held me, kissed my head, pulled me up, and sat me on his knee. "How about we get some breakfast and then maybe go for a swim later on?"

I nod. "Where are we?"

"Pendleton, Oregon. A long way from home—and a lot closer to happy." He smiled at me, a small but genuine smile, and I began to relax a little. "I'll tell you what: Why don't you watch some cartoons while I grab a quick shower?" He put me on the floor and then turned on the television. He flipped through a few channels until he found something with Scooby Doo. I crawled back onto the bed and listened to the water running in the bathroom. After a few minutes I went to the window and looked outside. Green trees dotted the brown hillside. In the parking lot, I could see our light-blue car, covered in a coat of dust and speckled with dots I guessed were caused by rain.

I stared at the car for a long time, wondering if Julia could find us here. I started to cry. Nothing made any sense. It felt like my head was swimming but my body was standing still. Dad came into the room with a towel wrapped around his waist and his hair dripping water down his shoulders. "You okay there, son?"

I sniffed and tried to sound convincing. "Yeah."

"You ready to get dressed and get some breakfast?"

I wiped my nose on the sleeve of my pajamas. "Yeah," I said again. I turned from the window and looked at my

dad as seriously as my five-year-old face could manage.
"We aren't going to live here, are we?" I didn't really ask;
I made it a statement.

"No, son. We're just here for a few days."

"Where are we going to live?"

"In North Carolina."

I had heard the name before, but I didn't know where
it was. My puzzlement must have shown on my face. Dad
sat on the bed and patted the space next to him. "We have
a long way to go. It's clear across the country, and it will
take us almost a week to drive there."

"What about Mommy? Where will she live?"

"Maybe in Seattle." Dad put his arm around my shoulder. "Maybe she'll move somewhere else."

I thought for a minute about my life without my
mom. I remembered what I'd heard her say the night
before, ". . . ruined my life, . . . you wanted him, not me."
Even as a five-year-old, I knew what she was saying. Even
at five. It wasn't the first time I'd heard her say things like
that. I had always tried to be extra nice, extra helpful, and
on my best behavior when she said things like that. I
would have done anything to make her love me, and even
when I heard her say mean things, I really believed she
loved me deep inside, that maybe her real feelings had
just gotten lost.

Dad pulled open a drawer in the beat-up, hotel dresser. He took out some shorts and a T-shirt for me and laid
them on the bed. "You get dressed while I finish. I'm a
little hungry. How about you?"

I started to take off my pajamas. "Yeah." Really, I wasn't much hungry at all.

We dressed and headed to the restaurant where I got pancakes with a smiley face made of fruit and whipped cream, and Dad got hash browns and eggs with a big slice of ham plus coffee. After breakfast we went swimming, but I couldn't enjoy the water. When dark clouds began to gather, Dad said we had to get out of the pool.

We passed a week this way, though it was a different hotel each night, a different place for breakfast in the morning, and so many fast food places in between that I didn't eat hamburgers for years after we got settled.

But with each day, I felt safer, calmer than the day before, and when we reached Wilmington, North Carolina, I was ready for anything. A few times I got my dad to let me call Julia. She would tell me she didn't want to talk to me because I chose which side I was on, and it wasn't hers. After a time, I didn't want to call her at all, though Dad made me try on holidays.

The years went by, and I honestly never thought about her other than those times when someone would ask where my mother was. I could go for months without thinking of her, and I was fine.

Now she stands over me like a dark shadow, a bad memory that has come back unbidden. She steps away from the door like she expects me to get out of the car and follow her.

"We need to talk," she repeats.

"I've got nothing to say to you," I say. "I don't know

you, and you don't know me."

"This isn't good for either one of us, and you know it. Let's not make things harder than they need to be." Her voice has a fake sweetness to it that grates on my already raw nerves.

"You're the one making them harder. Why don't you just crawl back into your hole and leave me alone? My life is perfectly fine without you."

Jayden reaches over and puts a hand on my arm. "Dude, what do you want me to do?" His voice is low and serious.

"Get me the hell out of here."

"What about Rachel?"

"She'll have to fend for herself."

Julia steps closer again, standing right inside the open door so I can't slam it shut.

Jayden revs the engine.

"You'd better move, lady, because I've got no problem taking you out with this door." I look up at her. Her jaw is clenched, and her feet are firmly planted. There is no sign that she is worried I will knock her over with the car door.

"I swear to God, Julia, you'd better get the hell out of my way."

"You won't go anywhere. You ran off on me before. Not this time."

"I didn't run off on you." The insanity of the remark makes my voice climb higher. "You *told* Dad and me to leave. You said *we* ruined your life."

She looks at me with a severe gaze. "Who told you that lie? Did Rich tell you that?"

I jump out of the car, barely able to keep myself under control. I'm taller than she is by a good four inches, and my shoulders block the sun and cast a shadow on her. "I was there, remember? I heard it from your own mouth."

Every muscle in my body is taut, ready to run. My fists tighten, then release. Despite the rage that seethes inside me, I could never hit her. I remember that night, all the banging and slamming. I remember my dad telling me later when I asked him that she kicked the walls, threw pans and books, and threatened to throw us both down the stairs. I remember being so afraid of that kind of anger that I swore I'd never go there. But here I am. My gift from Julia, my genetic inheritance from her: rage.

Her back is pressed against the door, and I see just the slightest bit of fear in her eyes. But it is the anger that shows most.

"What do you want from me. I was never good enough for you. I was never what you wanted, so why do you care now?"

"I'm your mother." She spits the words at me as if they are poison. "It's my job to take care of you now that Rich is gone."

Jayd revs the engine again, and behind me I hear hushed voices.

"So I'm, what, a trophy? You lost the game ten years ago, and now you want your prize anyway?" A sarcastic laugh leaps out of my throat. "I'm just really a toy to you, aren't I? Just a possession. You don't really love me, you just want something that my dad took away so you can say you won."

She looks me in the eye, her face defiant, obviously unmoved by anything I've said. "You don't understand," she says. "I paid child support all these years. It nearly broke me sometimes."

"Oh, so it's about the money?" I jump into the car and reach behind her for the door handle. "You'd better get the hell out of my way."

Julia stands her ground.

I look at Jayd. "Just go."

"I can't," he says, motioning to the door. "Dude, we can't do this."

Another figure comes to the side of the car. "Mike, you need to head out." It's Chuck, and he's taking Julia by the arm, but she's fighting him.

"I'm calling the police," she yells.

"Julia, you need to step away and let him go," Chuck says. He has her lightly but firmly in his grasp. "This will all be settled in the courts."

Julia spins, wrenching her arm out of his grip. Chuck steps out of the door opening and slams the door shut. Jayd sticks the car in gear and pulls away from the tangle of people who have now surrounded Chuck and Julia.

We speed past the cars in the lot. I see Rachel coming out the front door, but we don't stop. Her head flips as we fly by, a look of shock and confusion on her face.

"Where do you want to go?" Jayd asks when we hit the main road.

"Take me to the marina. I want to go to the boat."

chapter 16

The boat sways and rocks in its moorings, the water lapping against the sides. I climb into the wheelhouse and sit in the captain's chair. Jayd climbs up behind me and flops on the bench seat next to the wheel. The parking lot is almost full, so the marina is almost empty. Most of the boats are out on fishing or sightseeing charters. The *Lolly Gag* bobs gently in the next slip, and the *Cap'n Dan* is a few slots down, shifting with the wake of passing speedboats outside the harbor. Both of them are quiet and dark.

"You okay?" Jayd asks.

"Better." I spin the chair until it faces backward, looking toward the dock and the parking lot beyond. "I can't believe she showed up."

"Weird," Jayden says. "What's her deal?"

"She thinks I'm moving back to Washington with her. She thinks I'm some kind of trophy, some kind of prize she won."

Jayden runs his hand through his hair, leans back, and

spreads his arms wide along the rail behind him. "So how can I help?"

"Just being here is a help. Just getting me out of there."

Jayd lets his head drop back. The faded blue canvas awning is pulled up over the wheelhouse like an artificial sky. It shades the small space from the pressing summer heat. He lets his head rest on the railing, his body sliding out from the bench and under the captain's chair. "So what happens next? Do you really have to leave with her?"

"We have court sometime tomorrow," I say. "I have a lawyer; she's cool. She knows her stuff."

"You have a lawyer? Not Chuck?" Jayd sits up. "Why not Chuck?"

"Too much history," I say, spinning the chair around to face the bow. "He's afraid the judge will think I've been influenced by him because he knew my dad and because he's friends with Maggie." I rest my arms on the cool metal wheel and lay my head on my hands. "My lawyer's name is Ms. Young. I guess she knows Chuck, or she's a friend or something."

Jayd leans toward me, resting his arms on his thighs. "Can I go to court with you?"

"I don't know. I'll ask tonight and let you know." I turn the chair forward. From where I sit, I can look out from the marina to the open water, stretching miles and miles from where we're docked. The sun is high and the air is still. The sky is a blinding blue, and all the clouds from the storms of the past few days have moved along to pester some other part of the South. I want to take the boat out about twenty miles and just drift in the current for a while. I want to feel the rock and sway of being on deep water.

Jayd's cell phone rings, and he pops it out of his pocket and taps it with his fingertip. "Yeah," he says. "Just hang on. It wasn't like that." He moves the phone away from his ear and covers the mouthpiece. "It's Rachel," he says, then hands the phone to me.

I put the phone to my ear. Rachel is shouting something, but I can't understand her. "Rachel," I say loudly into the phone. She stops yelling. "Rachel," I say again, softer than the first time. "I'm sorry. I had to get out of there fast."

"Michael, what happened?" She sounds slightly angry, but mostly worried.

"Julia found me in the parking lot," I say. "She made a scene, tried to get me to go off with her or something."

"Are you okay? Where are you?"

I sigh. "I'm okay. I'm someplace safe." I don't want to let anyone know where I am. I can't take the chance that Julia will find out and come looking for me again.

"But where?" Rachel says. "I want to come and see you."

The sound of her voice is as soft as her skin. My body aches to have her close. "I'm at the boat," I say, figuring Julia doesn't know who Rachel is, so it's probably safe. "But don't tell anyone except Maggie or Chuck."

"Can I see you tonight?" Her voice is gentle, like it was at the house, like when I lay with her.

"I don't know. I want to, but I don't know if it will work." I feel a tightness in my chest, an anxiety about wanting to be with her. I want to feel her skin against mine. I want to touch her and kiss her and smell the soft perfume of her skin.

"Call me and let me know where you will be. Maybe I can come to you."

"Come to the boat," I say. I don't know why. It's the middle of the day and there is almost no privacy on the boat, but I just want her close.

"I'll see if I can get a ride."

We say goodbye, and I hand Jayd his phone.

"Is she coming?" he asks.

"She's trying to find a ride," I say.

"Do you want me to go get her?"

I think about it for a minute. "No, but thanks. I need you here, just in case." But I don't know what I mean by "just in case." Nobody would come over here. I don't think Julia knows where it is or even that we have a boat. Did Dad ever tell her about it? Did she look him up and find out? If she went to the funeral, she might have heard it, but how fast could she find it, and would she even look here?

Jayd looks at me. "Anything to drink on this tub?"

There is a small chance there are some cans of soda down in the galley. "I'll go look," I say. I climb down the ladder to the deck, then the four steps into the cabin. There's a small refrigerator in there that we sometimes put sodas or bottled water in. The power has been off at the boat for almost a week, so I doubt there will be anything cold. I pull it open and find two bottles of water. They are lukewarm, but I guess that's better than nothing—unless I want to walk to the fish market and pay tourist prices for a soda.

I come out of the galley and see Jayd standing at the top of the steps.

"How about I take you to get some food? We'll come back with lunch and hang out for a while."

"Better than this," I say, putting the bottles on the small table next to a big rubber squid lure.

We drive to the closest fast food place and grab burgers and drinks. Back on the boat, I move the squid, mindful of the big hook inside, and we sit at the table. I slide open the small windows to let some air into the cramped space. It smells like fish and cleanser and rubber lures. And it smells like my dad. I take a bite of the hamburger. There is no flavor to anything, but I eat and drink because I need something to do with my hands, to keep myself occupied so I don't have to talk.

Jayd takes slow, small bites from his burger and then pops a few fries into his mouth. He stares at his food and then looks out the little window to the left. The boat is almost still, but I feel nauseated for some reason.

"Mike?" Rachel calls from the dock. "Are you down there?"

I head out of the galley and up to the deck. Rachel is standing on the dock, arms crossed and hugged close to her body. She makes a move to climb onto the boat. "Take your shoes off," I say, looking at the heels she's wearing. "You'll break your neck trying to get on with those."

She slips off the shoes and holds them in one hand. I reach out and take her other hand as she steps over the back onto the cooler, then jumps to the deck. As she lands, the boat begins to sway in the slip. I put my arms around her and pull her close.

"Thanks for coming." A light breeze cools the sweat at the back of my neck. She smells like magnolias and sunlight. Finally she moves a step away from me.

"Let's get out of the sun," she says. We move to the covered part of the deck.

"Are you hungry?" I ask. "There's fries and a burger that I only took one bite out of." I motion down the stairs.

She shakes her head. "What happened?" she asks. "How could she just show up and think you would leave with her?"

I climb up and sit in one of the sailfin chairs that's mounted to the deck. "Chuck's secretary called Julia and told her what happened because she didn't know the situation, so I guess Julia contacted Chuck and told him she was coming to get me."

Rachel drops her shoes with a clatter and climbs into the other chair. Jayden emerges from the galley and stands in the shade in the doorway, sipping from the straw in his drink as he leans against the wall.

"So Julia thinks I'm moving back to Washington with her. We have to go to court tomorrow morning to get Maggie to adopt me and keep Julia from ruining my life."

"Maybe she's not so bad," Jayd says.

I turn backward in the chair, and it groans. "You saw her. She's a nut case," I say. "When I was five years old she told my dad that I ruined her life, that she never wanted me, that I was his fault." My throat tightens around the words as they burst out of my mouth. "We had to bail out in the middle of the night because she was slamming things and throwing things, punching holes in the walls . . ." I can feel the rush of heat and anger in my face.

Jayd's eyes are wide, like he's just stepped on a cottonmouth, and it tried to bite him.

"Mike," Rachel says in a firm voice.

I look at her—her brow is furrowed and her eyes are worried. "Don't you understand? Julia wants me to pack up everything and move to Washington. I'm a trophy that she is trying to win. She doesn't want me there because she loves me—she wants me there because she knows my dad would hate it."

"But you don't really think she's going to be able to just force you to move?" Jayd is leaning on the door frame, his drink in one hand, his free hand stretched above his head and holding the top of the opening.

"She can't force me to do anything," I say, though I'm not completely convinced of this. My head is starting to swim, and I am regretting that one bite of hamburger I managed to swallow. "That's why I have a lawyer. That's why we're going to court tomorrow."

The more my thoughts spin, the more my stomach churns. I leap off the chair and run to the side of the boat, spewing the few bites of food into the water for the harbor fish to find.

Jayd moves beside me, one hand on my shoulder. "You okay?" he asks.

I nod, trying to pull the pieces of my brain together into a solid thought. All I want is to lie down on my bed, in my cool, darkened room, and wake up a few months from now with all of this resolved.

"I need to go home," I say.

We clean up the boat and lock the galley. I decide I'll come back later in the week and pull the boat covers out until I know what to do with it. We drive the fifteen minutes to the house.

"Go slow," I tell Jayden as we get close to the driveway. I look around the bend to see if there are any unfamiliar cars around. No one is there.

I climb the stairs and fish my key ring out of my pocket. "You coming in?" I ask my friends.

"I'd better get home," Jayd says. "My mom doesn't know what's going on."

I nod. Rachel looks at the step she is standing on. "I need to go. I don't have another way home."

"It's okay." I'm disappointed, but I understand. I probably wouldn't be good company, anyway.

"I'll call you later," she says.

"I'll be online later tonight," Jayd says.

A bone-tired ache overtakes my whole body. "Talk to you later then." I put the key in the lock and shut the door behind me.

It's cool and dark in the house. I wander to my room, toss my jacket and tie on the foot of my bed, then lie down. Before I know what's happening, I feel myself rocking on the boat. It's an off-balance, awkward feeling that shifts me from side to side. I can smell the salty mist off the waves, feel it speckle my face with cool droplets. The sun bathes everything in a whitewash of brightness.

"Dad?" I call out. But there is no answer. I climb the ladder to the wheelhouse. No one is there. Beneath the blue canvas awning, I look out across the calm water sparkling like a million pieces of glass shattered on blue silk. The blue of the sky is deep and seems to reach out forever. I feel it pulling me. I climb over the railing on the second level of the boat. The wind picks up and whips around me, the mist shifts into sand that pelts and stings my skin. The boat bobs up and down, leaning farther and farther from one side to the other. I grip the railing in sweaty hands, looking for a way down. The boat dips as the waves swell, then surges back the other way, leaving my stomach in a ball in the pit of my abdomen. Another great swell pushes up, and the water draws open like a gaping mouth. I feel the boat tipping past recovery, so I dive into the churning ocean. The huge wave folds over me, and I sink beneath it, watching the last few rays of light grow dimmer as I drop into the silent, cold, blue ocean.

chapter 17

"Mike."

A cool hand touches my cheek.

"Mike, honey," says a soft voice.

I strain to figure out where I am. I take a deep breath. There is something familiar about the scent. My eyes roll around in their sockets, but the lids refuse to open.

"You need to sit up a little."

It's Maggie's voice instructing me. I try to raise up on my elbows and find that my left arm is pinned beneath my body and totally numb. As I move my torso, prickles of sensation work their way down my arm like a thousand needles. I force my eyes open, but they only move enough for me to see a thin line of a darkened room between my eyelashes.

"There you go. Try to sit up a little more."

Maggie's voice is patient. She sounds like the time she took care of me when I got chicken pox, telling me not to scratch and feeding me bologna sandwiches on Wonder

Bread with mustard and fresh lettuce from her garden. I use my right arm to scoot back against the wall at the head of my bed, then I blink my eyes hard and make them open half way.

"I thought I'd let you sleep a little while, but it's getting late, and we need to head to the house to get ready for tomorrow morning." She brushes a piece of hair from my forehead. "You were dead to the world. I almost started to worry."

I shake my left arm to get the blood flowing. "I didn't mean to fall asleep. I just laid down for a minute." I yawn and stretch my arms in front of me. "What time is it?"

"Seven thirty. I thought you might be getting hungry, so I came to get you."

"How'd you know I was here?"

"Jayden telephoned. He said he dropped you off here and that you were okay."

I swing my feet to the edge of the bed, careful not to knock Maggie to the floor. "I'm sorry. I meant to call, but I guess I just passed out."

Maggie smiles at me. "We're all a bit out of sorts. I'm sure that nap did you a lot of good. I may take one myself after dinner."

"Why not just go to bed?"

"I might at that," she says. "You may need to pack a few things. I don't know what's going to happen tomorrow or the next day, so we'd better be ready." She lets out a quiet sigh.

"I need to switch laundry loads," I say. "I left a load in the other day." I stumble from my room to the laundry closet, take the load from the washer, put it in the dryer, and head back to my room. I grab a few pairs of shorts and some T-shirts, boxers, and my gym shoes. I find an empty duffel bag and shove everything in. "What about tomorrow?" I ask. "What do I wear for that?"

"I'll press your shirt and slacks. The jacket looks like it's still okay." She picks up the jacket and tie from the end of the bed where I put them.

I follow Maggie out the front, making sure to lock the door. The sun is still high in the western sky.

The Subaru glides along the roads leading to Maggie's. We pass the arcade and the strand of trees I ran through during the storm. Everything is so familiar and yet so foreign. We pull into the driveway and head into the house. Rocket barks and begs for attention.

"Hush, dog," Maggie says, but there is little behind her words to convince the dog to settle. He licks my hands and barks again. I let him out in the yard and wait by the door for him to take care of business. As he trots back into the house, he stops to nudge my hand with his nose, as if he's trying to let me know that nothing has changed for us.

I head to my room and change into a pair of shorts and a tank top, or a "muscle shirt" as my dad used to say. He'd usually follow that by commenting about my lack of said muscles. Then he and I would flex our biceps, pestering Maggie to declare one of us the winner of the Best Muscles contest. I smile at the memory even though it's wrapped in sadness.

"Hand those to me," Maggie says, pointing to the pants and shirt I've just shed. I give them to her. She has changed into a long T-shirt that nearly reaches her knees, and I realize it's one that belonged to my dad.

"What time do we need to leave in the morning?" I ask.

Maggie heads to the small laundry room at the back of her little house, and I follow. She plugs in an iron as she drapes the pants across an ironing board she has set up. "We have to be at the court in Jacksonville by ten, so I guess we'll leave by eight forty-five, maybe eight thirty if Chuck feels we need to be there early." She quickly presses each pant leg, flipping the fabric and snapping it into shape.

I can smell the warm, humid scent of freshly pressed cotton. It calms me for some odd reason, like a reminder that Maggie is here for me. Then the familiar knot returns to my gut. "Julia will be there, won't she?"

"I assume so," Maggie says. "I'd guess she has to be." She slides the pants onto a hanger and sets them aside. She maneuvers the shirt onto the board and begins pressing it. "I'm sorry that happened today," she says, never raising her eyes from the task in front of her. "That was a shock to all of us to have her show up unannounced like that."

"Not to me," I say.

Maggie looks at me with an odd expression, one eyebrow arched high, the other tucked low over the socket.

"Nothing Julia says or does could surprise me. She's crazy."

"She's certainly got issues."

"I mean, I think she's really crazy. Like mental issues kind of crazy," I say. Suddenly I am flooded with memories. Julia held a bottle of something in her hand, a small brown bottle. I knew it was medicine, but I was only about four, and I didn't know what kind of medicine it was. She dumped the little pills down the drain in the kitchen, and I could hear the plink and rattle as they fell. Water ran in the sink. She pressed a finger to her lips as she looked at me. "Shh," she said, "don't tell Daddy."

Tell him what? I remember Dad coming home later, finding the empty bottle. Julia told him something about the doctor trusting her to know what's best for her. Dad was mad. He tried to call the doctor, but Julia grabbed the phone from his hands and hurled it across the room.

"What is it, Mike?" Maggie says as she slides the shirt onto another hanger.

"I swear I remember Julia having to be on some kind of medication, but she didn't like it so she told my dad she didn't have to take it anymore."

Maggie looks at me, processing the information. "What was it?"

"I don't remember, but I remember her pouring the pills down the sink and then making me promise not to tell."

"Hmm. You need to tell Ms. Young about that." She takes the clothes on the hangers and puts them in my closet.

I follow her from room to room, and we end up in the kitchen.

"Are you hungry?" Maggie asks.

I notice that the counter is full of plates and pans covered with plastic wrap or foil. Maggie opens the fridge. It is jammed with pies, and hams, and other mysterious foods covered in shiny foil.

"We've got enough to feed everyone in the next three counties," she says.

For the first time today I feel hungry. We fix plates of chicken and potato salad with homemade rolls and coleslaw. We each take a slice of banana cream pie, then sit at the table. I take a few bites and realize I'm starving. I shovel food into my mouth, one bite after another in rapid succession.

"There's plenty more," Maggie says.

I force myself to slow down. Maggie has barely taken a bite of anything. "Not hungry?"

"I ate a bit at the church," she says, but I know she's not being completely honest. "And I think the sight of so much food actually makes me lose my appetite."

"I think it helped me find mine." I bite a hunk of chicken from a leg bone and swallow, pausing to take a drink of water. "Where did it all come from?"

"Ladies from around town, people I work with, folks who knew your dad." She pulls apart a roll and takes a bite of the bottom half, chews slowly, and swallows hard as if the food is resisting her—or she's resisting it.

"You'll be there tomorrow the whole time, right?" I ask.

Maggie nods. "The whole time."

"What about Chuck?"

"I think he'll be there, but it's really up to Ms. Young. Chuck is just there for moral support."

"You think I should tell Ms. Young about the medicine thing?" I take another bite of chicken.

Maggie shrugs. "It's up to you, but it might be important."

We finish eating in silence, then clean up the dishes and put everything away. We sit in front of the television for a while, but neither one of us seems all that interested in what's on. Around ten o'clock, I take Rocket outside.

Crickets are chirping, and I can hear a big toad bellowing off in the distance. Rocket trots around the yard, poking his nose under vegetable leaves, pawing at a frog that leaps and startles him. I wonder if it's fair to Rocket to make him move. There's no grass at our house, no garden, no yard. It's mostly sand and shells, a few splotches of grass, with a couple of squatty oak trees to give shade. Behind that is a private street with another row of houses facing the beach; expensive places owned by people from New York or Illinois or other places I've never been. They try to push the locals farther up the island, but Dad and I have never budged. It's close enough to the beach that you can listen to the surf break against the shore at night. Then again, it's not close to the creek like Maggie's.

Rocket gallops toward me, his nose covered with a smudge of mud. "Goofy dog." We go back into the house. The air is chilly inside, and my arms prickle with goosebumps as I shut the door.

"I think I'm turning in," Maggie says. She wipes the mud from Rocket's nose with her hand and then goes to the sink to wash it off. She heads toward her bedroom but stops at the hallway and looks at me. "It's all going to be okay," Maggie says.

"I know," I say, but there is a familiar tightness in my stomach and chest because I don't really believe anything will ever be okay again.

chapter 18

The boat rocks from side to side and whitecaps crest each passing wave. Gulls hover overhead or land in the water and float through the frothy peaks. The water is dark, and I can't see anything beneath the surface as I lean over the portside edge. I can't find what I'm looking for no matter how hard I try to see.

Rain begins falling in heavy drops that splash as they break the surface of the ocean. I keep staring into the water, looking for it, but it isn't there. The rain gets harder and comes down in pellets that sting as they strike my arms. But I keep looking into the water—I'm certain it's in the water.

The boat rocks harder now, bouncing and twisting in the swells. Beneath the dark waves I can just make out a shape, rising to the surface so slowly that it almost seems as if it isn't moving. The wind whispers around me, pushing and pulling to get my attention, but I am only focused on the shape. I think it's what I'm looking for, but I can't be sure until it gets closer. The boat slides and dips through the churning water. I move around the railing, keeping my eyes glued to the shape that's rising.

I can almost make it out now. It's familiar but not recognizable—not just yet. It's a pearl color, long and thin, with dark hair that shifts and sways with the current of the water.

"Dad," I say, calling out to it. "Dad." I reach my hand out to help him, to pull him from the water. My heart is beating hard because I may be too late, but I know I have to try. "Dad!" He floats faceup in the blue-black water. The boat dips and I reach out to grab him, but I only graze his arm with my fingers. His body spins in the water, and he looks up from beneath the churning surface, his face white and carved by the giant scar that slices from the bridge of his nose to the back of his head.

"No," I say, desperation and anger bubbling to the surface. Tears splash like rain in the water as I strain to reach him and pull him to me.

"Ten years too long," says a voice behind me. I spin and see Julia in a Donald Duck T-shirt. She grabs for my arm, but I turn back to the water.

"Dad," I call again, but already he is slipping beneath the waves. His pale face disappears as the water grows darker and darker around him.

I sit upright in bed, panting and sweating. I look around my room, my eyes adjusting quickly to the absence of light. Through the window I can see the speckle of stars above the pines, but the sky is still black.

I check the clock; its glowing green numbers read 2:35 A.M. Rocket lies across my feet, snoring like a diesel engine. His paws twitch and paddle as he chases something in his sleep. I rub my hand across his side, and his tail wags instinctively.

Worry floods my mind. What if the judge sends me to live with Julia? What if I have to leave Maggie, my friends, Rocket? What will I do with the boat? My head aches with confusion.

I want to lie down and be sucked back into the darkness of sleep, but I am so afraid of my dreams that I resist closing my eyes. I move off the bed and make my way to the kitchen. The refrigerator hums softly as I tug the handle and open the door. The small light is almost blinding. Cool air spills out to the floor and snakes around my feet. I'm not really hungry, but I don't want to fall asleep again. I slip a chicken leg out from under a piece of tinfoil, then grab a bottle of soda that's been shoved to the back.

I hold the chicken leg in my mouth as I set the soda on the counter and open the cupboard to get a glass. Quietly, I twist the cap off the two-liter bottle. The hiss of carbonated pressure sounds as loud as a steam engine in the dark air. Rocket has followed me out of the bedroom in the hope I might let him share in whatever I've pulled out to snack on. He sits by the fridge, his tail sweeping back and forth on the linoleum, looking up at me with longing eyes.

I tug the door open again, and Rocket inches back so

as not to get his nose bumped. A flood of smells mingles together: potato salad, ham, chicken, banana cream pie, baked beans. It's almost overwhelming, though from the looks of it, it's a blissful torture for Rocket. I find another chicken leg, grab a paper napkin, then set both of the chicken pieces on the counter and finish pouring my drink.

Rocket licks his chops as I tear small pieces of meat from the bone for him. He follows me to his bowl as I drop the chunks for him to eat. I grab my snack and sit at the table, nibbling small bites from the chicken and chasing them down with soda.

"Can't sleep?" Maggie says behind me.

I jump, startled at the break in the quiet. I turn to see her leaning against the hallway entrance, a shadow in a white T-shirt, arms folded across her stomach.

"I didn't mean to wake you," I say.

"You were making a lot of noise a little while ago. Is everything okay?"

I yawn and stretch my arms above my head. "Weird dreams. Just stressed, I guess."

"I'm not sleeping so well myself," Maggie says. She opens the fridge and lifts the foil from another dish. "How's the chicken?"

I swallow another bite. "It's okay. A little salty, but Rocket liked his piece."

"Don't give him stuff like that. You'll turn him into a beggar." Her voice isn't serious, and I've seen Maggie feed Rocket leftovers at least a thousand times before.

"If you need something to help you sleep," she says, taking a plate from the sink, "I've got something that would be safe for you to use. It's all natural."

"Will it keep me from having weird dreams?"

"I don't know." She sits in the chair next to mine and pulls a hunk of chicken from the bone. "You're right," she says, licking her fingers, "it's a little salty."

I bite the last sliver of meat off the thick bone, toss it with the napkin in the trash, and sit next to Maggie again. "I can't go with Julia," I say. "I won't leave with her. I'd rather live by myself or be in foster care if I have to."

Maggie looks at me, her face shadowed in the darkness. "She's still your mom, Mike."

"She was never my mom. Not really." The smell of cold chicken begins to turn my stomach a little. "She didn't even want me around. She said that. So why would I want to be with her? I won't do it. I will take the boat and head for somewhere else, disappear if I have to, but I won't go with her—even if the judge says I have to."

Maggie has her elbows propped on the edge of the table. She pulls apart the chicken breast like she pulls apart her pizza: slow and methodical. "Don't worry yourself sick over things you don't have any control over."

"But why don't I have control?" It sounds like a stupid question when I say it, but it is a genuine concern. "It's my life. If I don't have control over it, then who does?"

Rocket moves to my side and sits again, resting his chin on my thigh. He looks up at Maggie hopefully, but Maggie isn't paying any attention to him. She looks thoughtful as she pulls another strip of meat from the bone and chews it slowly. "All we have," she says, then swallows, "is the illusion of control. We make plans, we make choices, we make decisions, but then something comes along and knocks us over and proves that all this planning and choosing and deciding is just for show." She reaches over and takes my glass, gulping the last of my soda. "What you want doesn't always matter," she says, and I can hear the sadness in her voice. "Life gives you what it gives you, and your job is to do the best you can with that. But really, there's just no such thing as having control over it."

Anger boils in my chest, matched by confusion. "Then what's the point?"

"The point is," she says, moving to the sink to throw away the bones and rinse her plate, "the point is that sometimes, just for a little while, you get the smooth, calm waters that let you see twenty feet down. You get the peaceful day, the cloudless sky, the moments that let you breathe so deeply it feels like your lungs might burst."

I'm not sure I'm really understanding any of what Maggie is saying, but for the first time in days, she smiles at something. "These are the things that keep you going, because just one day like that can erase months of all the other garbage." She heads down the hall toward her room, but turns back to me. "You can't control it, and that's what keeps you going. That's the point. You keep going because you don't know when you're going to get one of those amazing days again, but you know you will."

She shuts her door, and I move to the edge of my bed. I want to believe what Maggie says—that there will be other days that feel "amazing," but right now, I feel like I'm being sucked under the waves in the deepest, darkest part of the water—and Julia is waiting for me at the bottom.

* * * *

Chuck arrives at eight thirty sharp. I've had about three hours of sleep, and I don't think Maggie has done much better. We ride in silence to the courthouse. Ms. Young meets us at the steps to the rear entrance of the red-brick building. She has on a navy blue dress with large, gold buttons and wears dark shoes. She offers her broad, friendly smile to us.

"You look like a right respectable young man there." She wraps an arm around my shoulder and holds tight like I might fly away. "Let's get you inside and seated before the opposing counsel arrives." We walk past the white columns into the air-conditioned, two-story building. Ms. Young steers me down a hallway, our footsteps clicking on the tile floors and echoing off the walls. She pulls open a heavy, dark door to reveal a courtroom like you see on television.

A large desk made of dark cherry wood sits on an elevated platform, dominating the space facing us. Behind it are two flags posted like sentries. The desk is fully enclosed, so you can only see the judge's upper body. I can see a microphone arching from the top and the back of a computer monitor. To the left is a smaller desk with a high-backed chair behind it and another slim microphone curving toward the chair. To the right is a third desk, then a railing, and behind that are two rows of seats, like in a movie theater. The courtroom is well lit, and there are lots of benches, like polished wooden church pews, to the left and right of where we stand. It has a musty smell, like a library, but there are no books or shelves.

"You get the front row," Ms. Young says as she motions to a long table at the front of the benches that holds a clear, plastic pitcher of water and low stacks of files and papers. I follow her through a gate in a low fence that separates the rows of seats from the front of the room. She moves to the table, and I stand beside her. Maggie and Chuck sit in the first row behind us.

"Can't they sit with us?" I ask Ms. Young.

She shakes her head. "They have to stay in the spectator seats. But they'll be right here the whole time."

I know she's trying to reassure me, but my gut rolls and shifts like the boat in the storm.

"Now let's go over a few things." Ms. Young slides a chair back for me, and then she grabs a yellow notepad that rests on a manila folder. "The judge and the other lawyer are going to ask you a lot of difficult questions— questions about your father that may sound cruel." She flips a sheet of paper over and scans her notes.

I fold my hands and set my elbows on the armrests of

the chair. They are hard and press against the bones. I shift to one side, then to the other.

"Mrs. Mayers has made some pretty harsh accusations against Mr. Wilson. She accuses him of spousal abuse, kidnapping, and interference with her parental rights."

"She's a lying bi . . ." I catch myself. "She's lying," I say. My heart is pounding hard against my chest. "She's the one who said she never wanted me."

Ms. Young puts a cool hand on my arm. "I wish we'd had more time to prepare you for what may happen today, but we didn't have that luxury. It's critically important that you remain calm, Michael. It doesn't do you any good to get angry, and if you lash out in court, it will hurt your case." She looks down at her notes again but keeps her hand firmly on my arm. "She's likely to say a lot of things today that will sound ridiculous and even dishonest, but we have no control over what she says."

That word *control* leaps out at me. I hear Maggie's tired voice from the dark morning telling me that nothing is in my control. But I'm not comforted by it, I'm terrified.

"She's crazy, you know. She used to have to take medication because she was crazy, but she didn't like it and dumped it down the sink. I watched her do it."

Ms. Young takes her hand from my arm and begins writing. "I don't know that we can introduce that. Do you know what the medication was for?"

I close my eyes.

"Do you know what it was for?" Ms. Young asks again.

My eyelids fly open. "No," I say, "but I remember my

dad saying that it was like she had diabetes or asthma, that she could manage whatever it was if she took the pills." A surge of pain crawls up the back of my neck and pounds against the inside of my head. "He said Julia did better when she followed the instructions and that it was easier for all of us when she did."

"Have you ever heard her use the term bipolar disorder?" Ms. Young asks, scribbling quickly on the pad.

"Maybe. I don't know. It sounds familiar but I'm not sure."

She pulls a set of papers from under the notepad. "We found some information yesterday on that and on another disorder."

The pounding in my head continues, threatening to pop my left eye out of its socket. I turn and look at Maggie. "Do you have any aspirin?"

She digs through her pocketbook and pulls out a small plastic bottle. She pops off the lid and shakes two white tablets into her hand and gives them to me. Ms. Young reaches across the table for the clear pitcher that drips condensation. She takes a small plastic cup and fills it, handing it to me. I choke down the tablets.

"Breathe," Maggie says.

I hate swallowing pills. Big bites of hamburger, huge chunks of Maggie's chicken, I can handle those, but there's something about pills that makes my throat refuse to cooperate. Maggie rubs my shoulder, and I relax a little at her touch.

Ms. Young looks at me squarely. "Let's not pretend this

is going to be easy."

I nod.

"I'm sorry we have to do this so quickly without the time to work with a therapist or a family counselor. I can only imagine the difficulties you've faced over the course of this week." Her voice is firm but genuine in its concern. "If you feel like you need a break, you let me know. If you just need to get up and walk outside, let me know. We'll take whatever time we need today, but there are some important decisions to be made by the judge, and we'll need to get as much of it done as we can today."

The heavy door yawns open, and I turn to see Julia enter with a short, stocky man in a beige suit. Julia smiles at me, but I turn away. Again my pulse speeds up, and my head begins throbbing.

"What if I feel sick?" I ask.

"Tug my sleeve and make a run to the restroom. Halfway down the hall, turn right outside the door."

Ms. Young doesn't laugh, doesn't even seem surprised at the question. Weirdly, that makes me feel better.

An African American woman in a police uniform enters the room along with a blonde lady in a green dress, her arms loaded with file folders and papers. The officer walks around the railing and stands by the smaller desk to the right, where the blonde lady sits and begins shuffling papers. The two women smile and talk in quiet voices with each other. The officer turns and comes toward the table where we are sitting.

"This is *Wilson v. Mayers*?" she asks.

"Custodial rights," Ms. Young says as she nods.

The officer walks back to the blonde lady, then turns and stands up straight. "All rise."

Everyone stands. "First District Court of Onslow County is about to convene. Judge Elizabeth Rudy Crowther presiding."

A small, white-haired woman dressed in a long black robe enters through a door behind the large desk and sits in the big chair. She adjusts the microphone and then looks around the room. "You may be seated." Her voice surprises me. She looks so small, like someone's sweet old granny, but her voice is low and strong, like she could knock you over with a word if it crossed her mind you needed knocking over.

"I understand this is the custody rights case of Mr. Michael R. Wilson. Ms. Young?" Ms. Young stands, resting her long nails on the edge of the table like an eagle about to take off. "You are representing Mr. Wilson in this case." She makes the statement as if Ms. Young herself wasn't aware of why we were here.

"Yes, Your Honor." Ms. Young puts her hand lightly on my shoulder. I look up to see if I'm supposed to stand. She nods to me, so I do.

"I understand also that there is a dispute to the plaintiff's desire for adoption and change in custodial care." The judge looks at the table where Julia and her lawyer are sitting. They both stand at the same time.

"Your Honor, David McIntyre representing Mrs. Julia Hanson Mayers, the plaintiff's mother."

I flinch at the word, and Ms. Young tightens her grip on my shoulder.

"Please be seated." The judge slips on a pair of glasses and begins shuffling through some papers the blonde lady has handed her. "These proceedings are being tape recorded. I will assume there are no objections to that." She looks up from her papers. The two attorneys shake their heads.

"Ms. Young, would you like to begin?"

The judge scribbles on a notepad, flips through the stack of papers, and looks up every once in a while at Ms. Young as she tells the judge about my memories of Julia and my wish to be adopted by Maggie. The beige-clad lawyer next to Julia takes notes, underlining and making marks in loud, scratchy pen strokes. He doesn't look up, doesn't take his eyes off the white, lined paper in front of him.

"Your Honor," Ms. Young says, and she folds her hands on top of the papers on the podium, resting her elbows on the small surface. "My client is an intelligent young man. He is a young man who uses logic in his approach to problem solving. He is not an emotional or over-reactive teen who makes rash and improper choices. He is a thoughtful person who seeks only to have a stable future, a loving future, and the comfortable future he would have had with his father and Miss Delaney if his father had not been so tragically taken from him."

An invisible rope tightens around my middle, pulling the air from my lungs. I fight to draw a deep breath and feel my chest rise and fall as the air slowly escapes through my nostrils.

Damn it, Dad! I feel my chin twitch, so I grit my teeth hard and turn to look at the sweaty attorney and Julia. I focus all my anger, all my hurt on her. It's her fault I'm in this situation. It's her fault we had to leave, had to run away in the night. It's her fault I'm having to sit here and have complete strangers decide my life for me. *Why couldn't she just drop off the planet and disappear?*

Ms. Young sits down next to me as Mr. McIntyre grunts his way out of the chair and waddles to the podium.

"Good morning, Your Honor." He taps the large stack of papers on the podium, and it makes a loud banging sound in the microphone. Then he grabs the mic and forces it to twist and turn, causing it to squeal and whine as he relocates it almost exactly where it was to start.

"Just over ten years ago, Your Honor, Mr. Wilson took his son out of the family home and spirited him away in the night, abandoning my client and preventing her from seeing her child."

"What?" I say aloud without realizing it until it's too late.

"Shh," Ms. Young says. She puts a firm hand on my arm, holding me in place with her grip. I look at her, my eyes wide with disbelief. Mr. McIntyre has turned to look at me. I glare at him, but I stay put.

"Ms. Young?" the judge says.

"Apologies, Your Honor." She looks at me, her eyes warning.

I sit back in my chair, folding my arms across my chest and bracing for the obvious lies that are about to spring out of the lawyer's mouth.

"Over the years," McIntyre continues in his drawling voice, "my client made numerous attempts at contacting her son, but she could never be certain that her messages were received. She was concerned that Mr. Wilson, her ex-husband, was brainwashing her son and turning him against her."

I roll my eyes and try to look back at Maggie. Ms. Young takes hold of my arm again and whispers in my ear, "Keep your eyes straight ahead. Do not make faces, do not roll your eyes, do not look around the courtroom."

I sit up straight, lean forward on my arms, and glue my eyes to a spot on the front of the judge's desk. The wood is darker in one place, and it looks as though an eyeball is peering out from the center of the desk. I fix my stare at that eyeball, daring it to blink before I do.

"As you can see, Your Honor," McIntyre continues, "my client had reason to be concerned about the messages her son was being given."

The eye watches me, and I continue to stare at it as the attorney continues piling on more and more of Julia's crap.

"When Mrs. Mayers remarried, she sent notice to her ex-husband that she would like to have young Mike come for a visit to her new home. Mr. Wilson at first refused the visit, then said it would be all right if certain conditions were met. These conditions were not only unreasonable, they were quite impossible to meet."

Ms. Young taps my shoulder, and I break my staring match with the desk eye. She slides a notepad to me. *Do you remember that?* I nod at her. She writes another note: *What happened?*

I take the pen and try to explain.

Julia wanted me to visit, but I was still in school, and Dad didn't want me to miss two weeks. He asked Julia to come and pick me up when school was out. She said she couldn't afford two tickets, she wanted me to fly by myself. Dad said he wouldn't send me across the country alone. He couldn't take time off to fly with me because he had charter trips. She told him to just forget it, it was too much of a hassle.

Ms. Young nods and writes a few notes in the margins next to my note.

" . . . has paid thousands upon thousands of dollars in child support for a child she was denied seeing for ten years." Mr. McIntyre motions to Julia. "Even with her growing family in Washington, she continued to long for time with the son who had been forcibly taken from her."

Oh, please, I think. *Could this be any more melodramatic?*

McIntyre turns back to the judge. "Your Honor, all my client is asking for is the opportunity to be a mother to her son, an opportunity that was taken away from her by Mr. Wilson. It's a simple request: Allow her to do the job that is her right and her privilege." He picks up the stack of papers and nods to the judge and then sits next to Julia, who has been staring at the judge's desk the whole time.

"Ms. Young," the judge says as she looks over the top of her glasses at me, "is Mr. Wilson prepared to answer a

few questions?" Her voice sounds doubtful, and I'm
embarrassed that I acted so immaturely. I'm worried, too,
because I don't want to do anything that will mess up my
chances to be adopted by Maggie.

"Yes, Your Honor, he is." Ms. Young stands and moves
out of my way. She motions toward the chair on the left
side of the judge's desk. I walk across the empty space
between the podium and the desk. The officer, who has
been standing by the blonde lady this whole time, follows
me to the chair, and I'm afraid I've done something
wrong. I turn to look at her. She holds up her right hand,
palm facing out, and nods at me. I do the same thing.

"Do you swear that the testimony you are about to
give is the truth, the whole truth, and nothing but the
truth, so help you God?"

"Yes," I say, and then I add, "I do."

My heart races as I step up to the desk near the judge,
praying that I don't let my emotions get the better of me.

chapter 19

"Mr. Wilson," the judge says. Her voice booms through the room.

I look up at her, too afraid to say anything.

"I'm going to ask you a few questions, and I want you to tell me in your own words what you think. Is that fair?"

I nod.

"We are tape recording this, remember?" She points in front of me. "Please answer and speak into the microphone."

"Yes, ma'am," I say. My voice seems to echo off the walls of the courtroom. This is not at all what I had imagined was going to happen. I thought the two lawyers would ask me questions, and I would have to talk to them, not the judge. Maybe I watch too much television.

"Mr. Wilson, I'd like you to tell me what you remember about the night you and your dad left home."

"I was asleep," I say, picturing the room in Seattle with the red, yellow, and blue train cars circling their way around my walls. "I heard a lot of banging and yelling."

"Could you tell who was yelling?"

"Yes, ma'am, it was Julia."

The judge looks over the desk at me. "How could you tell?"

"Because," I say, "her voice always got really high pitched and squeally, like a cat when you step on its tail."

I hear a chuckle that dissolves into a cough, and I look back at Maggie. Chuck is sitting next to her, his hand covering his mouth like he has a cold. I feel a little lighter for a moment.

"Did you hear your father yell?" The judge taps a pen on the desktop. The steady tick, tick, tick, is like a bomb getting ready to go off, so I focus on her question and forget Chuck for the moment.

"I only ever heard my dad yell twice in my whole life. Once was that night when we were already in the car and ready to leave. Another time was when he accidentally stepped on a really big hook on our boat, and it went more than an inch into his foot."

The judge's eyes grow wide. "I bet he'd yell," she says, a little smile tugging at the corners of her mouth.

Chuck and Maggie both chuckle softly, maybe remembering the day we drove Dad to the emergency room with a big rubber squid lure hanging off his foot.

"What else do you remember about that night?" The judge's voice is back to serious again. "Was there any violence? Were the police called?"

"Julia was punching holes in the wall, throwing things, screaming at my dad," I say.

"Your Honor . . ." Julia starts to say something, but McIntyre puts a hand on her and tells her to be quiet.

"You'll have your turn, Mrs. Mayers," the judge says without looking up.

"Dad was trying really hard not to scare me," I say. "He tried to make it seem like he and I were going on a trip. He didn't want to make me worry."

"Were you scared?" This time the judge looks right at me.

"A little, at first. Confused. But I knew my dad would never hurt me, so I knew I was going to be okay."

"Did you think your mother might hurt you?"

My heart speeds up, and the words have to fight their way out of my mouth. "Yes, ma'am."

I cast a quick look at Julia. Her eyes are wide, as if I've betrayed her or accused her of being a witch. I look at Maggie. She gives me a soft smile, like she knows how hard this is for me.

"Why were you afraid that she would hurt you?" the judge continues.

"Because she had almost hit me before. And she hit my dad," I say, and a knot slips around my voice and tightens. I swallow and breathe out, trying to force my throat to relax.

The judge raises her eyebrows, but she keeps writing, keeps her eyes on the notepad.

"What did your father tell you about the reason you were leaving?"

"The thing is," I remember him saying, *"the thing is your*

mom doesn't want me around anymore. She doesn't want to be married to me anymore."

"Dad said Julia didn't want to be married to him anymore, that she didn't want him around."

"Did you ever hear her say anything like that?"

"A lot," I say, and the words leap out of my mouth. "She blamed me and my dad for ruining her life. I even heard her say that she never wanted me."

"Your Honor, please." Julia stands up. McIntyre wraps a pudgy set of fingers around her wrist and pulls on her, but Julia holds firm.

"Mrs. Mayers," the judge looks up from her notes, takes off her glasses, and stares at Julia. "I don't want to have to remove you from the courtroom, but I will if you can't control your outbursts. This is a court of law, not a TV talk show. We have rules."

"But Your Honor, it's not fair," Julia says, her voice a pathetic whine. McIntyre stands, putting his ample body between Julia and the judge. He whispers to her, and eventually she sits back down, propping her head in her hands.

Part of me feels triumphant, like finally I get to confront her after all these years. Another part of me is confused.

"Mr. Wilson," Judge Crowther pulls my attention back to her. "Do you actually remember these things, or did your father tell you about them?"

I guess I knew she would ask questions like this one, but I still feel anger burning in my solar plexus. "I remember them," I say. "And Dad never liked to talk about any of it, so he didn't have a chance to brainwash me." I add emphasis to the world *brainwash* so that I make it clear to McIntyre and Julia that I'm not playing their game.

"Did you ever ask about your mother? Ask to see her?"

"When we first left, I asked if I could call home and make sure Julia was okay," I say. "Dad never turned me down. In fact, one time he pulled off the freeway near Indianapolis so I could use a pay phone. He gave me about five bucks in quarters." I laugh remembering how I struggled to hold all the change. "Then when he realized I was too short to put the money in the pay phone, he held me up so I could drop the coins in the slot."

I picture the pay phone at the rest stop, the big trucks pulling in, the greasy smell of the diner mixed with the pungent smell of diesel. I hear Julia's voice as she answers the phone. And I remember her hanging up the second she realized it was me on the other end.

"Did you ask to see her once you settled into your new home?" Judge Crowther asks, leaning toward me on the big desktop.

"I asked once."

"And what did Mr. Wilson have to say?"

"He dialed the phone for me and said that it was okay with him, but that I'd better ask Julia if it was okay."

"And?" The judge looks at me expectantly.

The memory spills out. "When Julia answered the phone, I told her it was me, Mikey. She said, 'Mikey who? I don't know anyone bad enough to be named Mikey.' I tried to explain to her who I was, because I thought maybe she had forgotten me. I was only six or so. So I said, 'It's me Mikey, your little boy who was in your tummy.' Her answer," I pause as the memory floods back to my heart and the tears flood into my eyes, "was 'Oh, you must be that flu bug, that disease I got rid of. Quit calling me.' And then she hung up on me."

Maggie's hands cover her mouth, and I can see the red flesh surrounding her eyes. Julia's head is buried in her hands. I look at the judge. "After that, I stopped asking to see her or even talk to her. One time she asked if I would fly out to see her, but I was only about ten years old, and she wanted me to fly by myself because she said she couldn't afford two tickets. My dad couldn't afford to buy a ticket and take time off work, so Julia told him just to forget it."

The judge finishes writing and sits quietly for a moment, then she looks at me. "I think we should all take a short recess right now."

"All rise," says the lady officer. I head back to my chair.

A few moments later, I stand in the hallway outside the courtroom. Chuck and Ms. Young are talking quietly in a corner. Their faces and gestures are firm and serious. Maggie is standing by a window, looking outside at the gathering clouds. I stand beside her, watching as the sky shifts from a pale blue to a dark, menacing blue-black that is spreading like an ink spill.

"Mike," Maggie says, wrapping an arm around my shoulder, "I'm so very proud of how strong you are."

I lean into her, like Rocket leans on me in the morning. "I'm okay," I say, because I know she is worried. "I'm sure it's gonna get worse."

"Why do you think so?" Maggie asks. She doesn't disagree with me, so it's like she is just comparing notes with me on something inevitable.

"That McIntyre guy is gonna say all kinds of stupid stuff. Julia is gonna say I made it all up. But I didn't. I don't need to make stuff up. She was the crazy one. She wrote all the best material herself."

Maggie sighs. "I feel so sad for her."

"What for?" I ask. I pull away from Maggie to see if she is joking. She isn't.

"What a terrible position to be in, knowing that your own child would rather be raised by anyone else but you."

"It's her own fault," I say. "She's the one who didn't want me to call. She's the one who told me I was a disease." The muscles in the backs of my arms and my shoulders begin to tense, like I want to draw back my arm and punch my fist through a wall. I resist the anger, resist the rage. Those are Julia's qualities, and I don't want anything to do with her.

We stand in silence as the sky outside trembles with distant thunder. Chuck hands an envelope to Ms. Young and then walks toward us. "You're doing great," he says. "Sylvia said she thought you handled everything just right."

I don't feel any relief at hearing this. "It's not her I'm worried about. It's the judge." Every inch of my body prickles like sunburn. I ache, I'm tired, I just want this over with.

"The judge has to keep an open mind until all the evidence is presented." Ms. Young has moved next to Chuck. "She has to play devil's advocate, if you will."

"It feels like she's already made up her mind," I say. "I don't think she likes me."

Ms. Young smiles kindly at me. "It isn't about if she likes you or not. She just has to accept that what you want is what's truly in your best interest. You've done a fine job of showing her that you know your mind and that what you're asking for is not unreasonable."

"But what about that McIntyre guy?" I say. "He's going to try to make me look like I'm an idiot."

"But you're not," Ms. Young says. "So he can try, but if you stay true to what your heart says, as clichéd as that sounds, you'll be just fine."

The bailiff signals us to return to the courtroom. I practically run to my chair to avoid being close to Julia. Ms. Young takes her place next to me.

"All rise," the bailiff says.

The judge enters from the secret room behind the big desk. "You may be seated," she says as she takes her place. "Mr. Wilson, will you please resume your place on the stand." She motions to the chair I had been sitting in before.

I move toward the desk again.

"Let me remind you," the judge says in a serious voice, "that you are still under oath."

I nod to her as I sit. "Ms. Young, are you ready to proceed?"

Ms. Young steps up to the podium and nods at the judge. "Your Honor, I'd like to address the issue of custodial care."

"Proceed," the judge says. She picks up her pen, and I can see it has the pale blue of the University of North Carolina Tar Heels on it.

"Mike," Ms. Young says, "tell me about your dad. How did you two get along?"

I turn to look at her. "He was sort of like my best friend. Except he made me go to bed on time and stuff like that."

She flashes her broad, warm smile at me. "You were close to your dad, weren't you?"

"He was everything to me," I say. The ache in my heart forces a lump to move up my throat. I swallow against it and fight back the tears that threaten in the corners of my eyes again. "He took care of me, he gave up everything for me because he wanted me to be happy and safe."

"And you worked for him, too?"

"I worked *with* him," I said. "He taught me how to run the charters, taught me everything about the boat. He always said I was his partner."

"Did he pay you?" Ms. Young looks at her notes, like I haven't already told her all about this.

"Yeah, he paid me, but he also put a lot of my earnings into my savings account for college."

"How long did your dad and Miss Delaney know each other?"

I think back to when they first met, when I was about nine or ten years old. "Dad used to do a lot of handiwork around Indian Beach, Atlantic Beach, and Salter Path when the tourist season was over. Maggie called him to fix a hole in her roof. He asked her did she mind if he brought his boy and she said no." I look up at Maggie. She looks into my eyes like we are sharing the moment all over again.

"She had this cute puppy," I say, recalling when Rocket and I were both a lot smaller. "I played with the puppy and ate tuna sandwiches this nice lady made while my dad fixed her roof." The lump in my throat is choking the words from me, and I have to swallow hard several times so I can finish. "Maggie gave me crayons to play with and talked to me while Dad finished the work. When he was done, she tried to pay him, but Dad said he owed her more for babysitting than she owed for the roof."

Tears sparkle on Maggie's cheeks, but she keeps looking at me. Thunder grumbles low outside.

"How long did your father and Miss Delaney see each other for?"

"Five years, maybe a little more," I say. "He had gone to buy her an engagement ring when he got in his accident." The empty feeling that surges through my core is cold and draining. I want to put my head down and sleep for just a moment, but I keep my eyes glued to Maggie's.

"Your father intended to marry Miss Delaney?"

"He hadn't picked a date, but knowing Dad, it would have been soon. Once he made up his mind about something, he went to work getting things done."

"How did you feel about his decision?"

An inadvertent chuckle escapes like a cough. "I thought it was about time." I smile at Maggie. "I thought he should have asked her a long time before."

"And why do you think he took so long in asking?" Ms. Young asks. She thumbs through more papers in front of her.

"Because he wanted to be sure," I say. I slow down, unsure if I should add the rest or not. Ms. Young looks up at me and nods. I keep going. "He didn't want to make the same mistake twice. Julia really hurt him, and he didn't want to put me in danger again."

"Michael, how do you feel about Miss Delaney?"

The cold, empty feeling gives way to a spreading warmth. "She's totally the coolest. She's been like a mom to me for almost five years, watching out for me and my dad, taking care of me when I got sick, helping me with homework, talking to me about girls and stuff."

Chuck puts a hand on Maggie. Her head drops, and I can tell she doesn't want me to see her cry.

"Maggie is probably more strict than my dad, too, but I know she loves me—and she loved my dad."

"How did Miss Delaney react when you asked her to be your guardian?"

"I asked her to be my *mom*," I say, then I look at Julia. "Anybody can be a guardian, but not just anybody can be a mom."

"So how did she react to your asking her to be your mom?" Ms. Young looks up from her notes. Her broad smile hasn't faded a bit.

"She was scared, and she said we would both have to learn a lot about how to be a family, but she said she loved me. She said she would love to be my mom."

The thunder pounds against the window like angry fists. It startles everyone in the room, jolting us to attention.

"Michael," Ms. Young says in a firm voice, "why are you so resistant to seeing your real mother and to living with her?"

I knew this one was coming, but still it causes me to flinch. I take in a deep breath while the words organize themselves in my head. "Because this is where I live, this is my home here in North Carolina with the Wolf Pack and the Tar Heels, the beach, the boat. My friends are here," I say, "my life is here. This is where I've grown up and where I want to finish growing up." I look straight at Julia as I finish. "And just because she gave birth to me doesn't make her my 'real' mother. A real mother doesn't call you a disease and tell you to leave her alone."

Julia looks me in the eye, but her lower lip quivers, and I can tell she is afraid of what I'm saying because it's true.

"I believe that's all I have for Mr. Wilson," Ms. Young says.

The judge drops her pen on the desk. "Mr. McIntyre?"

The slime-ball attorney stands and makes his way to the podium as Ms. Young returns to the desk. My stomach folds back on itself and threatens to push what little is down there out onto the desk.

"Michael," Mr. McIntyre begins. He flips to a page on

his white notepad. "I'm so sorry about the loss of your father."

I want to remind him that he never knew my dad so how could he be sorry, but I hold my tongue.

"Do you remember much about living in Seattle?"

"Some," I say. "I remember our house. I remember my bedroom and my friends. I remember driving to the San Juan Islands for vacation and going to see my grandparents once."

"But you were very young when you lived there," he says. "You probably don't remember much about being so young."

"I remember my room had wallpaper with trains on it. I had a lamp with a little red, yellow, and blue train that ran around the bottom. And the drawers of my dresser were painted red, yellow, and blue." I know what he's trying to do, so I want to show him how much detail I do remember. "My friend Jeffy lived two doors down from us. He had red hair and freckles on his nose that his mom called fairy kisses. One time Julia told me I couldn't play with him anymore because Jeffy's mom had said something mean to her, so he couldn't be my friend."

Mr. McIntyre looks at his papers, takes a quick glance at Julia like maybe she forgot to tell him some things, then he flips through the notebook again.

"You say you remember *hearing* your parents fight, but do you ever remember *seeing* them have an argument?"

"Lots of times," I say. "When Julia wouldn't take her medication and they fought, I was standing in the doorway to the kitchen, but the table blocked them from see-ing me. When Julia spent all the money they needed for bills buying clothes and shoes, I was standing at the top of the stairs looking down into the front room."

Mr. McIntyre looks straight at me. "Do you remember this, or is this what Mr. Wilson, your father, told you?"

"I watched them. I remember seeing them." I can hear the slight quiver in my voice, like I'm suddenly four again and I am sitting behind the sofa, hiding from my parents as they fight. I remember Julia throwing something breakable at my dad, and I flinch as I hear it shatter again in my head.

"Your father didn't really want you to have a relation-ship with your mother, did he?"

McIntyre makes this a statement, like everyone in the room knows this to be gospel truth.

"He just didn't want me being hurt over and over," I say. My knee begins bouncing up and down, and I'm try-ing not to blow up at this guy. "He let me call whenever I wanted, but it didn't take long before I didn't want to call anymore."

"But if your father had continued to encourage you, then it stands to reason that your mother would have got-ten over her anger and been able to have a close relation-ship with you."

"So why didn't she call me, then?"

The judge sits up a little straighter, and McIntyre snaps his balding head to look at Ms. Young. She frowns at me, but it seems like if I don't ask a few tough questions myself, no one is ever going to know the truth, how it really happened.

"Mr. Wilson, you will limit your responses to answering the questions posed." The judge has put on her glasses again and is looking over the top of them at me. I half expect her to shake her finger at me and click her tongue in a *tsk, tsk* sound.

"Yes, ma'am," I say, and I try to fake politeness even though I'm so pissed off I could start throwing fists.

McIntyre has moved over to the table next to Julia and is having a whispered conversation with her. He nods his head and waddles back to the podium. Lightning rips past the only window and shoots a flash of light into the far corner of the room. Almost immediately, the window rattles again with thunder that seems to explode inside the courthouse.

"Mr. Wilson," the heavy guy in beige says, then "Mike," in a voice like he thinks the two of us are real buddies, "tell me about the trip you took to the San Juan Islands."

He catches me off guard with this request, so I have to take a minute to search through my memories and find the right ones. "It was summer," I say. I can feel the heat and humidity pressing on me as we loaded suitcases into the car. "We packed everything into the silver car we had and drove to the ferry. I know it wasn't all that far, but I wanted to see the boat, so it felt like it took forever. I remember thinking it was weird that you could drive your car on the boat."

"Do you remember where you went?"

"Orcas Island," I say, "named for the whales."

"And what else do you remember about that trip?"

Pictures shoot through my brain, and I try to grab something to go with them: a memory, an emotion, something to serve as a landmark. I let my eyes close and allow the images to solidify in my mind. "We played on the beach, but there were a lot of pebbles, and they hurt my feet. We drove around the island looking for someplace Julia wanted to go, but we couldn't find it, so we wound up going to a fancy restaurant for dinner instead."

"Were your parents fighting?"

I search deeper into my memory. "I don't think so."

"So there were some good memories in your childhood."

"I didn't say there weren't." My eyes are open now.

"Do you recall visiting your grandparents?"

"Yeah, I remember them. They had a big swing in back of their house, and my grandmother used to bake bread."

"In fact," McIntyre says, "if you stop and think about it, with your amazing memory, there are probably more good memories than bad ones, wouldn't you say?"

"No, I wouldn't say." I look at Ms. Young, wondering how to handle this. She is writing on her notepad. No help to me.

"Out of the five years that you lived with both your mother and your father, you can't recall one moment where you were physically harmed. You had a nice home in the suburbs with your own room, a mother who stayed at home to care for you, and by most measures it was a pic-ture-perfect childhood—until your father stole you away."

"Objection," Ms. Young says, rising in her chair. "Your Honor, that's a big leap in logic."

"Sustained," the judge says. "Mr. McIntyre, the late Mr. Wilson is not on trial today."

"Apologies, Your Honor," McIntyre says, then under his breath, "but perhaps he should be."

"Pardon?" Judge Crowther says.

"Your Honor!" Ms. Young leans hard on the table.

I look at Maggie and Chuck. Maggie is staring at the floor, and Chuck is holding her hand. He whispers some-thing to her that I can only guess at. I'm suddenly jealous, not because Chuck is holding Maggie's hand, but because I'm up here all by myself. I'd give just about anything to have Rachel here, or Jayd, or almost anyone to tell me that it's all going to be okay.

"Mr. McIntyre, do you have anything further for Michael?" The judge taps her pen on her big desk. She reminds me of Mrs. Sanford, my eighth grade English teacher, with her white hair and soft face but a voice as serious as a 911 operator.

"Just a few questions, Your Honor."

I shift my focus to the bald guy again. Sweat runs down the side of his face, and he rubs at it with his jacket sleeve. I shift my weight in the chair and lean for-ward. *Bring it,* I think. I stare at him.

"When your father took you away in the car that night . . ."

"He saved my life, and probably his," I interrupt before he can finish.

Ms. Young gives me a look of warning, but I don't care.

"Is that what he told you?"

"It's what I *know*. He didn't talk about it much, but there was life with Julia, and life after Julia, and the life after was a million times better."

"Were you aware that your mother hired a private investigator to find you?"

"I knew she tracked down our address a few years ago so she could send me a picture of her new kid."

"Were you aware that she spent thousands of dollars just to send you that picture?"

"Then why couldn't she spend thousands of dollars to come and see me herself?"

McIntyre looks a little flustered at this, but he keeps going.

"She spent thousands of dollars of her own money to locate you, to try and have a relationship with you."

I pause for a second. "You mean she spent thousands of her new husband's dollars to try and make up for those lost years."

"But were you aware that she had spent . . ."

"No, I wasn't, and why does the money even matter? If it was my dad, he would have spent everything he had, and he would have come himself instead of hiring some second-rate rent-a-cop to find me." The anger that races through my veins makes me clench my hands in fists, and I can feel the muscles across my shoulders pull tight.

"Mr. Wilson . . ." Judge Crowther says, turning to face me.

My skin is hot, and my heart pounds in my brain.

"I have nothing further, Your Honor." McIntyre stacks the papers in front of him and heads back to the chair next to Julia's.

"Take your seat, Mr. Wilson." The judge sounds tired. "We will adjourn for lunch and resume at," she looks at a watch on her wrist, "1:45 this afternoon."

"All rise," the bailiff says. We do. "This court is now recessed to reconvene at 1:45 P.M."

The judge leaves through the door behind her desk. The blonde woman and the bailiff follow. I make a beeline for Maggie. My heart pounds like a jackhammer, and I feel the urge to bolt down the hall, out the door, and into the gathering storm.

chapter 20

Ms. Young wraps an arm around my shoulder again. She puts her body between me and the aisle that leads to the only other door, out of the courtroom. We stand that way until we see Julia and McIntyre leave.

"Mike," Ms. Young says, grabbing my shoulders and turning me toward her, "I know this is difficult. I know you're angry." She grips my shoulders so tight I can feel her thumbs dig into the flesh under my collarbones. "But you have got to get your emotions under control."

"This guy is a jerk. Julia's fed him a string of bullshit that stretches across the entire country."

"And he's going to use your emotions against you, tell the judge that you've been lied to, and that your hostility is a result of being raised by an angry, vengeful father."

An invisible strap tightens around my chest, and I suck in air and try to fill my lungs.

"If you are not careful," Ms. Young continues, "you'll cost yourself severely, and you'll wind up with the opposite result from what you want." Her face is serious, and her eyes are fixed on a spot in the middle of my forehead like she is trying to drill the words into my brain. "Do you understand what I'm telling you?"

I nod. She drops her hands from my shoulders. "Let's wait here while Mr. Marshall pulls up the car, so we can be certain that Mrs. Mayers is not waiting in the hallway."

Maggie takes my hand in both of hers and turns me toward her. Her hands are like ice. "You did a great job," she whispers.

"I'm tired," I say. "I just want to go home and crawl in my bed and sleep until Christmas."

Maggie squeezes my hand. "It'll be over soon," she says. Her voice sounds as tired as mine.

Ms. Young backs into the aisle and leads the way to the door. She pushes it open with one hand; her long, polished nails click on the wooden surface, and she peeks outside to see if it's safe for us to leave. She motions for us to follow. The humid air outside wraps around me, sucking the energy from me and making me even more tired.

Chuck pulls up, and Maggie and I climb into the backseat of the VW. We wait while Ms. Young slides into her white Oldsmobile Cutlass, and then we follow her onto the street. My eyelids slam shut and I lean back into the corner, resting my head against the cool glass of the window. Chuck and Maggie talk in hushed voices I pay no attention to. An image of Rachel forms in my head, her thin body next to mine, her soft skin against my fingertips. I can smell her hair, sweet and clean like the air after a summer storm. I can hear her breathing quietly and feel the warmth of her against my chest. My whole body aches to be there, next to her, the rest of the world fading away into blackness. I want to call her, to hear her voice.

The Volkswagen jolts and bounces over a speedbump, and I open my eyes to see that we've pulled into the parking lot of Smithfield Barbeque. My stomach churns, and I can't tell if I'm nauseated or hungry, or both. I feel like I'm trapped in the bubble again, moving in slow motion, isolated from reality. I follow Maggie and Chuck into the restaurant, where Ms. Young is placing her order at the counter. I'm floating, not really moving under my own power. I'm trying to think about Rachel, but all I can see now is Julia: her face drawn, her lower lip quivering—not because she regrets what she said, but because I remember. I *remember*!

I give my order to the pimple-faced guy behind the counter, take my soda, and follow Chuck to a table where Ms. Young is sitting. They begin talking about what will happen next, but I don't care anymore. I just want to go home and sleep. I want to go home and call Rachel and Jayd. I close my eyes again and prop up my head in my hands. People talk, trays clatter, kids cry—but all the noises sound like they're wrapped in a towel before it reaches me.

"Mike?"

I look up from between my hands.

Maggie looks at me, her face twisted with concern. "You okay, hon?"

I want to scream about how NOT okay I am, but I nod instead because I'm too tired to yell.

"Are you going to eat?" she asks.

I look down at the plate of shredded pork and hush puppies she pushes toward me. I grab a fork and take a bite, but I can't taste anything. I chew because I know I'm supposed to. I swallow because I know I'm supposed to. Dad loved North Carolina barbeque because its tangy vinegar-based sauce appealed to him more than the sweet tomato-sauce type. He once spent hours roasting a pig in Maggie's backyard, telling me in great detail about all the differences between North Carolina barbeque and every other kind of barbeque. I was so bored then, and now I'd give anything to have him explain it to me again. I swallow to fight the ball rising in my throat, but water floods my eyes despite my efforts. *God, I miss my dad.*

Chuck puts a firm hand on my shoulder, squeezes, then takes a sip of his iced tea. Ms. Young continues eating as if nothing is more important in the world—or maybe because eating is how she deals with stress. I don't know. I don't care.

Maggie reaches across the table and puts her hand on mine. "What can I do?" she asks, and she is so sincere and so kind that the tears work their way out of my eyes and spill on my plate.

I shrug. "I'm just so tired, and I miss my dad so much." My voice is strained, and it doesn't sound like me at all. "I want to go home."

Maggie moves her hand away and looks at Chuck.

The dark circles under her eyes remind me for a second that I am not the only person who's having a hard time, even though it feels that way most of the time.

Ms. Young slides a notepad toward me. "Flip to the back page for me," she says. "Draw me a map, a schematic of the home you lived in with Mrs. Mayers and your father." She tosses a pen to me and goes back to eating coleslaw. I draw a rectangle for the first floor. I think about my ninth grade drafting teacher, Mr. Craighead, and I make the hash marks for doorways, half-circles for chairs, squares for tables and other furniture. I label each item: a small circle for the ugly green lamp, a rectangle with curved ends for the sofa. I draw a separate rectangle for the upper level, with an accordion shape to show where the stairs were. I separate the rooms with double lines, draw in the furniture for my bedroom, Dad and Julia's room, the bathroom. It feels like it's too small, but it seemed so big to me back then. I add a few details, like where the yard was, the garage, the long driveway, and the edge of the street. After a few minutes, I push the pad back across the table.

Thunder rumbles again. Ms. Young finally looks up from her lunch. "The worst is over," she says. "The rest is up to Mrs. Mayers and Mr. McIntyre."

Her words seem empty. I still have to sit there and listen to the crazy woman lie about my dad and what happened and whether or not I can remember what a bitch she was. I still have to listen to the sweaty attorney who put my dad on trial when he's not here to defend himself, and it's been made very clear to me that I'll get in trouble if I try to defend him.

I pick up my soda and take a few swallows of the cool, sugary drink. It tastes gross, and I nearly gag.

There is a flash of white light outside followed by the crack of thunder, and giant drops of rain begin to pelt the windows. The rain turns to hail that sounds like God is throwing marbles against the glass.

Ms. Young wipes her mouth with a paper napkin, balls it up, then tosses it on her cleaned plate. She glances at her shiny, gold wristwatch. "We still have about forty-five minutes before court begins again. We should leave sooner, though, to be sure we get there before Mrs. Mayers and Mr. McIntyre." She pushes back her chair a little, folds her hands on the table, and looks across at Chuck. "If it were up to me," she says, "I'd go for the attack on the father and the regretful mother act."

Chuck nods. "What do you plan for cross?"

"Diagnosis questions, medication questions. I'll ask her why, if she knew where her son was, she didn't come looking sooner."

"But won't Mr. McIntyre ask her that?" Maggie asks. "Isn't he trying to show that she tried to find her son?"

"He is, but he isn't being specific, so I'll press for answers. I doubt she'll have any details to offer. She'll say something to the effect that she tried many times, or that she tried and was turned away by Mr. Wilson. I'll ask her for specific details about when, how many times, who she hired." Ms. Young gives a slight grin. "She won't be able to provide verifiable information, and she'll say she can't remember important details like names and dates."

"What do I do?" I say from inside my bubble.

"Nothing. And I mean nothing." Ms. Young turns to me. "You are going to have to sit on your hands and keep your feelings under wraps, or you'll be asked to leave the courtroom."

Chuck puts a hand on my shoulder again. "McIntyre is going to say that your dad kept you away from your mother. He's going to say that Rich lied to you about her, planted these memories in your head about how bad she was."

"But that's crap. He never did that. I remember all of that stuff actually happening. I remember her saying all those things."

"No one here doubts that," says Chuck.

A desperate sort of feeling begins surging in my chest again: the feeling that I can't get enough air in my lungs, like I'm drowning and the water is pressing on me and pulling me under.

The rain continues to beat on the windows. The greasy smell of barbeque and deep-fried hush puppies is making my stomach fold up like origami. I look at Ms. Young. "If they're going to crucify my dad and say I'm an idiot, can't we just tell the judge she's crazy?"

"We still have a few special tricks up our sleeve," Ms. Young says. She looks at Chuck, and a faint twitch flickers at the corners of her mouth.

"Like what?" I ask.

"It's best you don't know right now. It makes the information more valuable and more powerful that way." Ms. Young breaks into a full smile now. "But when the time comes and we use the information, you'll understand why we couldn't tell you."

Chuck smiles, Maggie smiles—everyone but me is in on this. I am not happy at the concept that they are keeping secrets from me, but it would take more energy than I have to make an issue of it. A blast of thunder causes all of us to jump. Maggie gives a nervous giggle. A spot behind my left eye begins to throb, and I feel my stomach rolling and churning. I fight the urge to puke all over the table.

"Can we go yet?" I ask.

Ms. Young checks her watch. "Let's head out."

chapter 21

Things go pretty much as Ms. Young predicted. McIntyre blasts away at Dad, asking Julia crap like "How bad did he treat you?" and "How devastated were you when they left?" Julie gives the expected answers. She cries fake tears and tries to look pathetic and heartbroken. But I can see what she's doing. I can see through the act, and underneath I know she is smiling, thinking she is winning. Anger and nausea duke it out in my gut, each one slugging away at the other for dominance. Acid rises in the back of my throat, and there are a few times I think I might hurl all over the slick tabletop.

But I keep it together. I realize that if I give in, if I call Julia a liar, a lunatic, and all the other names running through my head, I'll tip my hand; I'll help her win. I watch her sitting in the chair and realize, with a little bit of shock and a lot of horror, that I sort of look like her. Everyone has always said I look just like my dad, but they never saw Julia to compare me to. Her hair is dark, too, but it's her mouth where I see it. My eyes, my cheeks, my jaw, that's all my dad. But the mouth and nose on her face are what I look at every day in the mirror.

After about an hour of listening to McIntyre blather on about what a jerk Dad was and about all the wonderful things Julia has done in her life since Dad and I left, McIntyre finally says, "Nothing further, Your Honor."

Ms. Young is slow to rise. She flips through notes on her legal pad, scanning them as if she might have nothing to say. Eventually she stands, makes her way to the podium in the center of the room, folds her pudgy fingers over the legal pad, and turns her head to Julia.

"Mrs. Mayers, why did it take you so long to attempt to reconnect with your son?"

"At first," Julia says, "I didn't have the funds to hire someone to track them down. When I finally did have the money, it was more difficult to find them because they had moved a few times."

I knew this was a lie. After the drive to North Carolina, we lived in one apartment in Wilmington before Dad bought the house in Atlantic Beach. We have lived in that same house for almost nine years, so it's not like we were that hard to track down.

"Did you hire a private detective?"

"Yes, I did. Two of them, actually."

"And who were they?" Ms. Young leans on the podium and looks right at Julia.

"I don't recall their names right now."

Just like Ms. Young said at lunch.

"And when did you hire each of them?"

Julia's eyes roll up to the ceiling. "The first one was about six years ago, after I married my second husband. He didn't have any luck tracking them down. About a year later I hired another one, and he found the address in North Carolina for me."

"But you don't recall their names or the dates you hired them?"

"I'm sure," Julia said, a smirk forming on her lips, "I have it at home somewhere."

"Mrs. Mayers," Ms. Young says in a voice that practically drips with sugar, "have you ever heard the term 'borderline personality disorder'?"

Julia blinks quickly, but her face doesn't change. "I'm sure I've heard it somewhere before."

"Have you heard it in any way applied to you?" Ms. Young's voice is still sweet and gentle.

"Absolutely not," Julia says, mimicking the sugary tone of Ms. Young.

"Could you explain to me, then," Ms. Young says, producing a few sheets of stapled paper from under the notepad with all the flair of a TV legal show, "why the Seattle Office of Child and Family Welfare ordered you to seek therapy and take medication for a diagnosis of borderline personality disorder ten years ago before they would grant you the opportunity to visit with your son without your ex-husband being present?" Julia hands the paper to the bailiff, who looks at it and hands it to the judge.

Julia's face doesn't flinch. "It was a misdiagnosis, one which I fought against for the next five years."

"I thought you just said you weren't aware of this diagnosis as it applied to you personally."

"It didn't," Julia says, her voice calm. "I was previously diagnosed with anxiety and depression, both of which I was treated for as part of postpartum depression after Michael was born."

"And for which you continued taking medication even up to the time that your ex-husband left and removed Michael from the home?"

"Yes, until Richard stole Michael from me."

"Only, you weren't actually taking the medication. Michael watched you dump it down the sink on at least one occasion."

"He was just a little kid. His memory is confused by the lies his father told him for so many years."

Ms. Young tears out the drawing I made at lunchtime and hands it to the bailiff, who hands it to the judge. The judge looks it over, then looks at Ms. Young and nods.

"Mrs. Mayers," Ms. Young says, "do you recognize this?" She hands the drawing to Julia, who takes it as if Ms. Young were handing her a snake.

"It's the floor plan to the home we lived in when Michael was very small."

"Would you say, then, that it's a fairly accurate representation?"

"Not to scale, maybe, but yes, fairly accurate."

"Detailed?"

Julia looks. She studies it.

I even drew in her bay window with the house plants and my toy chest in the closet of my room.

"Very detailed," Julia says, her voice faint as if she realizes she has been caught.

"Would you be surprised to know that Michael drew this from memory during our lunch break?"

Julia doesn't respond.

"Mrs. Mayers, does that surprise you?" Ms. Young says more emphatically this time.

"I haven't seen my son in more than ten years. I don't know him well enough to be surprised."

"But you're certain he can't have a good memory, that he can't remember you pouring medication into the sink."

"His father told him that so he would hate me." There is a hiss in Julia's voice, and I know she is frustrated at having been caught.

"Is that how you explain all the negative memories your son has of you?" Ms. Young says.

"Objection, Your Honor," Mr. McIntyre says.

"Sustained," the judge says. "Ms. Young, please continue without leading the witness." It's a warning, not a polite request.

"Let me rephrase the question," Ms. Young says. "Why is it that your son can recall pleasant memories with detail, but those that are not so flattering to you are lies implanted by his father?'

"Objection," McIntyre says again, almost yelling at the judge.

"Overruled," the judge replies. "Mrs. Mayer, answer the question."

Julia looks at her lawyer, her eyes reflect just a hint of panic. "I'm not a psychologist. I can't answer that."

"Would you agree that it is reasonable, then," continues Ms. Young in her syrupy sweet voice, "that some of those unflattering memories might just be true?"

"If you're asking me was I a perfect mother, then the answer is no. But I was not the monster I'm being made out to be." There is fear and frustration welling up in Julia. You can hear it in her voice, see it at the corners of her eyes.

Ms. Young walks to her briefcase and sets it on the table next to me. She flips the latches open and reaches inside, then pulls out a small tape recorder, which she carries to the podium.

"Your Honor," Mr. McIntyre says, "may I inquire as to what nonsense Ms. Young is preparing for?"

"It's in the disclosure I faxed to you yesterday, Mr. McIntyre," Ms. Young says. "If you'll look on page five, you'll see it there." She takes another set of stapled papers from under the legal pad and hands them to the bailiff. "Transcripts," she says.

The bailiff nods, walks the papers to the judge, and returns to her post by the blonde woman whose fingers are flying over some sort of typewriter.

The judge nods and sets the papers on her desk. "Proceed, Ms. Young."

Ms. Young looks at Julia, who is sitting up straight in

defiance of her frustration. "Do you recall a phone call placed on or about July 12, nine years ago?"

"I'm sure I don't," Julia says.

"Do you recall referring to your son Michael as a," she looks at her notes, then back at Julia, 'parasite who can't be far enough away'?"

"I would never refer to Michael like that."

From the corner of my eye I see McIntyre squirm in his chair as he flips through a stack of white paper.

Ms. Young switches on the small recorder, and it crackles to life in the microphone. There is a beep, like the sound of our old answering machine, and then a pause. Then it's Julia's voice, overlain with static and some unidentifiable noise in the background.

"Pick up the phone, Rich." There is a long pause and then a loud, obviously annoyed sigh. "Quit letting him call me, Rich. I don't have the money to change my phone number, so quit having that little brat leave me messages trying to make me feel guilty. He's nothing but a parasite who can't be far enough away from me, and I don't appreciate your trying to force me to interact with him."

There is the sound of a phone disconnecting with a violent slamming, then Ms. Young clicks off the tape recorder. The trick up the sleeve. Dad must have saved this, given it to Chuck years ago to keep in case something like this ever came up. *Got it under control.*

Julia is stunned. McIntyre is leaning back in his chair, patting his face with a white handkerchief.

I feel relieved. I feel like finally someone else knows

the truth about her. Every muscle in my body twitches with excitement, but I hold perfectly still and fight to keep the smile off my face.

"Nothing further, Your Honor."

Ms. Young collects her things and returns to the chair beside me. I want to jump up and hug her, but I hold completely still. She reaches over and pats my knee beneath the table, and then she scribbles something on the legal pad. She slides it over for me to read.

"McIntyre isn't stupid."

My enthusiasm dries up a little.

"Opportunity to redirect, Your Honor," McIntyre says.

"Go ahead, Mr. McIntyre," the judge says.

He lifts himself from the chair with great effort and returns to the podium. "Mrs. Mayers, how old is your son Steven?"

Julia has been crying softly. She sniffs, takes a long, shaky breath, and dabs at her eyes with a tissue the judge has handed her. "He's almost five now."

"The same age you lost Michael at."

"Yes," she says, her voice cracking with emotion that I can't decipher is real or faked.

"How is your relationship with him?"

"He's a wonderful little boy, and I do everything I can to be with him as much as possible. I volunteered at his preschool, and when he starts kindergarten this fall, I'll volunteer there, too."

"Do you work, Mrs. Mayers?"

"No, I'm very fortunate to have a husband who makes

a good enough living that I can stay home and be a full-time mother."

"And are you currently taking any medication?"

"No, I'm not."

"Can you explain to us, Mrs. Mayers, what would have caused you to say such a thing to your former husband about your son Michael?"

Julia begins to sob, her shoulders bouncing up and down. "I had postpartum depression, the worst kind. It lasted for years after Michael was born. I was angry, I was hurt, and I felt so guilty about not being able to be the best mother to him that I lashed out at him and at Richard." She is crying for real, and as much as I hate her, I feel a little sorry for her because this is the most genuine emotion I've ever seen out of her. "I would get these calls from him, I'd hear his little voice, and it was a terrible reminder of what a failure I was, and I couldn't take that pain."

"Mrs. Mayers, what is it you want to have happen out of this? What outcome are you looking for by showing up now?" McIntyre's voice is soothing, but I don't trust him.

"I just want to know my son. I just want the chance to be the kind of mother he deserves."

I nearly yell out "Bullshit!" but I grit my teeth so hard I think they might crack. Ms. Young puts a hand on my knee and squeezes tight.

"Thank you, Mrs. Mayers."

"You may step down," the judge says. There is a long silence as the judge writes on her notepad and looks over documents. "Ms. Young, are you prepared for closing statements?" The judge looks over the top of her glasses at us.

"Yes, Your Honor."

Ms. Young steps up to the podium and proceeds to tell the judge all the reasons why I should be allowed to stay in Atlantic Beach, and especially why I should stay with Maggie. "Removing this young man and placing him into a situation that is foreign, taking him away from his support system when he has just lost his father, and relocating him to a place and with a woman of whom he holds so many terrible memories would be a devastating blow to his development and well-being." Her voice is passionate and loud, echoing off the courtroom ceiling and punctuated by thunder.

"Michael has grown into a healthy, well-adjusted young man who has a strong sense of himself and his future. He knows he is making a choice that is in his own best interest by requesting these arrangements. He understands the consequences of this decision, and he is prepared to embrace those consequences fully. Ms. Delaney is a responsible adult, one who took on the role of mother when she had no obligation to do so. She accepted the job even with no commitment from Mr. Wilson himself, though that was clearly forthcoming before his untimely death. To take this young man away from the only other family member he has would be untenable, and would be akin to losing another parent. Your Honor, he has already lost two parents in very difficult and tragic circumstances. It would be a shame for him to lose a third."

Ms. Young takes her yellow legal notepad, her stacks of papers, and returns to the chair beside me.

"Mr. McIntyre," says the judge.

McIntyre heaves himself from the chair and heads to the center of the room. Sweat blotches darken the back of his beige suit.

"Thank you, Your Honor." He clears his throat and dabs at his forehead again with the handkerchief. "Mrs. Mayers doesn't claim to be perfect. She doesn't claim to be without faults that, in the past, have led to mistakes and most assuredly, to regrets. But she does claim something that no one else in this room can claim: a blood tie to Michael. She is his biological mother, and therefore, in the eyes of the court and the eyes of the law, she is his legal parent and guardian." He clears his throat again, and I wonder if he's going to cough up a wad of phlegm in the middle of his lecture. "Mrs. Mayers has the love and support of a husband, which Ms. Delaney does not. She has the means to provide a lifestyle of advantage for Michael, which Ms. Delaney does not. But above all, she has the love that only a real mother can provide, the love that only blood can provide, which Ms. Delaney does not and will never have."

Behind me I can hear Maggie taking deep, shaking breaths, and I know that she is crying. I want to turn around and let her know that it's going to be okay, but I'm too afraid to move. McIntyre is spinning a glass shell around us, and if I move wrong, it will shatter and fall in on us, and cut us all to shreds. I look at the judge to see if she is buying any of this crap. She is looking at the top of her desk, taking notes, giving nothing away.

McIntyre finishes. "Thank you, Your Honor," he says with a grandiose bow. She doesn't acknowledge him.

"We will reconvene tomorrow at one o'clock, at which time you'll have my decision." The judge looks up from the desk for the first time in a while.

"All rise," says the bailiff. We do.

"This court is now in recess to reconvene at one o'clock tomorrow afternoon."

The judge leaves. We sit still. Julia and McIntyre huddle together, their heads almost touching. Ms. Young stands, takes my arm and pulls me up, nods toward the door, and we all make a hasty retreat to the hallway.

It's dark outside, though it's only around four in the afternoon. The black clouds blotting the sky make it feel as if it's midnight. I'm so exhausted I could drop to the floor like a pile of rags.

Ms. Young pulls us into a knot and whispers, "I can't get a clear read on the judge. I'd like to say I'm confident, but I'll be honest, that last little stunt of Mrs. Mayer's may have won her a few points."

Chuck puts an arm around my shoulder, and I want to pull away, but I can't move. "What do you think she is likely to do?" he asks.

"She's a wild card," Ms. Young says in a hushed voice. "I've only appeared before her once, but I've been study-ing her cases. She's hard to figure out."

"I don't feel good," I say.

"I'm sure it's going to turn out fine," Chuck says. He squeezes my shoulder.

Maggie looks at me.

"No, I mean . . ." I duck from under Chuck's arm and find the nearest trash can into which to puke the soda I drank at lunch.

Maggie takes a paper napkin from her pocketbook and wets it in the drinking fountain. She puts it on the back of my neck. "Blood is thicker than water. That's crap," she says. I laugh in spite of the foul taste in my mouth and the feeling I might hurl again. We sit on a wooden bench in the darkened hallway.

"I think I've thrown up more in the past week," I say, my voice sounding like a little kid's, "than I have in my whole life combined."

"You goin' for some kind of record?" Maggie asks. She smiles as she hands me the wet napkin.

"Not on purpose," I say.

Maggie points to the drinking fountain on the wall near the door to the courtroom. "Go rinse out your mouth. You'll feel better."

I take a gulp of water from the fountain, swish it around in my mouth, and then spit it out. I do it again.

"Better?" Maggie asks as she moves beside me. She smiles at me.

"I just want this all to be over. I want to go home and sleep, and play with Rocket, and ride my surfboard." I want to see Rachel, too, but I leave that out.

The storm outside is raging as we make our way to

the car. We drive to Maggie's house and sit around the kitchen table. Rocket leans hard against my leg. The lights flicker overhead but stay on. My knees feel wobbly, like I just got off the boat for the first time after not being on land for months. I look at Chuck talking on his phone. A sudden surge of panic rushes through me like lightning, and my mouth opens before I know what I'm saying. "What about the boat?"Chuck stops. His brow furrows, and the lines of his mouth draw tight. He looks at Maggie.

"Let me call you right back," he says, then he slides the phone closed.

"What about the boat?" I say.

"What about it, Mike?"

"What's going to happen to it?" I don't know why this is suddenly so important to me, but it is, and I need to know.

"We haven't gotten that far yet," Chuck says.

"Are we selling it? Is Jack Sutton gonna buy it?"

Chuck lets out a sigh. "I don't know yet, Mike. We'll figure that out another day."

"We can't let it sit too long. It needs maintenance. It needs work. I need to know what we're gonna do with it, so I know what I need to do. Do I need to clean it up? Am I going to keep it and run charters? What are we doing?" My voice arcs.

Chuck looks at Maggie, frantic and confused. "Can you help him understand?" he says.

"Mike," Maggie says firmly, "let's get through tomor-row. We'll talk about the boat after that, I promise."

I look at her. She's not mad, but she has a serious look that says "drop it," so I take a deep breath and hold it. I let it out slowly and wait for my heart to stop banging around like a gorilla trapped inside my chest.

"If you try to take on everything at once, you'll drown," Maggie says. "Let's just deal with today. Then we can figure out the rest later."

I let the pounding in my chest die down, sucking in air through my nose and letting it drift out. I can't let go of the feeling that I need to deal with the boat. Then I hit on an idea. "I need to get out for a little while. Can I go with Jayd for a drive?"

Maggie looks at Chuck, who has his head down, scrolling through something on his phone. She looks back at me. "Only for a little while. I'm afraid this storm is going to get worse, and we have a big day tomorrow."

I grab Maggie's phone and call Jayd's cell. "How'd it go?" he asks without saying hello.

"Don't know yet," I answer. "We won't know until tomorrow."

"That's rough, dude. So what are you doing?"

"Hoping you can spring me for a ride. I need to get out for a little while. Can you take off for an hour or two?"

I hear Jayd cover the phone and ask his mom if he can go. I can't hear the discussion, but he comes back quickly. "Yeah, I can come for about an hour."

"I'm at Maggie's."

Jayd disconnects, and I hurry to change out of the suit and into black-and-red shorts and a T-shirt.

Chuck is heading out as I reappear in the kitchen. "I'll be here before noon," he says to Maggie, and then he pulls the door closed behind him.

"Are you hungry?" Maggie asks. "We still have all that food in the fridge."

"I'm good," I say, eager for Jayd to arrive.

Maggie walks down the hallway to her room, and Rocket follows. I decide to have a few bites of potato salad even though I'm not really in the mood to eat. It's cold and creamy, and I eat more than a few bites as I realize how hungry I actually am.

Maggie comes around the corner in a pair of jeans and a gray T-shirt that I know belonged to my dad.

"That looks good on you," I say.

"I helps me feel close to him," she says. "But if it bothers you . . ."

"No," I say, setting my fork in the sink and wrapping the bowl of potato salad in plastic wrap again, "I like it. I might try that, too."

I grab my wallet from the bedroom as I hear Jayd pull into the driveway.

"Not too late," Maggie says as Rocket climbs onto the sofa beside her. She clicks on the television, and I slip out the door and get into the white car.

"You want to head to the arcade?" Jayd asks.

"I want to go to the marina."

"I don't have a long time," he says. "I told my mom I'd be back by seven for supper."

"Just drop me off. I'll find a way back." The rain is easing, and a few streaks of light are slicing through the clouds. "I just want to feel close to my dad. I want to go to the boat."

We drive down the main island road to the causeway and over the bridge. Jayd is quiet, flipping the radio station to find something he likes. "So what happened today?" he asks as we start over the bridge to Moorehead.

"Julia told a bunch of lies about my dad and about how awesome she is." I feel my heart speed up a little recalling the events. "But my attorney nailed her with a phone message my dad saved from a long time ago."

"What did it say?"

"She called me a parasite and told my dad to stop having me call."

"Ouch," he says.

The words from the message and the total anger in her voice replayed in my head. *Quit having that little brat leave me messages trying to make me feel guilty. He's nothing but a parasite.*

We round the corner to the street that leads to the marina. "Are you just gonna hang out? I can maybe come back and pick you up later if you need." Jayd steers into the empty parking lot.

"I'm going for a ride," I say. "I need to feel close to my dad, and this is the only way."

"You can't take the boat out by yourself," he says in a loud protest. "There's a storm rolling in and—"

"Who do you think you are? My mom? You have to get in line for that job." I grab the door handle, determined and eager to get out on the water.

"Don't be an idiot. You haven't ever taken the boat out by yourself. Maggie will kill you."

I step out of the car and stare in at Jayd. "I need to do this." I slam the door and head down the walk to the slip.

chapter 22

I have taken the boat out of the slip more than once. Dad let me do it sometimes when it was just the two of us and we would go fishing for ourselves. I maneuver it out without a problem, and soon I am motoring past the channel markers and out into the open ocean. The water is choppy but not too rough, and the big craft bounces and lurches in the swells. The eastern sky has brightened; the clouds are breaking up into smaller and smaller clusters.

"Maybe this is what I'm meant to do," I say to the open sky. I sit a little taller in the captain's chair and guide the boat past the channel markers, heading toward deeper water.

The boat jolts and sways in the white caps, but I know I can handle it. When I get about ten miles or so off shore, I drop the anchor and move to the deck. The early evening light is trying to break free from the purple clouds. A cool wind is blowing across the deck. If I had any bait, I'd drop a line and see what I could find, but I didn't really think about it before I came. I walk to the rail and look over. The dream from the other night floods into my memory as I stare into the deep blue water. It's not as calm now as it was in the dream, and I can't see more than a few inches below the surface. Something silver cuts through the waves, maybe a barracuda or an amberjack. It darts under the boat, and another one follows.

"Dad, if you can hear me," I say into the wind, "just let me know you're there. Let me know everything is going to be okay, because right now it feels like my whole world is caving in, and I have no idea what's happening." I listen, but all I hear are waves slapping the side of the boat and the wind hissing across the deck.

In my head, Dad's voice calls at me to get someone's line. He cheers for a great catch and chats with guests about where they live. I sit in the galley and smell his coffee. I feel the boat sway and remember the times when I was younger that I would fall asleep here and he would carry me from the boat to the truck and drive us home. The memories flood into my head like old movies flickering on a screen behind my eyes. I remember the day Dad bought the *Mighty Mike*, the day he took me up the coast in the old truck we used to have, and I sat in the middle between Dad and Chuck as we went to pick up the boat.

"This is rockin'," Chuck had said. He was only in his twenties and had worked with Dad on another charter. When Dad bought the *Mighty Mike*, Chuck had begged to come and work for him. We climbed on board, and I explored every small space I could squeeze myself into.

Then Dad and I sailed back to Moorehead, and Chuck drove the truck back to meet us in the harbor. There were a lot of days with no charters and not much money, but the three of us would go out fishing, sell what we could to the market, and keep a little to help with the grocery bill.

I wipe the tears from my face with a paper towel and try to swallow down the knot that has slid up my throat.

The boat shifts with more force and draws my attention away from the memories. I look around and realize the sky and the water are all one color. I head to the wheelhouse and check the time on the instrument panel. It's 6:23 P.M. The gaps in the clouds have closed up again, and darkness has collected quickly around the boat. Even though I'm only ten miles from shore, I can't see the coastline or any hint of people, and a little jolt of panic pokes at my chest. The waves are hitting the boat harder and cresting over the sides. This rising fury of water is frightening, so I hoist the anchor and start the engines. I realize the radio is turned off, one of the biggest mistakes a captain can ever make. I flip it on and it crackles with static. I switch through channels until I hear the coast guard alert.

". . . High winds through midnight and increasing rain showers. There is a small craft warning for the Outer Banks, Beaufort, and Wilmington. High waves and wind continuing throughout the evening."

High waves and wind. That's a deadly combination for smaller boats. Even though *The Mighty Mike* is over thirty feet, it wasn't built for rough seas like this. And Atlantic

Beach, right where the harbor is, is right in the middle of the alert area.

Fingers of white light claw across the sky as I watch the compass and turn the boat to face the marina. My heart bounces around in my chest, and my palms sweat as I count the many mistakes I have made in taking my little trip: I didn't turn on the radio, no one knows where I am, bad weather, limited skills . . . "You dumb ass," I say aloud.

A huge wave washes over the bow, swamping the deck in frothy sea water. The boat rises with the swell, then slams down in the trough, jolting me sideways. Thunder bangs like it's inside my head. Another wave lifts the boat and sends it sideways. I rev the power in the engines and steer into the swells, but they are getting bigger and more frightening by the second.

Then a wave spins the boat sideways, and a huge crash of water hits the deck. I see it rush down into the galley, and the engines go quiet. The storm growls and howls around me like some crazed monster intent on sinking the boat that has invaded its territory.

"Shit," I say, low and almost growling. "Stupid, stupid, stupid." I grip the wheel and try to steer back into the swells, but without engines, I'm just a buoy on the water—totally out of control. I'm in trouble. And it's getting worse. I don't know how to restart the engines, and that means I'm a sitting duck. All I can think is *stupid*. The rain and the waves have soaked me, and it's hard to grip the wheel. I slide most of the way down the stairs and get to the pump. If I can work the pump by hand, I might get enough water out to try the engines again. Water sloshes around my ankles. I grab the lever and pump the handle. The sucking noise raises my hopes, and I crank the lever faster.

Steady and smooth. I hear Dad's voice when he taught me to use the equipment. *Not too fast or you might get air in the lines.*

I slow the motion of my arms and try to calm my breathing. The boat bounces and careens. It's hard to keep up a steady rhythm. My heart races, but so does my mind. Another big wave slams into the side of the boat, sending spray into the air and pushing the craft over to the side. Enough water below deck means it sinks.

A priming pump on the engine gets my attention. I press it a few times, nice and slow, then I clamber up the stairs to the wheelhouse and try starting the engines. They sputter and fight, but then they kick on, and I check the compass. I line up with what I think is the southwest and start negotiating the huge waves that are slamming me around like a cat swats a toy.

I fight the swells to keep the boat on a line toward home, toward safety. Time slows to a crawl, and I look back and forth, side to side, waiting for the wave that washes over the bow and sends me and the boat to the bottom.

"I'm sorry, Dad." Tears stream down my face, and the brisk wind is raising goosebumps on every inch of my skin. I don't know how long I fight the swells, but after what feels like hours, I can sense they are easing. In the distance, I can see the entrance to the marina. Finally. I let out a deep sigh, realizing that maybe I'd been holding my breath for a long time.

By the time I maneuver the boat into the slip, I can feel the exhaustion overtaking me. I don't know if I'll even have the strength to hose the boat off with fresh water like I should do. As I shut off the engines and climb down from the captain's chair, I see Maggie's Subaru in the parking lot. She jumps from the car and races toward me.

"Mike! Mike! Where did you go? Are you okay?" She looks frantic, then relieved, then furious. I can't say I blame her.

We drive back to her house in silence. I'm shivering from being drenched, but I don't dare ask Maggie to turn off the air. When we get to the house, Chuck is waiting inside. After hours of lecturing, everyone crying, and then more lecturing, Chuck finally calls it a night at close to midnight.

Maggie goes straight to bed, but even with the doors closed I can hear her still crying. I lie on my bed with Rocket until I can't take any more of the guilt. I walk to her door and knock.

"Go to bed, Mike."

"I can't sleep with you crying."

Things get quiet, then she opens the door and stands in the entry. "You need to sleep. Tomorrow is a big day, and I have a feeling we're going to be in for some huge changes." Her eyes are red and swollen. My stomach tightens, and I feel about fifteen different kinds of embarrassed and at least a dozen kinds of stupid.

"Maggie, I'm sorry. I was irresponsible. I didn't think. I just wanted to be close to my dad, and I didn't know how else to do it."

"So you thought nearly sinking the boat and drowning yourself was the answer?" Her voice gets shrill and a lot louder.

"I wasn't trying to sink it," I say, my voice getting louder, too. "I just wanted to be on the water, to be in his favorite place."

"His favorite place was anywhere that you were. You don't have to go find him, he's right here with you." She lets go of a big sigh and puts her hand on my chest above my heart. Her voice is softer. "Mike, I don't care about the boat. I care about you. You could have died doing that." Tears stream down her cheeks. "If I had lost you on top of losing your dad, it would be the death of me, too."

Shame floods my face with heat. "I'm sorry," I say, and tears let loose down my cheeks. "I didn't think. I was stupid." I take a few deep breaths. "If we get out of this okay tomorrow," I say, "I'm grounding myself until I'm twenty."

Maggie wraps her arms around me and pulls me close. I can smell Dad on the T-shirt she's wearing, and a deep sadness floods my chest, but it's comforting, too. "Maybe until your thirty," she says, and I look up at her to see a weak smile raising the corners of her mouth.

* * * *

In the morning we are silent. We dress for court, and Chuck arrives at eleven forty-five. It's clear he didn't sleep much after the previous night's events, and he doesn't say a word to me the entire drive. His hands grip the steering wheel so tightly, I can see the white skin tighten around his knuckles. I slink deeper into the seat and hope that Julia is the worst thing I have to face today.

We get to the courthouse, and Chuck finally breaks the silence. He looks me right in the eye. "It's a good thing the judge doesn't know about last night, or it'd be a sure bet this would not have a happy ending." He opens the car door, and we climb out. Heat rises from the pavement in waves, and the thick air makes me feel like I'm trapped again inside the bubble. The sound of the cicadas is muffled, and I more float than walk.

The courtroom is cool as I walk in and sit down at the table. Chuck and Maggie take their seats in the row behind me. Ms. Young doesn't seem to know about the boat, and I'm glad for that. I need someone on my side today.

chapter 23

We all stand. The judge enters. The judge sits. We all sit.

"I'm moved by both parties," the judge begins. She looks from Julia to me. "You each have a great deal at stake here, and I see so many possible resolutions to this particular set of circumstances."

I don't control this. Let it be, don't let it drown me.

"My primary concern, however, is for Michael." The judge looks squarely at me, and I'm afraid she may already have heard about the boat incident. I meet her gaze, but I don't smile, I don't flinch. "This young man has been through a terrible loss at a very young age, and he has barely had time to come to grips with that. It is clear that he has a strong support network in place and he is a young man who is responsible and confident in his decisions."

I flinch at the word *responsible*, and I sense the word *but* coming. It worries me. It's like Mrs. Sanford, my English teacher, talking about my research paper: "You've got a great idea, Michael, *but* you haven't executed it very well."

The judge looks at Julia. "Mrs. Mayers has made significant changes in her life in recent years, and it is clear she is sorry for what she has done in the past. Regret is a great teacher, and sometimes it offers us limited opportunities to reform our lives."

I look at Ms. Young, trying to get a read on what is happening, but she seems as unsure as I am.

"My decision is as follows," the judge says. She pauses. Everyone is silent.

I shift in my uncomfortable chair. *Here comes the* but *you've been waiting for.*

"I will award Ms. Delaney temporary guardianship of Michael pending the outcome of a full custody evaluation by the Department of Family Services. Should their recommendations be favorable, and after a six-month probationary period, I will award full, legal guardianship at that time.

Relief rushes through me, and I fight the urge to jump up and cheer. I hear Maggie suck in her breath behind me, and I almost leap up and cheer.

"However," the judge adds in a loud voice.

Here it comes.

"During this time, Mrs. Mayers is to receive visitation rights in accordance with the prevailing structure under North Carolina law. I believe this equates to alternating major holidays, and four weeks during the summer—unless the legislature has modified this without my knowledge." She smiles at her own joke.

I don't get it. Confusion swirls in my head like a cyclone. *I have to visit Julia?* How can the judge buy into that crap? She can't really believe that Julia is some reformed supermom. She can't be serious about me spending time with that psycho who doesn't even know anything about me.

The judge looks at me as if she can see into my head, reading my thoughts. "Michael, you need the opportunity to enjoy the stability and security that a life here provides for you. But you also need the opportunity to develop a relationship with Mrs. Mayers and with your half-brother."

I can feel the tears welling up again in my eyes, and they sting like salt water, like the spray from the waves. *You can't believe her, Judge. You have to be able to see she is crazy.*

"This is my ruling. This concludes our hearing." The judge raps her gavel on the big desk.

"All rise," the bailiff says. "This court is now adjourned."

The judge is out of the room before anyone can say anything.

I feel like I've been sucker punched. I can't move. I stand, leaning on the table, and wait for my lungs to inflate again. I'm lightheaded. I can hear Chuck saying something, I can hear Ms. Young answering. I can hear Maggie behind me, but I can't move, can't breathe, can't understand.

"Mike," Maggie says, taking hold of my arm, "it's okay, hon, it's okay."

Tears are flowing from my eyes, splashing on the table below me. I finally take a huge gasp of air, and my whole body shudders. "I won't go," I say. "She can't force me to go."

"Not now, son," Chuck says.

I wheel around, glaring at him. "I'm not your son. You were supposed to protect me. That's why my dad trusted you. You let us both down." My voice is low and full of anger that tastes like acid as I speak.

Chuck's eyes widen, and his face draws tight. He turns to Maggie, whispers something, then steps into the aisle and heads for the door.

Ms. Young maneuvers behind me and blocks my exit. Over my attorney's shoulder, Julia looks at me.

"I'll die first before I'll spend one freaking minute with her." I hurl the words at Julia, but her expression doesn't change.

"You don't have a choice," she says, her voice taunting like a bully's.

McIntyre hands a paper to Ms. Young. "A copy of the current statute on visitation rights for noncustodial parents."

"I have my own, thank you." Ms. Young hands the paper back to Mr. McIntyre.

"We will be in touch tomorrow before Mrs. Mayers leaves the state to make arrangements for the initial visit." McIntyre stuffs the papers into his satchel and begins waddling up the center aisle.

"Michael," Julia says from behind Ms. Young. I turn and look at Maggie. "The more you fight, the harder this will be for us all."

I turn and stare at her. "Maggie is my mother. Maggie has always been my mother. You never wanted me, and no matter what, you'll never be my mother."

"Michael, I am your mother, and not even the judge can change that."

I turn back to Maggie. Her face is pale and her eyes are red. "Let's go home," I say.

"In a moment," Ms. Young says from behind me. "There are some documents to be signed, and then we need to talk about some of the details."

Julia's footsteps gradually move toward the hallway outside. I hear the door open, hear it close, then I turn to look to make sure she is gone.

Ms. Young looks at me, her lips pulled in a thin line, her brow furrowed, and I feel like I used to when I was about to get laid into by Dad for doing something stupid.

"First, I want to tell you that you're very fortunate the judge didn't hear about your boating trip, or she may have changed her mind. Second," Ms. Young brushes a stray piece of hair from her eyes with dagger-like fingernails, "you are fortunate the decision was for the standard visitation schedule. You could have been told to pack immediately and fly to Washington with Mrs. Mayers, or the judge could have said that it would be a shared custody, and you would have to live half the year here and half the year with Mrs. Mayers." She draws a breath and looks at Maggie. "As for attitude, I'm afraid that will now be yours to take care of."

Maggie looks freaked out.

"I'm sorry," I say to Maggie. She volunteered for this, and so far I've done nothing but act like a jerk to her— well, in general.

"We've all been through the ringer," Maggie says, and the lines in her face are so deep that I wonder why I've never seen her look this way before. "It's too much for a lifetime, let alone just a week."

Ms. Young motions to Maggie, and they head over to the blonde lady's desk to sign some papers. The weight of the past few days feels like lead in my veins, and I have a hard time even holding my head up. When they are done, they come back toward the table and go through the little gate. They walk up the aisle toward the door, talking in hushed voices. I try to follow, but it's like I'm encased in wet cement. They wait in the hallway as I slog my way toward the exit.

Ms. Young hands a flyer on pale blue paper to Maggie. "This is the information for beginning the evaluation process. Once a caseworker has been assigned, you can expect weekly visits, and when school starts, you'll be expected to provide progress reports and copies of grades." She hands another paper to Maggie. "This form needs to be filed with Social Services so that you can be given the proper documents to show your guardianship for things such as school registration, insurance, medical and dental care, etc."

Maggie looks at the papers, but I can tell she's too tired to pay close attention to what Ms. Young is saying.

We leave the courthouse and stand on the steps beneath the arched portico. Rain drums on the pavement, and the air feels heavy on my skin.

Ms. Young shakes hands with Chuck and then turns

to me. "It's a good outcome, better than we might have expected."

I'm not sure I agree with her. My brain spins like it's in a blender, and I can't sort anything out. Maggie takes my hand and holds it with firm pressure. Her fingers are cool on my skin.

We stand at the doors while Chuck pulls the car up.

"I'm here to help," Ms. Young says to Maggie. "If you run into anything you can't resolve, or if things should become—complicated?—give me a call." They shake hands.

"Michael," the lawyer says to me, "let go of this anger you have. It will only cause you more pain, and you've had enough of that for a while. Holding on to anger is like drinking poison and waiting for the other person to die."

I nod. "I know," I say. I pause, then add, "Thank you for everything. I really appreciate all you did for me."

Ms. Young extends her hand. I take it, and she shakes it firmly. "You really will be fine."

Chuck honks and we say goodbye, running to the car as the black sky pours down.

"Is the bridge going to be open?" Maggie asks.

"Won't know 'til we get there," Chuck says.

We drive in silence, tension battling with exhaustion as we make our way along the flooded streets. It takes twice as long as usual to get back to Maggie's. The bridge from Moorehead to Atlantic Beach is flooded with water, and no one can go faster than about ten miles an hour, and Chuck keeps complaining about not being able to see anything out the windshield. It reminds me of the night Dad and I drove to Maggie's; the night he told me he wanted to go to Raleigh and buy the ring. My heart pounds in my chest, but then it slows, and I lean my head against the side of the car and watch the sky pour.

Rocket meets us at the door and wags his tail like he thought maybe we weren't ever coming back. I get a can of dog food out, open it, and dump it into his bowl. He wolfs it down and then looks at me like he's expecting more, so I grab him a bone, and he takes it from my hand, crunching it happily on the kitchen floor.

Maggie has disappeared into the bedroom. She comes out dressed in a pair of cotton shorts and another one of Dad's T-shirts. She gets a glass of water from the tap and moves over to the sofa. I head to my room, the judge's words ringing in my brain. . . . *you also need the opportunity to develop a relationship with Mrs. Mayers and with your half-brother.* I don't want a relationship with either of them. I have all the family I need in this little beach house. I shed my suit and tie like the cicadas shed their outer skin. I flop onto my bed and wonder why every inch of my body hurts.

Even though it's only around four in the afternoon, I decide I'm done for the day. *In fact*, I think, *I could sleep for a week, as long as I don't have any more weird dreams.* I close my eyes and wonder at how my life doesn't feel like my life anymore.

chapter 24

The sun streams in the window. Rocket fidgets by my feet, which probably means he needs to go to the bathroom. I pull on a pair of shorts and a tank top and head for the kitchen door. He runs into the yard, darting behind trees. I lean in the doorway, enjoying the feel of the sun on my skin, the sound of the mockingbirds in the trees, and the relaxed feeling that more than twelve hours of sleep gives me.

Rocket returns, his nose covered in mud. I let him in and follow him to his food and water bowls. I fill the water bowl and set it on the floor. As I listen to the slurping noise he makes while drinking, I get his dry food from under the sink and fill his food bowl a little more than usual.

Maggie sleeps until around ten. She gets up, makes coffee, and sits quietly at the table, reading over papers I assume she got from the court yesterday.

"I have to take parenting classes," she says.

"Oh." I can't really think of a reply.

Around noon, the phone rings. It's Jayd. "You never called me yesterday to say what happened." He sounds more worried than upset.

"I came home and crashed," I say. "I fell asleep around four in the afternoon, and I didn't wake up until just a little while ago."

"You were totally wiped out."

"Yeah, you could say that."

"Any chance you can hang out at the arcade tonight?"

I turn to Maggie. "Can I go to the arcade with Jayd tonight?"

"The arcade, not the marina." It's a statement, not a question.

"I swear. I'll be home by nine. I promise." I hold up two fingers like a boy scout, even though I was never in a scout troop.

"Is Jayd driving you, or do you need a ride?"

I lift the receiver to my ear again. "Can you drive, or do I need a ride?"

"I'll get you and bring you home. And I'll baby-sit you and make sure you don't go anywhere you're not supposed to."

"Oh, you heard that." I laugh and then look at Maggie. "Jayd is driving, and he promises not to let me off my leash."

Maggie smiles just a little. "Then I guess it's okay."

We make the necessary arrangements, and I hang up the phone. I take a shower and get dressed, then I sit at the table where Maggie is still reviewing papers. "If I had known there was this much work and frustration involved, I wouldn't have asked."

Maggie lets out a burst of laughter. "Michael," she says, and she looks me right in the eye. "If I'd have known you were going to put me through so much in the first few days, I would have declined the request." She giggles a little. "I'm teasing. This isn't so bad. I go to a few classes, we get visited by a case worker, and I sign a few documents."

I look at the stack of papers on the table. "Looks like more than a few."

"Not so much." She fans through the pile. "We are going to be okay. Both of us. It won't always be easy, but it will be okay."

Something in her voice convinces me, and I feel a little lighter as a result.

I waste most of the day playing with Rocket, hunting through TV channels, and eating some of the many leftovers still in the fridge. Jayd picks me up around five o'clock, and we meet up at Jungleland with Rachel, Trevor, Caitlyn, and Bryce. It's good to be with my friends, but as much as I want to see them—especially Rachel—I'm still so tired from the past week that I ask Jayd to take me home around seven.

Rachel walks out to the car with us. "I wish you weren't leaving," she says. "I feel like I haven't seen you in forever."

"I'm so tired that I am not fun. Give me a few days, and I promise things will be more normal. We can hang out, go to the Rusty Bucket, maybe go to the boat."

"Um, maybe not the boat," Rachel says with a laugh. "I heard about the last time you went to the boat."

"Man, does everybody know about the boat?" I look at Jayd.

"Yeah. Pretty much. It's a small island and word travels fast."

Rachel wraps her arms around me, and I feel that same content, calm feeling that I had the night she let me hold her. Her hair smells like spring flowers and her skin feels like silk. "I'll call you tomorrow, I promise." I tuck a strand of her hair behind her ear, and I kiss her softly.

Jayd drives me back to Maggie's. Rocket meets me at the door with his usual enthusiasm.

"You're home early," Maggie says from the sofa.

"I'm beat. I didn't want to hang out anymore, so Jayd brought me home." I sit beside her. She has a book spread open in her lap. "I don't mean to interrupt," I say, pointing to the book.

"I can't concentrate, anyway," she says. She moves to the kitchen and fixes a glass of soda to drink.

The phone rings and I pick it up. I don't recognize the number, so I figure it's probably for Maggie.

"Hello," I say, using my most polite voice.

"Michael. I didn't expect you to answer." It's Julia. Immediately I regret not letting it go to voice mail. My palms grow sweaty, and I think about hanging up, but I figure she'll probably just call back.

"What do you want, and how did you get this number?"

There is no reply. I can hear a television in the background, with fake laughter and fake music like every TV sitcom has and that sound weird and out of place coming through on this call.

Maggie looks at me. Her face is screwed up with the same confusion I feel.

I mouth the word "Julia" to her. Her eyes widen, and she motions for me to hand her the phone. I shake my head.

"I just called to tell you not to bother making any plans to come and visit until you can speak to me in a civil and respectable tone." She lets out a loud, quick breath, and I can almost feel her frustration—or maybe it's anger. "I will not let you poison Steven with your hatred the way your father poisoned you."

I hold the phone, silent and confused. "Um, okaaay," is all I manage to say. There are so many things I could say, but I take a deep breath and realize that she will never be my mom. My real mom is right here with me, offering to help but still letting me deal with this on my own.

"My dad didn't poison me," I say. "You poisoned me. You called me a parasite. You told me I ruined your life." My heart races, but I'm too tired for anger and too tired for tears. "I tried to call you, but you never wanted to talk to me." Her voice from so many years ago echoes in my head with hateful words I couldn't understand when I was little. "I hope your son Steven can give you what you want. I'm sorry I couldn't, but I tried."

"I tried to reach out to you," she says, her voice straining as if she's trying to make it sound like she's crying. "I spent thousands of dollars I didn't have to find you."

"Why is it always about money for you?" I ask.

She makes a noise almost like a growl. "Your father kept you hidden from me. He isolated you and lied to you so you would grow up hating me, and obviously it worked!" She is practically screaming at me, but I keep my voice low.

"My dad never tried to stop me from having a relationship with you. You did that yourself. You hung up on me. You called me a brat. You called me a parasite. My dad didn't have to lie to me and teach me not to love you. I figured out who and what you are all by myself." The words bypass my brain and roll straight out of my heart. I let out a deep sigh and wait for the barrage of insults and lies I'm sure are about to fly at me.

"You disappoint me, Michael." There is emotion in Julia's voice, but it sounds hollow and as fake as the laughter coming from the TV in the background.

I pause for a moment, but then the truth finds its way out. "You can't disappoint me anymore, because I won't let you." I disconnect and put the phone back on the base.

"What did she want?"

I stand by the hallway, unsure where to move or what to do. "She wanted to tell me I can't visit because she doesn't want me to poison her son like my dad poisoned me." The words feel odd coming out of me, strange and uncomfortable—and a little sad. "She said I disappoint her."

"You disappoint her?"

"I told her she was the one who poisoned me," and I realize that Maggie had been looking at me the whole time, so she knew what I'd said. "I did love her," I said, my voice softer and more gentle. "I tried very hard to keep loving her, too."

"That's because you're a very loving person, Mike, and you were just a little boy then. You know you didn't do anything wrong. Right?"

I nod, and I really do know it's the truth, but maybe for a long time I believed I wasn't a good kid and that's why she didn't like me. "I didn't do anything wrong," I say, and I let the truth of it weave around me and through me.

"Come here, Mike," Maggie says in an exhausted voice.

I sit next to her, ready to be bawled out for taking out the boat, for losing my temper, for mouthing off at Chuck, and for whatever other sins I committed without knowing it. "Whatever it is I did," I say, "I'm sorry." I figure it's better to get it done up front and maybe soften the blow a little.

"You don't need to say you're sorry, sweetie," she says. "After the week we've had, I'm surprised one of us hasn't been arrested or shipped off to the loony bin." She takes a sip of soda. The glass is slick with condensation.

I rock my head from side to side, trying to loosen the muscles that are bunched up defensively there. "What's up," I say. My neck strains, and my face tenses in a mix of pain and relief. I wait for whatever she's going to say to me. I don't care if she's mad, or sad, or whatever. I'm tired, and all I want is to sleep for a week and figure out the rest later. I sit beside her and wait for what's coming.

"I know that what we got wasn't perfect," Maggie says. "But we were never going to have perfect, anyway. You know that, right?"

Rocket noses in between us and sits on my feet. I pet his head and rub his ears. "I know," I say. I want to add a "but" in there, but I think better of it. The weight of time and too many emotions is pulling my body down and making me feel paralyzed.

"So now we have to figure out how we go forward from here. We have to figure out how we're going to be a family, just you and me."

"And Rocket," I say. He thumps his tail on my feet, and Maggie reaches over to rub his nose.

"And Rocket," she says.

"And Dad," I add.

Maggie nods. "In his own way."

"And what do we do with the boat?"

"That's a subject for another night," she says.

I wait for what is coming next, but Maggie is silent.

We sit like this, Rocket between us, Dad present somewhere in the room, and nothing being said. It is dark outside, but the rain has slowed. Finally we stand, and I make my way to my room, slip into a T-shirt and my boxers, and crawl into bed. Rocket hops up with me, curls up by my feet, and begins softly snoring. The cool sheets and the faint smell of rain-soaked pine comfort me. It feels like home. My eyes close on their own, and I sink into the darkness and let it wrap around me.

I find myself on the deck of the *Mighty Mike*, the sun beating down but a cool breeze lifting off the water. I call out for my dad, but he doesn't answer. I look all over the boat, but he isn't there.

But I can feel him. I move up to the bow and look over the edge into the deepest part of the water. It fades from clear, to pale blue, to the deepest blue, and I can just see his face. The breeze stops, and the water turns to glass. I can see him as plain as if he were right in front of me.

"I wanted to go with you," I say. "I almost wanted the boat to sink so I could be with you."

I can hear his voice, feel it resonating in my head and in my chest. "I'm glad you didn't."

"But I miss you, Dad," I say, and it is my five-year-old voice that sounds scared and lonely.

"I'm right here, son."

I turn and there is Dad, standing behind me. He is alive and perfect, except for the long, white scar that curves across his nose and back toward his scalp. I reach out for him, eyes closed and arms wide, and I feel him, warm and strong, close to me, moving through me. When I open my eyes, he is gone. The ache in my body is so strong that I turn back to the water and prepare myself to dive in. I will allow the water to close in over my head, pulling me down, and then I will inhale, taking the salty liquid deep into my lungs. I'll sink down until I can't see the boat, or the sky, or the surface anymore.

"No, son." I hear in my head again.

I look everywhere, but I can't see him. "Please," I beg.

"I miss you so much. *Please* let me come with you."

I feel the warmth again. "You *are* with me. You will *always* be with me. No one can take you from me. No one can take me from you."

I smell the salty mist from the breeze mingled with the pines. I can sense Rocket beside me and Dad close by. I'm crying again, and I know I'm dreaming, but I don't care. I feel a calmness move through me, feel Dad's voice vibrate in my head and in my heart.

"I love you, Dad."

"I love you, too, son."

Rocket thumps his tail on the bed. Finally, I let myself fall into the deepest sleep.

The End

acknowledgments

Special Thanks:

To Mike, for your unending patience and support of my dream, even when it isn't easy to believe.

To Amanda, for your music, your humor, and your awesome T-Rex impersonation.

To Carson and Emery, for showing me the wonderful and complicated minds of teenage boys, and for helping to bring Michael to life. Your insights were invaluable, and the assistance you gave me helped to tell a story that I believe in with my whole heart.

To Peggy, for seeing in this story what I saw when I wrote it, and for always believing in my ability to do better and to go deeper.

Author Kim Williams Justesen is a Salt Lake City native who now lives in Sandy, Utah. In third grade she wrote her first book, **A Pony of My Own**, and then wrote a book report about it. Her amazing teacher, Mrs. Saenz (now Shirley Lohnes), saw promise in the work and encouraged Kim to consider being a writer. Mrs. Saenz also made Kim choose a book from the library and write a new book report.

Kim earned a B.A. in English from Westminster College and an M.F.A. in Writing from Vermont College. She spent twelve years as a writer in the advertising and public relations field, has written for various Internet sites including *City Search* and *Utah Parent*, and has taught numerous English and creative writing courses at local colleges for more than 15 years. Many of her former students have gone on to become published writers themselves. Her first novel, *Kiss Kiss Bark*, was published in 2006 by Tanglewood Press.

When she isn't writing, Kim enjoys movies, snow shoeing, and knitting. One of her favorite things in the entire world, however, is sitting down to enjoy a good book with some really good chocolate nearby.